LOVE IN
Linna
BOOK ONE

secret SMILES

LAURA JOHN

Independently published.

Editor/Interior Formatting: CPR Editing

Proofreader: Kierra McKay

Cover Designer: Dark City Designs

Trigger Warning

Secret Smiles talks about depression, drug abuse, and suicide.

There is an attempted suicide in this story.

If you struggle with depression or thoughts of self-harm, this book may not be the best for you to read.

If you feel like reading about an any of these things would be triggering for you, please tread with caution.

If you or someone you know is thinking about suicide, or dealing with addictions, please reach out. There is help available. You are not alone.

<u>Canadian Resources:</u>
Canadian Suicide Prevention Services: 1-833-456-4566

Crisis Text Line: Text **TALK** to **686868**

Addiction Services: https://www.canada.ca/en/health-canada/services/substance-use/get-help/get-help-problematic-substance-use.html

<u>U.S. Resources:</u>
National Hope Helpline: 1-800-SUICIDE (1-800-784-2433)

National Suicide Prevention Lifeline: 1-800-273-TALK (1-800-273-8255)

Crisis Text Line: Text **HOME** to **741741**

Addiction Services: 1-877-221-1396

I WANT TO DEDICATE
THIS BOOK TO DANNY.
I LOVE YOU, BABY.

PATRICIA MARIE DAGGEN
FIFTEEN YEARS AGO

"Hey, Fatty Patty, what are you doing in my fucking way?" my tormentor calls.

Ugh! My name is Patricia, *not* Patty, but I don't say anything. I just try to grab my stuff as fast as possible.

This school is full of beautiful people, and I'm just a short, chubby nerd who doesn't fit in. I wish I was like them. Maybe one day. I try to stick to myself as much as possible. I eat lunch outside, away from everyone else. I keep my head low and avoid drama as much as possible. I just want to finish school and be invisible.

Being twelve sucks, especially when you're twelve and already in high school. Being a December baby, I was already the youngest in my class. But then my teachers decided that I wasn't challenged enough, so they had me skip fifth grade, which put me in middle school, and then high school, a year early. Because being a year and a half younger than everyone else in this school makes the bullying better. *Not.*

Having my locker right below the most popular guy in school is just the icing on this craptastic cake. Especially since he seems to hate me. He's always yelling at me to get out of his way or making fun of me in one way or another. I've studied his patterns and try to avoid my locker at those times.

Today, I'm running late and end up at my locker at the exact same time that Johnny Crown needs to get into his.

This is nothing new. I remember one time when I was in his way, he pushed me over and I hit my face on my locker. I got a nasty shiner. I told my dad I tripped and he seemed to believe it, or at least he didn't question the lie. That day, Mikey Ecosta and I shared one of our first secret smiles.

I remember his face when Johnny pushed me. It was a mix of panic and concern. I looked up into his beautiful eyes and gave him a smile, as if saying I was okay, and he smiled back and nodded.

I can tell he doesn't want the other guys to know he's nice to me, so he doesn't talk to me, but those smiles make the days easier.

Normally, Johnny just laughs with his buddies at his "Fatty Patty" joke and moves on, but today he takes it one step further by kicking my stuff all down the hallway.

"Did you not fucking hear me, Fatty?" he barks a bit louder, but not yelling, because he doesn't want the teachers to hear.

I gasp and scramble to get my stuff, trying not to cry. He kicks more books out of my hands and high-fives one of his buddies. All of his buddies are laughing. Well, all of them except for Mikey.

"Come on, Johnny, let's go. We're going to be late for class," Mikey urges, giving Johnny a slight push, and they all move on.

He looks back at me and smiles. Sometimes I feel like I can read what he's saying. It's like he's telling me everything will be alright.

Mikey has always been the one who doesn't laugh at Johnny's jokes. He's the nicest of them all, but he's still friends with that asshole, and that makes him not my friend. But oh, how I wish he was my friend. I have had a crush on Mikey since the moment I first laid eyes on him. Our secret smiles are what have kept me going strong this long.

As I'm picking up my stuff, I decide this is the last straw. I'm done. I don't need to be bullied anymore. I'm done with this school. There will be no more secret smiles, but at least I won't ever have to see Johnny Crown again.

I grab everything out of my locker and head home. This is the last time I will set foot through the doors of South Sienna High School. My dad won't be the happiest, but he'll also be pissed at the guys for picking on me, so he'll understand.

As of today, I'm no longer Patricia. I'm Tia, and no one is going to fuck with me again.

TIA MARIE DAGGEN
PRESENT DAY

The past six months have been the worst of my life, and that's saying something. I lost one of my best friends and clients, I broke off my engagement three days before the wedding, and I think I'm about to lose my job. Life has been a real bitch. I'm sure it could be worse, but I wish things would just turn my way.

God, if you're listening, or even real, I could use some help here.

I let out a sigh. Yeah, I'm sure God has better things to do then to help me out.

I'm sitting in my office when I see this super tall man walk into the main lobby. I can't quite make out who he is, but I can tell he's gorgeous. He has to be over 6'4" and is built like a Greek god. He has dark brown hair that is long and shaggy. I briefly wonder what it would feel like to run my fingers through, and I feel my cheeks heat at the thought.

I've always been a girl who likes long hair on a guy, something I can pull in the heat of the moment. My ex had a short business cut; it was cute, but not the same.

I keep staring at the guy, wishing he would turn slightly so I could see his face. His outline is somewhat familiar, but I don't know why.

Finally, he turns, and I see his ice blue eyes. He has perfect cheekbones, a strong jawline, and full kissable lips. Biting my lip, I realize I know exactly who he is.

He is major rock star Mikey Ecosta. I heard through the tabloids that he was looking for a new manager, but I had no idea he was coming to Eaststreet Consulting to do it.

Michael William Ecosta, the guy who never made fun of me. The one who offered a smile when everyone else was kicking me while I was down. My childhood crush, and maybe that crush lasted far longer than I care to admit. When his first album came out, I was obsessed with it. Everyone thought it was because he was cute, and obviously that didn't hurt, but no one knew about my past and what Mikey meant to me.

Mikey used to be this gangly, awkward-looking kid. He's still cute, but I'm happy to say that he's changed for the better. He's grown over the years, put on lots of muscle, and filled out nicely.

I've seen him a few times since I left school, whenever our paths have crossed in the music world, but I've never talked to him. My eyes were always drawn to him whenever I saw him, like our secret smiles continued. I know he didn't recognize me, but it was nice to pretend we still had a connection.

I'm not a short girl. At 5' 10", I'm taller than all my girlfriends, but that also means when I wear heels, I'm taller than a lot of guys. And I love to wear heels. It makes me feel powerful. But I could wear my favorite stilettos next to Mikey and still be a few inches shorter than him.

My ex, Thomas, was 5'11" and refused to let me wear them. He always told me it would make him look stupid if his fiancée was taller than him.

Looking back, there were so many red flags in my relationship with Thomas, but I didn't see any of them until right at the end.

Why does Tom never clean up after himself? I feel like I live with a teenage boy and he thinks I'm his mom.

Grabbing his shirt, I pick it up and get a waft of perfume. I don't wear perfume, and if I did, it wouldn't smell like cat piss. I almost gag.

I look closer at the shirt and see a red lipstick mark on the collar. I don't wear red lipstick. Tom told me it was trashy.

I see red. Tom has been out a lot lately. You'd think he would be home with me, trying to cheer me up. I did just lose my best friend.

"What the fuck is this?" I yell, throwing the shirt at Tom.

He looks at me like I'm stupid. "Um, my shirt?"

"Well, no shit, Sherlock. I'm talking about the red lipstick. Are you sleeping with someone else?"

This isn't the first time I've suspected it, but it's the first time I've had proof.

"Who are you to fucking judge, Tia?" he spits at me. "You're the biggest slut I know. You've been sleeping with Travis for our whole relationship and I don't say shit."

I take a step back. I feel like I was slapped across the face.

"I never slept with Travis," is all I can manage to choke out.

How could he think that? Travis was my client and best friend. He was like a brother to me. And now he's gone.

"Yeah, right, Tia. You've been crying for fucking weeks. You never get out of bed; you aren't there for me."

I'm not there for him?

"My best friend died, Tom! Of course, I've been sad."

"You don't grieve that hard over just a friend," he insists stubbornly, as if it's some sort of excuse for his behavior.

"Get out of my apartment!" I scream.

"It's our apartment, and I'm not going anywhere."

"It's my name on the agreement. You didn't want to sign. So, it's my apartment." I take my ring off and throw it at his face. "The wedding is off. Get the fuck out! I never want to see you again."

"You can't do that. I won't get my money back from the deposits."

Seriously? That's what he's mad about? He isn't pissed that I just broke up with him? He's mad that he can't get his money back. Typical.

"Tough shit. Maybe you should have thought about that before you cheated on me and called me a slut. Now, GET OUT!" I scream at the top of my lungs.

I don't care if my neighbors hear. Maybe they'll call the cops and they can help me kick this piece of shit out of here.

"Whatever, Tia. I'll be by tomorrow to get my stuff."

"Good. You'd better get it all, because I'm changing the locks and never want to see your face again," I tell him.

That day was horrible, but I'm glad I got Tom out of my life.

I wasn't unhappy with Tom in the beginning, but now I realized that I'd been slowly losing myself. I loved him and forgot to love myself. I stopped doing a lot of things because Tom didn't like them.

Our whole relationship was all about Tom. He was always talking about getting married and having kids right away. He talked about our life without listening to what I wanted. He told me I should quit my job and just be a stay at home mom, but that's not something I want. I loved my job, but when the band broke up, I thought maybe that was what I should do.

I'm glad I saw him for what he really was before it was too late.

I've been working for Eaststreet Consulting since just after they opened. They were a small consulting company then, but they've since grown to be one of the biggest in Sienna, Oregon. I was nineteen when I first started and was supposed to just be working as a receptionist. But they didn't have enough managers and this new band needed a manager and was willing to sign a ten-year contract with the company. (That is unheard-of in this industry. What if they hated the manager? They would be stuck with that person, or at least that company, for ten years.) So, I convinced Greg Hastis to give them to me. I'm pretty sure he didn't have faith in the band or me, but he gave them to me anyway.

That band was the Broken Hearts. Over the last eight years, they have sold over two hundred million records and have had two albums go multi-platinum. I helped them get to where they are today, and they will go down in history as one of the best bands ever.

Now that the Broken Hearts are no longer together, I'm in need of a new client. And seeing Mikey Ecosta in our waiting area gives me a brilliant idea.

Now I just have to convince Greg that this big idea is best for the company.

I take a look at myself in the mirror and run my fingers through my hair. I look amazing in my six-inch heels and skinny jeans, with a cute tank top that shows a bit of cleavage, but not too much. My long white-blonde hair cascades down my back. My bluish-green eyes look fantastic with this new eye shadow I bought. I never had confidence as a kid, but I have it in spades now.

I can do this.

Walking to Greg's office, I take a deep breath. I am the best manager this company has; he would be a fool to not give me this client. But Greg is a fool, and this is going to be a fight. His best friend also works for the company, and hasn't had good luck with keeping clients, but Greg still tries to throw him a bone, even if it isn't good for the client or the company.

"Hey, Greg," I say, knocking on the door and walking into his office with my shoulders squared and my head held high.

Greg gives me a nod but doesn't say anything.

I can do this, I remind myself.

I close my eyes and take one more deep breath.

"I saw Mikey Ecosta in the lobby. Is he signing on with Eaststreet Consulting?" I ask.

"Yeah," Greg murmurs, not even looking at me.

Okay, so this isn't going well.

"Well, as you know, I don't have a client right now, and I was thinking I would be the perfect fit for a client like Mikey. I know the industry better than anyone here. I have a great track record and took a band from being unheard-of to being a household name with two multi-platinum records."

Greg knows all this, but I am going to have to sell myself hard to even get a chance at managing Mikey.

He finally looks up at me and sighs, his shoulders slumping. "Listen, sweetheart, I know you're good, but I think Carl would be a better suit for Mikey. You could be his personal assistant. You know, give yourself some time before you take on the full job of manager again."

Is he fucking kidding me? Personal assistant? I've been doing this job for eight years and am the best manager this company fucking has. Hell, I used to have my own personal assistant of sorts. But Greg wants to give his biggest client to Creepy Carl just because they're friends? What a misogynistic pig.

"You know I'm not a personal assistant, Greg," I argue, trying not to sound pissed off. "I don't need time. I know I can take Mikey's career to the next level *now*."

"It's already settled, sweetheart. Either you're his personal assistant or you can walk," he says smugly.

Oh, my God. I have given this company eight years of my fucking life, made them a hell of a lot more money than they paid me, made this company what it is today, and he's telling me to just fucking walk if I don't want to be demoted to being the person who fetches Carl's coffee in the morning?

"Fine," I spit out.

"Great! You can start next week; I'll send you a link with everything you'll need."

"No, Greg," I snap as I walk towards the door. "I'm walking, and you can go fuck yourself."

I slam the door behind me and head towards my office.

These idiots have *never* appreciated what I've done for them. They didn't know what I was going to bring to the company when I first started, so my contract is pretty basic. I didn't even sign a do not compete clause, so I can work for another company or even just go solo tomorrow. I don't need this piece of shit company to succeed as a talent manager. *They* need *me*, and now they've lost me.

I don't keep much personal stuff here, so it doesn't take me more than ten minutes to throw everything I have into a box and walk out of my office.

I see Mikey sitting on the couch looking at his phone. I freeze for a moment, thinking back to who we were as kids. I get a little nervous, and some of those old feelings come back, but my adrenaline kicks in and I know what I need to do.

I could technically poach him if I want to. And oh, do I want to. I grab my notebook from the box write my personal cell phone number and my name on a sheet of paper, then tear the paper out and walk over to Mikey.

"This company is a piece of shit, and they can't handle your kind of talent," I tell him. "If you want a real manager, you'll hire me. I'm the previous manager of the Broken Hearts, so you know my track record is good. If you want references, I'll give them to you. But I can guarantee you, I'll be a much better fit for you than Creepy Carl."

I hand him the piece of paper and strut out. Fuck this place.

MIKEY ECOSTA

I don't want to be looking for a new manager, but Chris can't manage me anymore. His wife recently got diagnosed with cancer and needs all his focus on her.

So, here I am at Eaststreet Consulting. I look around at the white walls and off-white furniture, unimpressed. It looks kind of dingey and dated in here, like they haven't kept up with the cleaning, or with building maintenance at all, really.

Honestly, Eastsreet has a shitty track record for the most part, and I wouldn't even be here if my buddy Jay hadn't recommended this one, as he put it, badass manager. I mean, he should know. She was his manager and took his band, the Broken Hearts, from being nobodies to being a worldwide success.

I've had a great career so far, but my last album was a huge flop. My fans hated it, and I got into a real slump with all the bad stuff that was said about my music. But with a top-notch manager like Tia, I feel like I could get back on track and take my career even further than it's already gone.

I look at the time on my phone and realize I've been sitting on this awful couch for an hour, still waiting on the CEO to come talk to me. This is shit service. I'm not even sure I'll stay. I mean, without the Broken Hearts anymore, this company will crumble. They need a big-name client to keep them from going under, and not to sound arrogant, but I *am* the big-name client they need.

I've worked my ass off in this career and have a pretty awesome fan base. Chris has been with me since the beginning, and I've been doing this for about ten years now. I would not be where I am today without Chris, and I'm so grateful for everything he has done for me. But now I need to move on, so hopefully, I can get Tia as my new manager.

Out of nowhere, this tall, beautiful blonde comes storming out of an office. She is sexier than anyone I have ever seen. She stops at the reception desk to write something down, and I can't help but admire her ass. Fuck, this woman is gorgeous. With fire in her step, she struts up to me and shoves the piece of paper in my hand. I am taken aback by her mesmerizing blue-green eyes. These eyes…I feel like I've seen them before, but I can't place where. Her lips are plump, and for some reason, I really want to kiss her.

I'm not even paying full attention to what she is saying because I can't stop staring at her. God, she looks so hot when she's mad. Maybe I could put that same flush on her face in my bed.

After my mind returns from its momentary vacation in the gutter, she's already storming to the elevator.

"This company is fucked without me!" she yells as the elevator doors close.

I look at the paper and see her pretty writing sprawled out across the page.

Wow. So that was Tia Marie.

Jay told me she was a firecracker, but he didn't mention how drop-dead gorgeous she is. I have to adjust my pants with all the thoughts I just had about Tia in my bed, under me, on top of me, on all fours… Fuck, that was a super-hot image.

What I don't know is why this company let her go. She was clearly their best manager, and now I have no reason to sign with them. If I were them, I would have been groveling at her feet for her to stay. But their loss could still be my gain. I'm not going to let Tia get away this easily.

I'm just about to walk out when some dude in a shitty suit comes walking up to me.

"Mr. Ecosta! So nice to finally meet you in person. I'm Greg Hastis, the CEO here at Eaststreet Consulting," he says with a sleazy smile that makes me want to punch his lights out.

So this is the fucking idiot who let Tia walk out of here. Yeah, I'm even less impressed now than I was before.

"I'm so sorry for that little show." He waves his hands around a lot when he talks and it's really fucking annoying. "That was just one of our minor assistants, and she's angry that we had to let her go."

Is this guy for real? Does he not know that I know who she is and what she has done for this company? Just as I'm about to confront him, some dweeb in big glasses comes walking out and slaps Greg on the back.

"Hi, Mr. Ecosta. I'm Carl and I'll be your new manager," he says smugly, like he thinks this is already a done deal when I haven't even signed a damn contract yet.

This guy has got to be fucking kidding me. I am so done here, but I think I want to have a little fun first.

"Gentlemen, it's so nice to meet you, but I was actually just coming here to tell you that I've found a manager. And, shitty for you, she just walked out that door." I get up, put my phone in my pocket, and slide my sunglasses on. "So, if you'll excuse me, I have to go catch my new manager."

Their wide-eyed, deer-in-headlights expressions are almost identical. I have a perfect shit-eating grin plastered on my face as I head to the elevator. Like I told these idiots, I have to go catch a manager. A super-hot, tall, curvaceous, bombshell manager. And maybe I can convince her to mix business with pleasure.

TIA

I'm fuming as I head towards the parking lot. Those jackasses will regret letting me go.

I mean, who the fuck do they think they are? I may not have been a founding member, but I helped build that company. Fuck, this is so frustrating.

I just hope I can do this on my own.

I get to my car and the panic attack comes. I hold the steering wheel and try to take some deep breaths, anything to help calm myself down. Did I seriously just quit my job?

Will Mikey call me? Probably not. He doesn't even know who I am. Why would he quit a big-name company for some girl who just lost her shit in front of him, and told the whole office to get fucked?

As I'm hyperventilating, my phone starts ringing. Unknown number. That's odd.

"Tia Marie speaking," I say, trying not to let the caller know how upset I am.

"Hey beautiful," this dark raspy voice croons on the other line.

The voice goes straight to my girl parts. God, I didn't even know that was possible.

"Um, who is this?" I ask. Not many people have my personal number.

"Well, you just gave me your number and told me you would be my manager so I'm just calling to ask when we start."

Oh, my God! It's Mikey! And he called me beautiful? Maybe my panic attack has caused me to hallucinate. Or, more likely, I'm probably actually passed out on the pavement outside my car, and this is all a dream.

"You there?"

My eyes go wide. This isn't a dream. It's actually happening, and I'm not even responding.

"Um, yes, Mr. Ecosta," I quickly recover myself. "You will not regret this decision, but can I ask why you didn't stay with Eaststreet Consulting?"

Most people don't leave a big organization to chase after a manager who's never gone on her own and has only ever had one client. Yes, they were a huge client, but still. You would think Mikey would want to go with the safest option, and the safest option is being in the hands of a company like Eaststreet.

"Because I was only there for you, sweetheart," he says.

Well, fuck. How do I respond to that?

"Meet me tomorrow at noon. I'll text you my address and I'll have lunch ready," I tell him.

I can't afford to take him out for lunch because I just quit my job. And now I have to figure out all the legal shit so I don't get screwed over, and to protect the client of course.

"Sounds great, beautiful. I can't wait."

And just as fast at the conversation started, it ends.

Oh. My. God. This is really happening. I've always thought about going on my own, but the plan was always to manage the Broken Hearts. We only had two years left and then were going to do our own thing. The guys and I talked about it a lot. But the Broken Hearts are a thing of the past now, and here I am going on my own, alone. Damn, it feels great.

I throw my keys on the counter when I get home and call my best girlfriend, Leah. I know, I know, Leah and Tia. We get jokes about it all the time. But thankfully, Leah is a lawyer and can hopefully help me out with a contract for Mikey and get me started on the right foot.

"Bitch, why are you calling me at two in the afternoon? Shouldn't you be busy trying to land a new client?"

I smile. Leah has never been one to actually say hello, and she loves her caller ID.

"Well, funny you should say that." I pause for dramatic effect. "I just landed a huge client, but I also quit my job."

Silence. I for the first time ever, have shocked my friend speechless.

"Which is why I'm calling you; I need your help," I continue.

"Are you fucking serious?" she shrieks. "You finally did it? You're going on your own? Oh, my God! I'm so happy for you!"

She squeals into the phone for a bit and I giggle. I can practically see her jumping up and down. Yeah, this feels right. And it's about time. I know what I'm doing. I just need to stop doubting myself. Sometimes that small part of the old me pops up and my self-doubt shows, but I know I'm damn good at what I do.

"So, are you going to help me or what?" I ask. "I won't be able to pay you at first, but once things get rolling, I'll definitely pay you back for whatever you do for me and my client."

"Oh, my God, Tia. Of course I'll help you! And we can figure out fees later. I trust you!"

God, it's nice having friends. And it's even nicer having friends in high places. I tell her all the details she needs to know to draw up the contract for me. Then I sit down to start planning everything I need to do to get ready for my meeting with Mikey.

I set up a list of questions I need him to answer and a list of things I think will help his career move forward and upward.

By the time I finish everything, it's ten p.m. and time for a glass of wine and some reality TV. I also send a text to Jay, one of my best friends and the former lead guitarist of the Broken Hearts.

Me: Guess what I did today?

Jay: Got laid?

I shake my head. Leave it to Jay to take it there.

Me: OMG I wish. Nope… Quit my job.

Jay: About fucking time! And Mikey is your new client?

Oh, my God. *That's* how Mikey knew about me. He must be friends with Jay. Makes sense. They run in a similar circle, and Jay always had my back, so I shouldn't be surprised.

Me: Yes! I guess I should thank you?

Jay: You're welcome, sissy. You know I always have your back. I just told him the truth. You're the best there is and if I didn't have Melly I would want you for myself.

Melly is Jay's wife. She was previously working for a different managing company but has since gone on her own to manage Jay's solo career, and to help him with setting up his own record label, Broken Ax Records. He named the company after Travis and their old band.

Melly is so amazing and treats Jay like a king. I loved her the moment I met her. Jay was always the sex symbol for the group. Had a different woman every night. I never thought I'd see the day he settled down.

I still remember the first time Jay brought Melly to meet the band. Jay was being his usual cocky asshole self and she put him right in his place. I knew from that moment she was a keeper. You couldn't be with Jay Coldheart without having a backbone. I smile at the memory.

I would have loved to manage Jay's solo career, to stay with familiar and family. But I know he's in fantastic hands with Melly and that makes me happy.

Me: Thanx Jay. I'm nervous but super excited! Thanx for always having my back. Love you, bro.

Things are finally feeling good after so much bad. Tomorrow is a new day and I'm going to rock it!

Before heading to bed, I decide to text Mikey and ask him a couple of questions.

Me: How long did you know your previous manger?

His response is pretty quick. He must be on his phone a lot.

Mikey: I met Chris in college and we became instant friends. Do you have anyone in your life you just jived with super-fast?

My thoughts go to Leah. The moment we met, I knew she was my person.

Me: Yeah, my best friend Leah. She's my person.

Mikey: Leah and Tia? Really?

Me: Yeah, we get that a lot. But it's not like we can change our names.

I mean, I could go by Patricia, but she doesn't exist anymore.

Me: So where do you see your career going in the next 5 years?

Mikey: Can we talk about that tomorrow? I want to get to know you more. We are going to be working closely together. We should at least be friends.

Friends? There was nothing I wanted more when I was younger. Can Mikey and I really be friends now? I guess only time will tell.

Me: What do you want to know?

Mikey: What's your favorite color?

Me: Easy, blue. Yours?

Mikey: Red. I bet you look really good in red.

Tia: Wouldn't you like to know? Next question.

Mikey: Do you sleep naked?

Me: Mr. Ecosta, can we please keep this PG?

Mikey: Fine. Are you close with your family?

Wow, I wasn't expecting that question. I am close with my dad, but my mom isn't in the picture.

Me: With my dad, yeah. What about you?

Mikey: Yeah, family is very important to me. My parents are the best people. I want my marriage to be like theirs.

Me: A romantic, huh? That doesn't suit the persona I've read about.

Mikey: Don't believe everything you read, sweetheart.

Shivers run down my spine. Ugh! Did he have to call me *sweetheart* of all things? Every time I hear it now, I think of my sleazy ex-boss. Thank God I don't have to listen to his derogatory comments anymore.

Me: You're right, I should know better.

Mikey: So, are you sure you won't answer the sleep naked question?

Me: It's getting late. I'm going to email you some paperwork that I need you to bring tomorrow. Goodnight, Mikey.

Mikey: Goodnight beautiful.

I still can't get over the fact that Mikey Ecosta is calling me beautiful. Little Patricia would die right about now.

The morning light shines through my blinds and I wake up with a smile on my face.

Today is the day!

Leah got the contracts all sorted out and gave me some pointers on starting my own business, which is technically what I am doing. She gave me phone numbers for a few PA's and an accountant for when I need them in the future.

Right now, I'm happy just managing one client by myself, but I'm not afraid of one day opening my own consulting firm and hiring people to work under me for other clients.

As I'm finishing making my famous lasagna and putting it in the oven, I hear my phone ring. I run to the living room and grab it without looking at the caller ID.

"Tia Marie speaking." I surprise myself with how happy I sound.

I've spent so much time the past 6 months being depressed and couldn't see the light at the end of the tunnel for the longest time. But now I'm out of the tunnel and the future is looking bright!

"Hey, beautiful!"

God, that voice is so sexy, and man what it does to my body. But I have a rule, and that is no mixing business with pleasure.

"Hello, Mr. Ecosta. How are you today?"

"So much better now that I've heard your voice," he croons.

How am I going to keep things strictly professional with him when he is clearly a huge flirt? It's probably how he talks to everyone though; he's known for being a player. That's it. I'll just keep reminding myself what a player he is, and it will make things easier. At least I hope so.

"Are you still coming over for lunch and our meeting?" I ask, trying to keep things professional because one of us has to.

"Yes. I'm looking forward to it, sweetheart. I was just calling to ask if you wanted me to bring anything over."

"Just yourself and the paperwork I emailed you yesterday." I smile; it's sweet of him to offer.

"Sounds great, beautiful. I'll see you in an hour."

And just like that, he hangs up again.

I'm smiling so wide, and I'm not sure if it's because I'm happy to have a new client or if it's Mikey himself that makes me happy. I'm going to have to tread very lightly with this situation.

Exactly one hour later, Michael William Ecosta is standing at my front door, and oh my, does he pull off the fitted dark jeans well. He has flowers and a bottle of wine. My favorite wine to be exact. That has me wondering if he's been talking to Jay again.

"Thank you, but you didn't have to," I insist, taking the flowers and wine to the kitchen.

I'm putting the flowers into a vase when Mikey comes up behind me, and whispers into my ear.

"I saw them and thought of you, so I had to buy them."

I get shivers down my spine. He's so close that I can feel his breath on my neck, and my body is reacting. I close my eyes and take a deep breath before I turn around. Once I'm facing him, he puts his hands on either side of me on the counter, causing me to glance up into his beautiful ice-blue eyes. Those same eyes that used to smile at me as a kid. The ones that told me I would be alright. I'm having trouble catching a full breath. I was not expecting this today, and I don't know how I feel about it.

"You are so beautiful. These flowers can't even touch your beauty," he says, staring into my eyes as he traces a finger over my arm.

I take a deep breath and his scent surrounds me. He smells like pine and peppermint. Such a manly smell. I don't know what is happening or what I even want. This man has just met me and wants me? Or does he just want in my pants?

I put my hands on his chest and push him away. The second I do, my heart hurts. I had a crush on Mikey when I was younger, and I remember so much about him. I didn't know those feelings would come back the first time I was around him in close to fifteen years.

"Thank you for the compliment, but I think we should start the business meeting," I whisper, pushing past him. "The lasagna still needs a bit so we will have time to go over some of the details and look at the contract."

I move to the dining area, trying not to look into his eyes, because I know if

I do, I will want to kiss him.

I sit at the table, where I have my stuff set up, and motion for him to do the same.

"So, I had my lawyer draw up a contract last night. It's pretty straightforward, giving us both protection. I have a figure which I think is completely fair for my salary in there, and what costs will be covered by you and what I will cover out of my salary," I tell him.

I hand him the contract, and he smiles at me. It's very much like the smiles he used to give me at school when no one was looking.

He takes the papers, but doesn't even look at them. "I'm sure it's perfect, sweetheart, but I'll have to send it to my lawyer to go over because I never understand all the legal mumbo jumbo."

"Of course," I mumble, giving him a shy smile.

God, he's gorgeous, and when he smiles a genuine smile, he has a dimple on his left cheek. I forgot about that.

"Can we go over what your previous manager has been doing for you and where you want your career to go now?"

He gives me that panty-melting smile again. God, this is going to be a long afternoon.

"Sure. Or you could just call Chris and talk to him about all that shit. We already talked and he said he would help transition you into the position," he tells me.

That is so kind. I would love to get inside Chris's head and discuss what he has been doing, what was going well and what wasn't, where he was hoping to take Mikey's career next, all of it.

"That would be amazing!" I say enthusiastically. "As you know, I was with the last band I was managing since the beginning, so I've never started a job in the middle before. Also, I've never done it all on my own before, so if you could bear with me while I work out some of the kinks, that would be awesome."

I bite my lip. I do that when I'm nervous. His eyes automatically zoom in on my lips, then quickly back to my eyes.

"Chris could probably help you with some of that as well. He's been with me from the beginning, but he never worked for another company, so if there's anything you need help with, ask him. He feels shitty about leaving me, but with his wife's cancer and all, he just can't give me the attention he wants to."

Mikey's smile drops. I know he and Chris have been friends since college, so it must be really hard for him to work with someone else. Also, it must be hard to see your best friend's wife go through a cancer struggle. I can't imagine what Chris must be going through, dealing with that.

"I'm so sorry to hear that, but it makes you a really good friend to let him have the time he needs with his wife," I say quietly.

I reach across the table and touch his hand. I'm trying not to be awkward, but I just don't know how to respond in situations like this. Hell, I laughed at my best friend's funeral because I didn't know what else to do.

Mikey looks at our hands, but doesn't pull away. "They say she'll get through it; she has good odds. But Chris told me life's too short and even after she's in remission he just wants to be with her and do everything together."

"That's so sweet of him. She's a lucky girl to have found someone who loves her so much."

Maybe one day I'll find that kind of love. A love that accepts me for me. But I highly doubt it. My last relationship didn't pan out too well, so I don't have entirely high hopes for future relationships.

Just then, my timer for the lasagna goes off. I pull my hand away as if Mikey has burned me. Saved by the bell. I don't want to be talking about relationships with Mikey Ecosta of all people.

"I'll go get the lasagna. You stay here and make yourself comfortable," I say, disappearing into the kitchen before he can respond.

MIKEY

I did *not* mean to come on so strong. I know I've pushed her away. Fuck.

When she opened the door in her skin-tight jeans that showed off that perfect ass and low-cut top that gave me just a glimpse of her huge tits, I couldn't help but make a move. This girl has it all. Curves for days and the longest blonde hair. Hair I can see splayed out across my pillow.

I was going to play it cool. Maybe make a comment about how beautiful she is, a little bit of light flirting. But when she started to put the flowers in a vase and I got a good glimpse of that ass, I couldn't stop myself.

I groan just thinking about it.

I wanted to take her right there in her fucking kitchen, and I don't even know her. But there's something about her that I'm just drawn to. Like the universe is telling me this woman is for me.

I'm your typical rock star. I don't do feelings. I fuck 'em and leave 'em. It's what I'm known for and it's what I'm good at. I did feelings once and that fucked me over, so never again.

At least that was what I told myself before I walked into Tia Marie's house. When she turned in my arms and our eyes locked, I could have sworn I knew her. I lost my breath. Those blue-green eyes dug into my soul. I know I haven't ever met Tia personally before, besides seeing her at some events here and there.

I've never even talked to her until yesterday. But I could swear those eyes look like someone I used to know. Except her name wasn't Tia.

Now I'm sitting in Tia's dining room, working very hard to get my erection under control. I might have fucked up earlier by coming on too strong, but I can still fix this.

I'm Mikey fucking Ecosta. I always get what I want. And right now, I want Tia Marie. If that has to be as just my manager for right now, I can deal with that.

While she is getting the lasagna, I quickly go over the papers she gave me. I smile at her little sticky notes and highlighted parts. She's definitely an organized girl. Her ideas for the future are awesome and the contract seems fine. I do need to send it to my lawyer for a double look, but the figures seem to be on par, except that I think I want to give her more money than what she is asking for. I paid Chris way more than that, so it only seems fair.

She comes back in with the most delicious-smelling lasagna ever.

"God, that smells good." My mouth is literally watering.

She gives me another of her gorgeous smiles and sets down the food. As she bends over, I get the best look at her tits. Fuck, I want to see those in the flesh. She goes back into the kitchen to get the wine I brought and some glasses. I adjust myself again once she leaves.

Down, boy. Now is not the time to play, I scold myself.

"This is my favorite wine," she admits, pouring us both a glass. "How did you know?"

I'm not going to admit that I called Jay and asked for some help, so I decide to tell a white lie instead.

"Just a lucky guess."

I wink at her and help myself to some lasagna. I can tell by the look on Tia's face that she isn't buying the lucky guess comment, but she *is* letting it go.

"The contract looks good," I choke out after a couple bites. Fuck, this is amazing lasagna. "But why are you underselling yourself? Don't you think you're worth more?"

I'm curious. She has an amazing track record and great references. The figure that she put in the contract is nowhere near what she could ask for.

She stares at me for a little bit.

"I *know* I'm worth more than that, but I just figured since this was my first time going out on my own, I shouldn't shoot too high of a figure," she finally says.

Avoiding eye contact, she twirls the wine in her glass before taking a sip.

"Sweetheart, you're worth so much more than the figure you quoted, and I only want you, so there is no way I'm paying you what you quoted. I'm doubling it," I tell her.

She chokes on her wine and covers her mouth; I can't help but chuckle. God, she's even more beautiful when she blushes.

I'm dead serious about doubling her figure. That's how much I was paying Chris, so it doesn't bother me to pay her the same.

"Don't even think about arguing about it. You and I both know how much you're worth, so you can just thank me and we'll move on."

I know I'm coming across as cocky and forward, but it's who I am.

"Thank you," she agrees, giving a shy smile.

"I really like some of these ideas you have, Tia. I know you are going to be great for my career."

She blushes again and takes another sip of her wine. "Although it's not written down, I think you could use a revamp on your social media accounts. Whoever is running it right now is seriously lacking. It feels very blank and vague. Even if you aren't posting yourself, it should still feel like you. And your website needs an overhaul as well."

Wow. She's forward, and I love it.

"Um, I run my social media myself," I tell her, lifting an eyebrow.

I thought I was doing a good job, but I guess not. I mean, I know I don't post a lot, but I didn't know it was coming across as "blank and vague."

"Well, maybe we should appoint someone to do that," she blurts out, not even phased by my comment.

"Okay. Do you have someone in mind?" I ask.

I don't know if Tia knows, but I don't have a personal assistant. My whole team was Chris and one girl who helped sometimes when I was on tour. Chris did so much work. I was always telling him to hire someone, but he's too much of a control freak to give up control to anyone else.

"I can do it for now," she tells me after a couple bites of her food. "But I'll eventually want to hire someone."

"That's fine by me. I told Chris to hire more people, but he didn't like giving up control to anyone."

Tia giggles. God, I love that sound.

"I thought I was a control freak, but I know when to get help and when I can't do it all myself," she says.

After we finish lunch and go over some of the paperwork, I know it's time to go.

Standing at her door, I so badly want to kiss her, but I know I'm already pushing my boundaries.

"I'll call Chris tonight and then text you so we can set up a date to go over and finalize everything," she tells me, smiling.

God, she has the best smile.

I lean down and give her a kiss on the cheek. I get a whiff of strawberries and vanilla; I wish I could bury my face in her hair.

"Sounds amazing, sweetheart. Can't wait to start working with you," I say, flashing her another smile.

And then I leave. I know I'm not going to be able to get this girl out of my head. I need to make her mine. I don't entirely know how yet, but when I want something, I get it. And I want Tia Marie.

Five

TIA

Well, that went well.

But why am I disappointed that Mikey didn't kiss me?

I lean against the wall and throw my head back. I know this wasn't a date. It was a business meeting, and I don't mix business with pleasure. But it felt like he *wanted* to kiss me, and I wanted him to.

How am I going to work with this man when feelings are clearly going to be in the way? He may not remember me, but I remember everything about him. It's kind of impossible to not develop feelings for the only person who was kind to you as a child.

I start cleaning up, and I can't stop thinking about Mikey in my kitchen. The way his light eyes darkened when he was staring at me. The way I wanted to offer my body to him.

I slap the countertop in frustration. I need to stop thinking about him.

I think my brain is fucked up because I haven't had sex in around six months.

Maybe the best thing to do is to go out and get laid. Maybe then I'll be able to think about something other than sex.

Grabbing my phone from the counter, I call the man with a plan.

"Hey, sissy! What's up?" Jay answers after the first ring.

"I need to blow off some steam. Care to throw me a party and invite a bunch of good-looking single guys?"

He chuckles on the other end of the phone. "I can arrange that. I was just talking to Melly about possibly having a party anyways."

"Yay!" I cheer. "I'll see you tonight."

"See you soon, sissy."

I hang up, beaming slightly. Now it's time to get ready.

A few hours later, I am in the middle of an awesome party. Jay has pulled out all the stops. The DJ is amazing, and there are a *ton* of good-looking guys.

When I first arrive, I see Tyler Shepherd, the former drummer of the Broken Hearts.

"Tyler!" I shout before launching myself into his arms. "It's so good to see you! How is Cali treating you?"

Tyler's smile could light up any room. "So good, but I miss you all."

"How long are you in town for? We should go for dinner."

"I'd really like that, sissy. I'm in town for a week. Just sold my house and I'm moving out the last of my stuff. Corey is actually here too, helping me move. He couldn't make the party, but we should all go out together."

I smile and nod. "Oh, my God! It's like a band reunion."

"Yeah, everyone except Travis," he says, his smile faltering.

I frown; I can't let myself think about him. I need to change the subject and move on. I close my eyes for a second, trying to push the feelings down.

I force a smile on my face. "I'll text you tomorrow to set everything up."

Giving Tyler one more hug, I move farther into the house, towards the thumping of the music. I've always loved to dance and right now, I'm in the mood to just move.

I feel great today; I'm wearing a bright red, skin-hugging dress. It's short and shows lots of cleavage. I feel so sexy, and my heels make my legs look like they go on for days.

I am in the middle of the makeshift dance floor working up a sweat, letting the music take control of my body, when I feel hands on my hips. I don't look to see who it is. I don't care. I've got a good buzz going and those strong hands are doing things to my body. Maybe this will be the lucky guy I take home with me tonight.

I start grinding my ass into the guy's crotch, and his hands drop lower on my hips. As I lean back into him, I can tell he is tall. Even in my six-inch heels, this guy is still at least a couple inches taller than me.

This guy can *dance*. I spend 2 songs not even looking at him, just dancing and being lost in the music.

When the song changes to a slow one, I decide it's time to turn around and see who the mystery guy is. I'm frozen as I look up into sky-blue eyes. I don't know who I was expecting, but it was definitely not Mikey.

"What the hell are you doing here?" I shriek.

I was just grinding up on my client. The guy I'm slightly crushing on. The one I'm here to forget about.

"Whoa, beautiful. Is that how you talk to all the guys you dry hump on the dance floor?" he smirks.

Fuck, he has the cockiest smile.

There are so many things I want to yell at him, but I need a drink. So I just turn and walk away instead of saying any of them.

Why in the hell would Jay invite Mikey? I pretty much told him I wanted to get laid, and he knows Mikey is my client. Why would I want him at my party?

I get my drink and go to find Jay. When I enter the living room, I find him and Melly making out like a couple of horny teenagers. They are a nauseatingly cute couple. They have been together for five years, but still act like they are in the honeymoon phase.

"Hey, you two," I call out so they'll acknowledge my existence.

"Hi, Tia!" Melly beams as she breaks away from her husband.

She is a gorgeous woman. Her light brown hair with blonde highlights stops just above her shoulders and frames her oval face perfectly. Her super bright green eyes captivate everyone, and they glow when she is really happy. Being a whole foot shorter than Jay, you would think they would look awkward, but they fit perfectly together.

"Why did you invite Mikey?" I ask Jay.

"'Cause he's my friend," he says slowly.

I roll my eyes. Leave it to Jay to just make it seem so simple.

"Why? Are you mad at him or something? I thought you guys were working together."

"We are working together, *Jeffery,*" I bite out his real name. He's been going by Jay for so long that everyone thinks that is his real name, and I don't blame him for having everyone believe that. Jeffery is a pretty awful name. "Which is why it's awkward to have him at a party I asked you to throw me, where I wanted to hook up with some guy."

I can be completely honest with Jay. He's always treated me like one of the guys, so I talk to him the same way.

Jay starts laughing, and I get even more mad. Fuck! This is so not funny.

"Whatever, *Jeffery,*" I shout, throwing back my drink.

I storm off. I don't need Jay making fun of me anymore. I take a deep breath letting the air fill my lungs and cool me down. I can still have a good time; I just have to find a guy.

I enter the backyard and relish in the feel of the fresh air on my body. It's June, so it's nice and warm outside tonight.

Jay has a beautiful backyard, and a fire is going. Looking over, I see a few good-looking guys sitting around the fire-pit on the comfy lounge furniture. I saunter over to them and sit down.

"How are you guys tonight?" I purr, sitting down and crossing my legs in a way that shows off a bit more thigh, but is still kind of classy.

The guy sitting next to me is gorgeous! He has shaggy blonde hair and light brown eyes. He told me his name, but I already forgot it. Not that it really matters. I'm not here to find a boyfriend. Just a fun one-night stand.

As I sit there drinking the beer he gave me, I start to relax. I almost forget about the super tall rock star that had his hands all over me earlier. Almost.

"So, this is a pretty awesome party," sexy stranger says to me, leaning in and resting his hand on my bare thigh.

"Mmm-hmm," I answer, smiling.

This guy is great, but my mind keeps wandering. Finally, I say fuck it and climb into sexy stranger's lap. I smash my lips to his and taste the beer, and I think cigarette smoke. Gross. I hate cigarettes. He doesn't complain about my forwardness. He just lets out a chuckle and starts groping me as we make out. I can feel his erection pressing against me in all the right places and I'm getting wet thinking about what could happen. Just as I am thinking about taking this guy to a spare bedroom, I'm ripped from his lap.

What the fuck?

As I turn around, I see Mikey's red face. He looks *pissed,* and fuck, it's hot.

MIKEY

I've been wandering around the party, hoping to find Tia. She looked pissed when she figured out it was me she was grinding against on the dance floor.

Jay told me that Tia has a rule about not being involved with clients, but when I saw her lost in the music, I knew there was no way I could keep my hands to myself. And there are always exceptions to a rule, right?

When she looked up into my eyes, I could see something. Lust? Want? I wasn't sure what. But then I saw anger. I swear, those eyes remind me of a girl from long ago. Eyes like hers aren't common. But it can't be her.

After she leaves me standing on the dance floor alone, I go to find Jay. I had been talking to him earlier and he said he was throwing this party for Tia and told me I was more than welcome to join. He didn't know I had a thing for her, so I agreed to come. I wasn't even planning on making a move. I just wanted to see her again.

Finally, I find Jay. He is with Melly, cuddled on a couch in one of his lounge rooms.

"What the fuck is going on with you and Tia?" he asks as soon as he sees me.

"Nothing," I lie.

Well, it isn't totally a lie. There *isn't* anything going on. Yet.

"Yeah, so that's why she came yelling at me because you're here," he presses.

Fuck. She's mad that I'm here?

"I don't know. I thought everyone was having a good time. Want me to leave?" I ask.

Please say no, I silently plead. I really want to apologize to Tia, get things back in good standing.

"Nah, man. She'll get over it." He turns his attention back to Melly, and it's as if I'm not even there anymore.

I have to come up with a plan to get back on Tia's good side.

After grabbing a beer, I wander around inside for a while. She's nowhere to be found. Maybe she isn't even here anymore. Finally, I make my way outside and breathe in the fresh air.

The yard is big. How long is it going to take me to find her?

The flicker of the fire draws my eye and then I see her. Her bright red dress is like a beacon. But her lips are attached to someone else's.

I see red. I am fucking pissed, though I know I don't have any right to be. I know I should just walk away. She isn't mine, and clearly, she doesn't want to be. But I can't just stand by and watch her get groped by some random guy.

Storming over, I pull her off his lap. She looks stunned, but also really turned on. Fuck, that makes my dick hard immediately.

As I hold her, just staring at her and not saying a word, I'm more and more drawn to her. I can't help it. I lean down and kiss her.

Our mouths smash together, and she is putty in my hands. Her taste is like nothing I have experienced before. I want to take the kiss deeper, but quickly she pulls away and slaps me hard across the face.

"What the fuck, Mikey?" she shouts. "How dare you kiss me like that? You are *not* my boyfriend! You don't fucking own me! You are my client and that is all I want."

And with those words, she storms off.

You are my client and that is all I want.

Those words float around in my head.

As soon as she storms off, I call for an Uber. I have no idea if she ended up hooking up with the guy she was kissing or not. I guess I'm not allowed to care. She doesn't want me, which is very clear.

Still, I want her. I can't help it. There is a connection between us. It's something I've felt only once before, but that girl fell through my fingers. I can't let Tia do the same. I have to respect her if I want her to be my manager. If I keep pushing my luck, she won't want me as her client, and I won't have any part of her in my life. And that would kill me. I realize I *need* her in my life, and if it's only as my manager, then so be it.

Me: Sorry about everything. I know I acted like an ass.
Tia: It's fine.

I leave it at that. If I keep texting, I'm likely to make an ass of myself again.

TIA

Fuck me.

That kiss was everything! It reminded me of what I wanted to happen when I was a kid. I wanted to melt into him. To let him make sweet, passionate love to me, right there in front of the sexy stranger. But I also know he was being possessive, and frankly, that pisses me off.

I feel kind of bad for slapping him, but at least it got my point across. I don't date clients. I don't sleep with clients. Work and play are separate. I hope he got that message now. Hell, I hope *I* got that message now. I can *not* let feelings get involved. I need to put these feelings into check and move on as a professional.

I go home alone, sad and unsatisfied, and have a wet dream about Mikey.

I keep telling myself that eventually this crush will go away and Mikey and I can just be friends. Have a working relationship and nothing more.

I just really hope that's true, and that I can make that work.

Me: Sorry for slapping you last night, but I don't hook up with clients. If you would like to continue with me as your manager, we need to have a

strictly platonic relationship. Feelings make things difficult and I choose to keep them out of my work life.

I have been drafting that text all morning. If I want to be the manager I know I'm capable of being, I have to keep feelings out of my professional life. I want to be Mikey's manager; I'm not going to fuck that up with feelings or emotions. I am going to call Chris next and pick his brain.

Mikey: I'm sorry too. Can I see you today?

Me: Let's wait until Monday, when your lawyer has gone over your paperwork. At least then we will have more to discuss. Have a good weekend, Mr. Ecosta.

Mikey: You too, beautiful.

Ugh. He can't make anything easy, can he?

I write down all the questions I have for Chris and make the call.

We end up talking for three hours and I am so happy with the way things are turning out. I want the best for Mikey's career, and clearly, so does Chris. He gives me some great pointers on software to use and also gives me tons of files on Mikey that he has made since the beginning of his career, including his rider, which is going to save both me and Mikey a ton of time because we won't have to draft a new one for him.

I can't thank Chris enough for everything he tells me and gives me. It is going to make my job so much easier.

After I sort things out and send out a few emails, I am ready for lunch and some girl talk, so I call my bestie.

"Hey, bitch. Did you get laid last night?" she greets me.

I laugh. Leave it to Leah to be so blunt.

"No," I tell her. "I could use some good food and good talks. You free?"

"Always! Come here at one. I'll make your favorite."

I love having a bestie who loves to cook. It especially makes up for the fact I kind of hate cooking. I'm not a bad cook. My food tastes good. But I would totally prefer to pay someone else to cook for me.

I put on my favorite comfy pants and shirt and go over to Leah's. Since we're having homemade waffles and bacon, I need my fat pants.

I pull up to her condo and park in my spot. Since Leah lives alone, but has two parking spots, I always have a personal parking place. Considering this is such a popular area of the city, I would probably end up having to park two blocks away if I didn't have this spot to park in.

"Are my waffles ready?" I holler as I walk in.

I hear a glass break and some swearing as I turn the corner to the kitchen.

"Fuck off and die!" Leah yells into her phone just before she chucks it across the room.

"Looks like I'm not the only one who needed some girl time," I announce, looking at Leah, who is on the verge of tears. "Oh, honey, what happened?"

She takes a deep breath as I wrap my arms around her.

"It's nothing," she whimpers, pulling away and wiping her tears. "Guys are assholes and I'm so done. Want to be my lesbian lover?"

I laugh and give her another hug.

"You know we don't swing that way. You'd miss the dick in a week, I promise you."

That earns me a giggle.

"You're right, but I'm done with relationships," she sighs. "I'm sticking with fuck buddies only."

"Chad didn't work out?"

Chad was Leah's longest relationship. Before him, she hadn't dated anyone in a long time. She told me she was going to invite him to move in, but clearly that isn't happening anymore.

"I guess he's been cheating on me and got his other girlfriend pregnant." Leah sighs, grabbing the bottle of vodka from her cupboard.

"Shit!" is all I can manage to blurt out.

I never particularly liked Chad, but I didn't think he was the cheating kind.

"Yeah, I guess they're getting married and moving to North Dakota, where she's from. He just called to tell me to get my shit from his house." Leah takes a big swig from the bottle of vodka and passes it to me.

We've been here before, but last time it was me ending a relationship, not Leah. She drank with me and let me wallow in self-pity when I broke up with Tom, so now it's my turn to return the favor. I take a small swig from the bottle and grimace a little. Straight vodka is not the best, but desperate times call for desperate measures.

"Sounds like what we both need is a good lay, and to forget about relationships," I tell her. "I know it's only one in the afternoon, but it's Saturday. We are going to get dressed, look fucking amazing, and go out and get laid!"

I take another swig from the bottle and pass it back to Leah, who finally has a smile on her face.

"What's that quote everyone says? The best way to get over someone is to get under someone else?" she says.

I laugh; Leah is sounding like her old, happy-go-lucky self again.

"Since none of your clothes will fit me, grab what you need and we'll get ready at my place," I insist.

Leah goes to her room to grab a bag and her stuff.

"And don't forget your condoms," I yell from the living room.

This earns me another laugh from Leah. Today is going to be a good day. At least I don't have to worry about seeing Mikey. I'm positive he doesn't go to the same clubs we do.

MIKEY

I can't help but think about Tia. I made a complete ass out of myself and she really put me in my place. But I can't fuck this up. I *need* her as my manager.

Now, if only I could get the picture of her hot body in that sexy dress out of my mind.

She made it very clear we were going to have a strictly platonic relationship, and friends don't jerk off to the thoughts of friends. I need to get laid if I am going to get this girl out of my mind.

I don't really want to go to another party, since the one I went to last night didn't pan out well, but the numbers in my phone aren't what I want either.

I figure my best option is to call Johnny.

Johnny Crown has been my best friend since kindergarten. He can be a complete ass and really fucks with people's heads, but he's always been good to me. And I can guarantee that without me in his life, he would have gotten into a lot more trouble than he already has. I might have gotten into less trouble without him in my life, but we're brothers and we always have each other's backs.

Me: Where's the fun tonight?
Johnny: Clare's Palace. 10 p.m.
Me: Seriously? A strip joint?

Johnny: Fuck yeah! Put all the tits in my face! Then we'll head over to All That Jazz for some dancing. Hopefully pick up some hot chicks.

Me: I'll just meet you at All That Jazz. I don't need to pay for what I can get for free.

Johnny: Fuck you. TTYL.

Normally, I'm all for the strip clubs, but something in my head is telling me that I need to grow up. I'm not twenty-one anymore. I'm pushing thirty and don't need that shit anymore. Johnny never grew up, though. He's got a different girl every night, strippers most weekends. I shouldn't be surprised.

Johnny has never had a girlfriend, and I doubt he ever will. He is definitely not the "settle down" kind of guy.

I've had a few serious relationships, but being a rock star comes with a certain persona, and I have lived that persona well. Dating models and actresses, having lots of one-night stands. But I'm ready to move on with my life. I just need one night to get Tia out of my head, and then things are going to change.

The bass is pounding when I walk through the doors of the club, and the place is packed. But I know Johnny will be in the VIP section, so I make my way to the back of the club. Since I know the bouncer, I give him a quick first bump and he nods and lets me in.

"About time you made it!" Johnny shouts from the couch, where he has three girls hanging off of him.

"Hey, man! Seems like you're already having a good time," I answer, checking out the girls with him.

One is sitting on his lap, kissing his neck and biting his ear.

Maybe I shouldn't have come out tonight. I'm really not feeling this scene.

"Fuck yeah. Want me to share? I'm sure these bitches wouldn't mind," he laughs.

I cringe at the way he talks about women. He's always been this way, and I've tried to straighten him out over the years, but it's never worked. Maybe one day he'll find someone to straighten him out and turn his life upside-down.

The blonde on his right is pretty cute, and she gives me a shy smile. She looks really young—I'm not even sure if she is legally allowed in here—but she seems like she's having a good time.

"I'm good, man. Maybe later," I tell him. "I'm going to grab a drink. You guys want anything?"

Everyone shakes their heads and Johnny goes back to making out with the brunette on his lap.

As I go to the bar, I see a bombshell in a smoking-hot black dress. Her ass is barely covered by the dress and her legs look fucking perfect. Maybe it wasn't a mistake coming out tonight. If I can get that woman in my bed, I will definitely forget about Tia.

I keep an eye on mystery girl as I wait for my drink. She is clearly here with the girl in the red. Her friend is shorter, with black hair. Cute, but not what I'm looking for.

They are dancing and clearly having a good time. I finally get my beer and make my way towards them.

"Mind if I cut in?" I shout over the music.

Then she turns around and I see her piercing blue-green eyes. The eyes that keep haunting my dreams. I instantly see how pissed off she is.

"Are you fucking kidding me?" Tia yells. "Of all the fucking clubs in Sienna, you had to come to this one? Great! Just fucking great."

She storms off, and I'm left standing there like an idiot.

"You must be Mikey," the friend says, with a big smile.

"Yep. And you're Leah?" I guess.

"Yep. The best friend," she adds, reaching out her hand.

I give it a quick shake and start to walk away, wondering how I'm always pissing Tia off. Leah stops me before I get too far.

"She's been through a lot," she tells me. "Give her some time and be her friend. Maybe she'll come around. She does like you; she's just made rules for herself and doesn't want to break them."

Leah seems like a great friend. I can tell she really cares for Tia.

I didn't mean to upset Tia. Fuck, I didn't even realize it was her. I mean, I should have; no one has an ass like Tia's.

"Thanks, Leah, but she's made it very clear she just wants to be friends." I sigh. "I guess I'll have to settle for that. Let her know I'm leaving. Didn't mean to ruin your night."

"It's all good, Mikey. Have a great night."

I don't need to say goodbye to Johnny, but I still send him a quick text letting him know I'm leaving.

Me: Bailed early. Have a good night, man.

Tia clearly doesn't want me around, but I am so fucking hard and need to blow off some steam.

I leave the bar and drive home. Halfway there, I take out my phone and make a quick call.

"Hey, sexy. Want to come warm my bed?" I ask.

"Be there in five."

Amber is always a sure-fire bet and she never makes things complicated.

The next morning, my head is fucking hurting. Amber wanted to play some strip poker with shots. I drank way too fucking much, and with all the coke we did, I was really out of it. Hell, even I knew the sex was shit, but she still pretended like it was earth-shattering. She gave me a quick kiss and left before the sun even came up.

My phone died shortly after I got home last night, so I'm getting a bunch of texts this morning, quite a few from Tia.

Tia: I'm so sorry for acting like a brat, Mikey. Are you still around? We should talk.

Tia: Leah told me you left. I'm really sorry. Friends don't lose it when they see other friends out.

Tia: Why are you so fucking sexy?

That one makes me smile. She was obviously getting progressively more drunk as she sent these texts.

Tia: Clearly, you're either ignoring me or having sex with someone else. I wish it was me.

I gulp. Now her secrets are coming to light, with the help of that truth serum known as alcohol.

Tia: This is Leah. Please ignore all previous messages sent. Tia should not be allowed to drink and text.

I start laughing. Got to love when your friend has to take over for you when you're drunk. I get one more notification saying I have a voicemail, so I listen.

*"Why are you what I want but I can't have? I've had a crush on you for forever. I want you." *burp* "Oops. Excuse me." She giggles a little then continues. "It's career suicide to date someone you're managing, and I wish things were different. Call me? No, Leah, I'm not calling Mikey. It's my brother."*

"You don't have a brother," I hear Leah say in the background.

"Oops. Got to go."

And then the message is over.

I sit on my couch, running a hand over my face. This woman wants me as much as I want her. Now I just have to show her that a relationship is worth the risk.

I know a girl like Tia isn't going to put up with the way I've been acting. Yes, she is surrounded by rock stars all day, but I know if I don't clean up my act, she won't even give me the time of day. She'll keep pushing me away, and I don't blame her.

TIA

Why do I drink? I always end up doing stupid things.

"I'm never drinking again!" I groan.

"You said that last time," Leah argues groggily from my couch.

"I mean it this time. I confessed my feelings to Mikey! Now I'm going to be jobless, and soon homeless," I whine while falling into my comfy chair.

"You are not jobless, and no one is losing their home. Besides, even without a job, you've made enough sound investments. You'd be fine for a while. But, seriously, Mikey is into you. Why don't you just give it a try?"

"It never works, Leah. You've seen it, same as me. He is my client! What happens when we break up?" I argue.

"If," Leah buts in.

"What?"

"*If* you break up. You're already dooming your relationship before it even starts, thinking like that."

Leah is always the voice of reason, and I get it, but I don't know if I can take the risk.

I want to be friends with Mikey. Maybe we can both agree there is an attraction, but that a platonic relationship would be the best. I'll stop freaking out every time I see him, and he won't go all caveman on my ass when he sees me with another guy.

I'm lost in thought when my phone buzzes. I look at the ID.

"Oh, God, it's Mikey," I moan, refusing to look at the text.

"Oh, let me see," Leah says while swiping the phone. "Looks like things might be turning in your favor, after all."

She raises an eyebrow while handing me back my phone.

Mikey: Hey, I'm hoping we can forget everything that has happened since we first met. Can we be friends? I'll forget your messages, you forget my forwardness, and we just move on.

I sigh. This is exactly what I wanted. Why does it make me sad at the same time?

"I think I'm broken, Leah," I say dejectedly.

"Well, no fuck! Aren't we all?" she counters.

I laugh and throw a pillow at her.

"Okay, no more wallowing. Let's go get some greasy burgers and move on with our lives," Leah exclaims after tossing the pillow back at me.

"You look so good!" I beam at Tyler. "Where are Corey and Jay?"

I've been fighting off a massive hangover and trying to deal with my emotions, so I haven't checked in with the guys.

"Corey didn't want to leave Alyssa. The long-distance relationship isn't really working well for them," he explains.

I nod. I couldn't imagine being so far away from the person I loved.

"And Melly has the flu, so Jay stayed home with her," he finishes.

"Well, I'm glad we're still getting together. Life has been so different with you guys gone." I stare at my glass of water. "I feel like my family was torn apart."

Tyler reaches for my hand and I smile at him. "I get it, sissy, but I'm still your family. I'm just a phone call away if you need anything."

I nod.

The bell of the diner rings and I turn my attention. I gasp and drop my glass, making water spill everywhere.

"Fuck," I swear and grab for some napkins.

Tyler laughs. "Always so graceful, T."

I can't help but laugh too.

Why does it feel like Mikey is fucking stalking me? Always at the same places I am. Up until I started working with him, I never saw him, except at some parties. Now, I'm suddenly seeing him all the time.

Tyler grabs my hand, stopping me from cleaning. "What's going on?"

Instead of looking at Tyler, I look at Mikey. His eyes zoom in on mine and Tyler's hands.

"I'm about to ask you to do something that might not be comfortable, but I need your help," I say, turning back to Tyler.

"Anything, sissy. What's going on?"

I lean across the table and press my lips to Tyler's. He gasps a little, but he doesn't break the kiss. After a few moments, I hear the diner bell chime again. When I look up, Mikey is gone. I giggle and sit back in my seat.

Tyler puts his hand to his mouth. "What was that, Tia?"

"Sorry. That was my new client, Mikey Ecosta. He's been trying really hard to get to me, so I just wanted to make things clear. I can see whoever I want, and he has no say in it."

The waitress comes over and cleans up the rest of the water.

"So, you used me?" He places his hand on his chest in mock horror. "I'm offended."

I laugh. "Um, remember all those times you would drape your arm around my shoulders when the crazies were out? Maybe it's not quite the same, but I would say you owed me."

We both laugh and I realize we are drawing a lot of attention from the other customers.

"Maybe we should quiet down. People are staring," I giggle while making a face. "So, Cali is going well?"

"Yeah, I'm drumming for a new band. It's going well, but I'd love to come back. Sienna is home," he sighs.

"I get it. I don't think I could ever leave."

"If you hear of anyone needing a drummer, let me know."

I smile. "I will. It would be great to have you back."

"You did what?" Leah giggles.

"Yeah, not one of my proudest moments. I never thought I'd be kissing my brother."

Leah is in full-on hysterics now. "And you thought that would make things less awkward between you and Mikey?"

I put my hand on my head. "I clearly wasn't thinking." I check the time and realize it's almost noon. "Look I have to go; I'll talk to you later."

"No more kissing your best friends." Leah giggles and hangs up.

Mikey's lawyer sent everything back to Leah this morning with all the correct signatures. All the I's are now dotted and the T's are crossed. I am officially his manager, and I want nothing more than to be the best manager I can be.

I spend a good chunk of the morning revamping Mikey's social media accounts. I can't believe it was actually Mikey running his account this whole time. The fans were even making comments about how it felt like a fake account and they wanted to connect with the real Mikey. With all the photos and files that Chris sent over to me, I was able to make posts about Mikey's personal life and career that had people really engaging.

His Facebook and Instagram are blowing up, and I am so happy I had a hand in it. Now I just have to talk to Mikey, so we can get on the same page about the direction his career is heading in.

I take a deep breath and make the phone call I have been dreading all morning.

"Hey. What's up?" he answers after the first ring.

Why does his voice have to be so appealing? Maybe if everything about him didn't ooze sex appeal, this would be a whole lot easier.

"Hey, Mikey, what are your plans for today? I have a few things I need to go over with you," I say, trying to remain professional.

"You don't have plans with your boyfriend?" he bites out.

"No, and that wasn't my boyfriend. Not that it's any of your business. I was hoping we could get together and go over some business stuff."

The line goes silent. Did he hang up on me?

"I just got done with a radio interview, but I'm free this afternoon," he finally says.

Oh, right. I totally forgot about that. I wanted to tune in and listen, but I was too busy chatting with Leah.

"Great!" I exclaim. "Sorry. I forgot about that, or I would have put it on your social media pages. Which, by the way, are doing amazing since I updated them this morning."

I'm thrilled with everything so far. I can see a bright future for Mikey. He just needs a push in the right direction.

"Can I stop by your place in like an hour? I'll bring coffee," he says.

"Coffee sounds fantastic," I tell him. "See you soon."

He sounds off. It probably has to do with seeing me kiss Tyler. Hopefully everything works out. I guess I'll see soon.

Mikey arrives a little over an hour later, and I have the plans all drawn out.

"Oh, my God. Thank you so much for this coffee, I ran out this morning and have been dying." I let him into my apartment and move to the living room.

Of course, he has to look fantastic. Ugh. Why is he the sexiest man I've ever met?

"Glad I could make your day," Mikey chuckles, giving me his famous smile that shows off that dimple and makes me feel all warm and fuzzy inside.

I stare into his eyes; they're bloodshot. I've heard through the rumor mill that Mikey likes his drugs and washing them down with a drink or two, and judging from the way he looks right now, I'd say those rumors are true. That should make it easier to push him away. I hate drugs. I've seen them fuck up too many people's lives, and I've lost one friend to them already.

But everything about Mikey reads comfortable and familiar. I want to cuddle up with him and just spend the day watching TV. But friends don't do that. And if I don't want drugs in my personal life, then all we can ever be is friends.

Why does life have to be so complicated? If things were different, I feel like Mikey and I really could have a good chance at being together. There is clearly chemistry between the two of us, but maybe it's the wanting what I can't have that makes him so desirable.

"So, I want to get you back in the studio as soon as possible," I start. "Chris told me you've been working on new stuff and I know your fans are going to want to hear it."

"That sounds great!" he says enthusiastically. "I'm really happy with my new stuff. It's a different direction, but I think my fans are going to dig it."

Mikey looks so at ease when he's talking about his music. It's so obvious that this is what he lives for.

"I wanted to set up a private event for only your die-hard fans. We can give them a tease at your new music and really get the buzz going that you are back and ready to do big things," I tell Mikey while grabbing my phone. "Is there an app you and Chris use to sync your calendars? I want us to both be on the same page, so I don't miss anything like your interview this morning again."

"Yeah. I'll send you the link for the app now. And don't worry about missing the interview. You didn't miss much."

"Thanks for making things easy here, Mikey. I'm really sorry about everything that happened this weekend."

I didn't want to bring up the past because we both agreed to leave it there, but I also want to thank him for being great about it and not making this awkward.

"I need to apologize too," Mikey adds, reaching forward to grab my hand. "I respect you so much and would never want to make you uncomfortable. I'm sorry for how I acted and I really want this to work."

His hand feels like fire and is sending shocks right to my heart. He is holding eye contact with me and I can feel the heat of his stare. I glance at his lips and want to know what they would taste like. I'm the one who made it very clear we could not have a relationship, and now I feel like I'm regretting that.

Pulling my hand away, I stand up and grab the empty coffee cups, but as I bend to grab his, I get a whiff of peppermint. Every time I smell it now, I think of him.

"Thanks. I'm glad we can be friends." My voice sounds coarse, and I can almost hear the tears wanting to break loose.

I excuse myself to the kitchen and take a deep breath.

I wanted things this way, I remind myself.

I don't date clients, and I don't deal with drugs.

MIKEY

I am so confused after Tia excuses herself to the kitchen. She looks genuinely upset, but this is what she wanted. Isn't it? And besides, she's clearly seeing someone.

Women are fucking confusing. I wish there was a manual on them. Fuck, who am I kidding? Men don't read manuals.

I love the plans that Tia came up with. She's even planning a huge tour for the end of the next year, plus a few small events just for my hardcore fans.

I'm itching to get back into the studio so I can release the new album before the tour starts.

I grab Tia's notebook and start flipping through the pages. Her ideas are fantastic, and well thought out. She thought of things I never would have dreamed of. I'm super artistic and love writing music and being creative that way, but when it comes to planning things, I'm lost.

While Tia is still in the kitchen, I call my friend A.J., who is also a great producer, and book some studio time. I've finally written a good amount of songs for the new album and feel comfortable getting back into the studio.

Finally, Tia comes back into the living room and she looks a lot less upset.

"I just got off the phone with A.J., and he said he can fit me in this week to start recording the new album," I tell her.

"That's fantastic! I can't wait to hear your new stuff," she says with a smile. "I've actually been a pretty big fan since you first started, but if I'm being honest, your last album wasn't the best."

Her smile does weird things to my heart, but I'm glad it's back.

"I agree. My label was pushing for me to do something *out of the box*, and it just sounded like trash." I let out a laugh.

That's an understatement. I usually listen to my gut, but with the last album, I let the label push me in a crappy direction. I'm proud of everything I've done, but that album was my biggest flop and all my fans hated it.

"Well, I should probably get going," I blurt out, standing and turn to grab my coat. "I love the idea of that small event. I think we should do it in the next couple of weeks to get the buzz going about the new album. Maybe we can send out an email to my fan club forty-eight hours before, and then if it's not sold out, post it on social media twenty-four hours before to sell the rest of the tickets. But I want it super intimate and maybe acoustic? What do you think? Does that sound doable?"

"That sounds great!" She beams at me. "I can definitely get it done. I downloaded the app and will send you all the details once I get things set in stone. I'm so excited!"

She is jumping up and down and gives me a giant hug. I love seeing her this excited; it makes me want to do my best and never let her down.

"I'll keep in touch, and let me know how recording goes," she says.

I stand awkwardly at her door, not really ready to leave. "Do you want to come to a party I'm having tomorrow? It's just a little get-together."

She stares at the floor, twisting her foot. Looking up at my face, she tucks her hair behind her ear.

"I'm not sure if that's a good idea." She bites her lip.

She really has to stop doing that. Does she not realize it makes me want to kiss her so badly that I can't think straight?

"Come on, I thought we were supposed to be friends. It's just casual. At least just make an appearance," I plead.

Her beautiful eyes search my face. Those eyes. They're perfect.

"Okay, I'll make an appearance," she finally agrees.

Yes! I'm sure my smile is fucking huge right now.

"Great. I'll see you tomorrow then," I say, reluctantly turning to leave.

TIA

As I walk into Mikey's house, I'm struck by how *huge* it is. There are pictures of him and his band, signed guitars, and a few pictures of his family. It's homey, but clearly a bachelor pad.

There are a lot more people here than I thought would be, and I don't really know anyone. I recognize a few faces from other parties I've been to, but no one I would really call a friend. I should have brought Leah.

I tuck my hair behind my ear and make my way to the kitchen. After I pour myself a drink, I take a small sip and turn around, looking for anyone I would know.

Then I see the man who keeps making appearances in my dreams and I smile as his eyes meet mine. His smile lights up his face, and his dimple appears. That damn dimple is going to be the death of me.

Mikey picks me up and spins me around. I shriek and laugh.

"I'm so glad you came." He leans down and kisses my cheek.

I feel my face heat. His touch sends tingles through my body.

"I thought I would know more people," I say, looking around at all the strangers.

"Everyone's awesome. You're going to have a great time," he says.

"Hey, Mikey!" someone yells from the living room.

He leans down and kisses my cheek again. "I'll be right back. Make yourself at home."

He runs over to his buddy, and I'm left alone again. I lean against the counter, not really feeling like moving. This party might have been fun if I had someone to talk to.

"He's mine," says a skinny woman with fiery red hair.

"Excuse me?" I ask, taken aback.

"Mikey's mine, and if you don't want bad things to happen, you'll back off."

She gets right up in my face, and I can smell the liquor on her breath. Is this really Mikey's girlfriend or just some groupie with the wrong idea? Either way, she has crazy eyes and I don't want to stay around her for a second longer than I have to.

"Noted," I say before walking away.

I'm pretty sure I hear Mikey's voice coming from a side room, so I make my way over there. I think it's time for me to go home, but I want to say goodbye.

When I enter the game room, I almost stumble. Mikey's standing there snorting a line of cocaine off the counter.

I close my eyes and take a deep breath. I can hear my heart beating in my ears. I should not have come here. It's one thing to hear about Mikey doing drugs. It's an entirely different thing to see him doing them.

I quickly leave the room before Mikey even sees me. He was way too caught up in what he was doing to notice me enter the room.

Calling an Uber, I leave Mikey's house. There are tears streaming down my face, but this is a good thing. Now that I've seen this, it will make it easier to keep Mikey at arm's length.

The car ride home is quiet. Mikey probably hasn't even noticed I've left. I kind of thought he invited me tonight to try something. I know I'm crazy. I keep pushing him away, but still want him to chase me.

I'm almost home when my phone buzzes.

Mikey: Where did you go?

Me: Sorry. Got a headache and headed home. TTYL.

I hate lying to people, but I don't want to have this conversation over text.

He doesn't respond. He probably went to find the redhead. He definitely doesn't have a shortage of girls available to him. Since I'm not there, he'll just move on.

Eleven

MIKEY

It's been a hell of a day. Nothing sounded right in the studio. It was all garbage in my head. Everyone was telling me how "fantastic" it was, but I know that wasn't the truth.

I've been home for a couple hours and have thrown back more than a few drinks. And a couple of lines of coke. I just want to forget this shitty day. At first, I think about calling Amber, but I know that would be a bad decision, so I decide to text Tia instead. I haven't seen her since the party, and she has been a little distant.

Me: How was your day, princess?

Tia: Princess? Really? What am I, 5?

I laugh. She's right. She's a badass. Princess is way too cute of a term for her.

Me: Sorry. If anything, you are a queen.

Tia: Damn right. Anyway, what's up?

Me: Was just replaying my shitty day through my head. What are you doing?

Tia: Just getting ready for bed.

Me: Nice! What you wearing?

Tia: Seriously, Mikey, not appropriate.

Damn. Shot down again. I know I'm drunk, but can't she give me just a little?

Me: Come on, admit it. You've been thinking about me.

She doesn't reply for a minute. Shit. Did I go too far? I don't want to push her away.

Tia: Okay, you're right.

Wait. Seriously?

Tia: I've been thinking about you all day. I just can't get you out of my head.

Me: Tell me more…

Tia: I mean, it's super hard to get my annoying client out of my thoughts.

Damn. Not the response I was hoping for.

Me: I can't stop thinking about you.

Tia: Stop it, Mikey.

Me: I'm serious. Give me one shot! I'll prove to you I'm worth it. Or is it that guy you were kissing at the diner stopping you from being with me?

Tia: I told you, I'm not seeing anyone. He was just a friend. And don't you have a girlfriend?

Me: Just a friend who you kiss? And I don't have a girlfriend. Where would you get that idea?

I haven't had a girlfriend in a long time. Why would she think that?

I pause for a second, thinking back to the diner. Was she just trying to make me jealous?

Me: Did you kiss him because you saw me?

She doesn't respond.

Me: Seriously, Tia, I care for you.

Tia: Enough, Mikey! You promised you wouldn't push this anymore. I'm putting my foot down.

Me: I don't give up easily, sweetheart.

Tia: You need to drop this. I'm not changing my mind.

Me: We'll see about that.

Tia: Even if you weren't my client, I don't let drugs into my life.

Fuck. Did she see me at the party? Maybe that's why she left and has been distant.

She doesn't respond anymore, and I don't know what to say. This woman keeps pushing me away every chance she gets, but I need to give it one more try. This connection is so strong. I never would have pursued a girl this hard in the past. Hell, I never would have had to. Most girls throw themselves at my feet, but Tia is different. Maybe that's why I want her so badly. Badly enough that I'm willing to clean up my act for her, if it would make her give me a chance.

The next few weeks fly by. I've been in the studio a ton and am still hating everything I'm putting out.

I haven't touched any drugs since that drunken text conversation with Tia. My brain is really fuzzy and I'm fucking exhausted. I have no idea how long I'm going to feel like this. There's not a day that goes by when I don't crave a hit to make it stop, but my pull to Tia is stronger. I've apologized to her and we have been talking a lot. And she makes everything I'm feeling worth it. At night, I get the chills and I can't stop shaking, but if I picture Tia, it makes it a bit better. It reminds me that I'm doing this for a reason.

The email was sent out for the private event this morning, and the tickets are already sold out. I couldn't thank Tia enough for everything she did. She booked an awesome venue that only held a hundred people. It was exactly what I had envisioned.

I decide to give Tia a call and touch base since the concert is only two days away now.

"Hey, beautiful," I greet her. "How are you doing?"

"I think I'm dying." Tia's voice is hoarse; I can barely make out the words.

"Are you okay? Do you need anything?"

"Just a cold," she sniffles. "I'll be fine for your concert, but stay away. I don't want you getting sick. You can't risk not having a voice."

She sounds rough, and I have this weird feeling inside me that I just want to take care of her. I've never felt like this about anyone before.

"Can I at least bring you some chicken noodle soup and then leave?" I try.

"That's sweet, Mikey, but I think it's best if you just stay away. I'll talk to you tomorrow. I'm going back to sleep now."

"Sweet dreams, sweetheart."

I know she's just trying to make sure I don't get sick, but the idea of her being all by herself doesn't sit well with me. Tia sent me Leah's number a while back since Leah's her lawyer. I know it's probably crossing a line, but I decide to call her anyway.

"Leah Gulfson speaking."

"Hey, Leah. It's Mikey. I don't know if I should be calling you." I pause and grab the back of my neck, nervous about the possibility that I'll piss Tia off by making this call. "But I just wanted to let you know that Tia is really sick."

God, I sound like such a loser. Why did I call Tia's best friend? I'm sure she already knows Tia is sick and is giving her space like she asked for.

"Seriously? I was just texting her and she didn't say anything," Leah huffs out. "This is so typical of her. She never wants help with anything. She thinks she'll be a bother, so she deals with most things by herself."

That makes my stomach sink a little. Tia deals with most things all by herself? Why wouldn't she let her friends take care of her? Maybe it's one of the reasons she doesn't want to date me. She likes to be Miss Independent and doesn't like to let people in, by the sound of it.

"Yeah. I asked if I could help her, but she said she didn't want me to get sick before my concert," I tell Leah. "But I hate the idea of her being by herself. She sounded horrible. Would you mind going over and checking on her when you get done with work?"

"You're so sweet, Mikey. Of course I'll go check on her. I'll let you know how she's doing when I get there. Talk to you later."

Well, that makes me feel a lot better. Now at least I know that Tia is going to be taken care of. But I just wish it were me holding her and making her feel better. Being friends with Tia is great, but I want so much more. I'll just have to make her see that we are worth the risk.

Twelve

TIA

I'm lying on my couch feeling like I'm dying when I hear my front door open.

"Hello?" I pause the TV, thinking maybe I'm hearing things.

"I have chicken soup, ginger ale, Powerade, essential oils, Echinacea, and DayQuil. What do you want and how can I help?" I hear my best friend's voice from the foyer.

Leah is like a fairy godmother with her goodie bag of get-well items.

"How did you know I was sick?" I ask.

"I'm a mind reader. I know all." Leah chuckles, lifting her eyebrow and giving me a smile as she walks into the living room.

"Nice try. It was Mikey, wasn't it?"

"He was just concerned. He cares about you," Leah sighs. "And he was right. You sound like death, and you look even worse."

This is what friends are for: to take care of you and give you a hard time. But I hate being taken care of. I have taken care of myself for long enough. I'm good at it.

My dad is an awesome dad, but he worked two jobs while I was growing up to give me everything I wanted. My mom was never in the picture. She left when I was three days old. I haven't ever talked to her, but that's fine. If she didn't want me, I don't want anything to do with her. At age seven, I was cooking and cleaning for both my dad and me, taking care of things I could do to help out and make things easier on Dad. At thirteen, I started homeschooling myself. I graduated at sixteen and got a job to help out as much as possible. I moved out on my own as soon as I turned eighteen. I'm not jaded. My life has been great for the most part, but I just have a hard time letting other people take care of me.

I didn't go to college because I just didn't want a repeat of high school. I was smart enough and was even offered scholarships to cover the cost, but I didn't think I could survive more bullying.

"You know, it's not going to kill you to let someone take care of you every once in a while." Leah sets the chicken noodle soup down on my coffee table and helps me sit up.

"I know, but when you've pretty much taken care of yourself for your whole life, it can be a challenge to let people in."

I take a small sip of the soup and sigh. It tastes so good. I have barely gotten off the couch, and I was starving, but every time I stood up, I got lightheaded and had to immediately sit down. It was actually a huge blessing that Leah showed up.

"Thanks for being here for me," I sniffle.

"I'm always here for you, chica. You just have to ask." Leah leans over and gives me a tight squeeze.

Maybe it's because I'm sick, but I start to cry. I've spent the majority of my life pushing people away, wanting to act strong and not let people know how broken I am on the inside. I was the victim for far too long and I never wanted to feel that way again, but not letting people in clearly isn't working either. I can still be a strong, independent woman and let other people help me when needed. I was able to do it in my professional life. Now, I just need to learn how to let people help in my personal life.

"I'm so sorry," I mumble between sobs. "I've been a shitty friend, not letting you in and always keeping you at arm's length. I promise to try harder from now on."

Leah gives me a tight hug. "That's all I'm asking, hon. I'm always here for you. Just let me in. And maybe let Mikey in too?"

Ugh. She had to bring him up, didn't she? But maybe she's right. I was dead set on pushing him away because I thought there was no way a relationship between him and I could work. But what if it could work? Yes, it could make things awkward if we tried and failed, but what if we didn't fail? What if we had the most epic of love stories? I would be a fool to not at least give us a chance.

But fear is still eating at me and I'm not sure if I can push it aside and not sabotage things even further. And then there's the matter of the drugs. Those are a hard no for me. Would he be willing to give them up?

"I'll try, Leah, but you know it's hard for me." I grab a tissue and wipe my eyes. I'm an ugly crier. Good thing Leah's my best friend; otherwise, she might get scared off. "If it's meant to be, it will be. I don't think I can pursue him after how much I've pushed him away, but I won't fight it anymore either. If he still wants me, and if he's willing to stop the drugs, I guess I'll give it a try."

Leah starts bouncing up and down on the couch. "Yay! You guys are going to make such a cute couple."

I laugh and roll my eyes at her. "Stop bouncing! I'm going to throw up."

She stops and gives me another tight squeeze.

Maybe, just maybe, Mikey and I can be perfect together. If he still wants me.

Tomorrow is the concert. I'm still exhausted, but for the most part, I'm feeling a lot better. I know I should touch base with Mikey and make sure he doesn't need anything at the last minute, so I give him a quick call.

"Hey, beautiful. How are you feeling?" Mikey greets me. It's so nice and refreshing to know he cares.

"A lot better," I tell him. "Thanks for asking."

"Glad to hear. You sound much better."

"I was just calling to check in. Is there anything last minute you need from me for tomorrow?"

"I think I'm good. You've already done a lot."

I decide I want to do something special for him, but don't want to come right out and ask him, so I come up with the idea of twenty questions.

"Want to play a little game?" I ask.

"What kind of game?"

Is it just me or did is voice drop an octave? That's hot. I have to catch my breath before responding.

"Twenty questions, but the rule is you have to answer the question you ask first."

"Okay, sounds interesting. Do you want to start, or shall I?"

I don't know why, but I giggle a little. God, I sound like a schoolgirl.

"I'll start," I tell him. "What's your favorite TV show? Mine is *Survivor*. My guilty pleasure is definitely reality TV."

He lets out a chuckle. "Reality TV is trash, but if I was forced to watch, *Survivor* is probably the best of them." He pauses for a second. "My favorite TV show is *E.R.*, but like old school with George Clooney."

I can't help it; I bark out a laugh. "Way to take it way back."

"What can I say? Clooney made that show. I'm pissed it's not on the air anymore."

"Okay, your turn."

"Right. Hmm…what's your favorite tea? Mine is chai."

"Random much? I had no idea you drank tea."

"Yeah, I drink a cup before every show. Helps open up my vocal cords. But I can't have anything in it. Just straight tea."

"Interesting. Well, I'm not the biggest tea drinker, but I'll say Earl Grey, because that's what is in London Fogs."

"You are such a girl," he chuckles.

"Guilty as charged, but you wouldn't want me any other way," I flirt back.

"Correct you are, Tia Girl. Your turn."

"Who is your favorite actress? Mine is Blake Lively. She is so amazing and, I mean, she's married to Ryan Reynolds, and he is *so* dreamy."

I hear Mikey make a gagging noise and I giggle.

"Blake Lively is my favorite actress as well, but it's because she's hot as fuck."

I laugh so hard I start to cry. "Oh, my God. You are such a guy." I take a second to compose myself. "Okay, your turn."

"Hmm. What's your favorite movie of all time? For me, it's *Forrest Gump*. It's a classic. Everyone loves that one."

I pause. Should I admit I've never seen it? I've heard wonderful things, and I've seen bits and pieces, but never the whole movie. I decide to leave that little bit of information out.

"My favorite movie is *Space Jam*. You can't beat Michael Jordan and Bugs Bunny."

I hear Mikey's boisterous laugh. It makes me smile. His laugh is fantastic; it's deep, but so full of life.

"Are you twelve?" he teases.

"Har-har," I mumble. "Now it's my turn. What is one thing you couldn't live without? For me it's my dad. He's always been my rock. We aren't as close as we used to be, but I still know he would do anything for me."

Mikey mumbles something under his breath but I can't make it out. At first, I think he says "you," but it can't be.

"What was that?" I ask.

"Um, my family," he responds quickly. "They have been super supportive of my career, even when other people said I would never make it as a musician, they were there pushing me to do my best."

"That's so sweet, Mikey. I'm glad you guys are close." I look at the clock and realize it's getting late. "Well, time for me to get to bed. I need my beauty sleep, you know."

"You're always beautiful, whether you get enough sleep or not."

I know he can't see me, but I blush. Mikey is so charming. I'm really glad I called tonight.

"Goodnight, Mikey."

"Goodnight, beautiful."

Today is the day of the concert, and I'm mostly feeling better. The antibiotics I got from the doctor helped a lot. I still took a big shot of DayQuil this morning to make sure I was one hundred percent, because today is going to be a busy day.

I have been at the venue all morning, making sure things are going according to plan. The bar is set up exactly how I wanted and the stage is getting set up with all the band equipment and Mikey's logo. Everything is looking perfect.

I haven't seen Mikey since we started planning all of this. We've talked on the phone every day. Even when I was sick, he still called to check in, but we haven't seen each other in person. Last night's game of twenty questions was fantastic. I felt like we really connected and I got to know him a little better.

Me: Everything's perfect! Can't wait for you to get here and amaze your fans!

Mikey: Can't wait to see your beautiful face. ;-)

I roll my eyes. Always the flirt. I know he cares about me, as a friend, but I thought I had finally pushed too much and now that was all he wanted. But that text seems like more than just banter between friends. Maybe I'm reading into it too much, though. He could just be excited to see me as a friend. God, life is difficult for people like me, who can never get out of their own heads. I overthink everything. I wish I could just live in the moment.

I take a couple of deep breaths and get back to work. I have to focus; this is a very important event. It is the beginning of Mikey's reboot. His fans have been all over social media, posting about how excited they are. If this show is a flop, I won't be able to live with myself. But I'm confident in my skills, and everything seems perfect so far.

"Can you please make sure Mikey's dressing room is all set up?" I ask one of the assistants, and move on to other things that need attending to.

The day passes by in a blur and before I know it, it's time for sound check.

When Mikey arrives, I stop in my tracks. He looks ridiculously hot. His grey sweatpants sit low on his hips, and his sleeveless black shirt rides up slightly, revealing that perfect V. His hair is that perfectly mussed mess it always is, and I want to run my fingers through it. He looks like heaven on a stick, and I want to take a bite. His eyes seem brighter too. Every other time I've seen him, they were cloudy, but today they are just pure blue. I wonder why that is? I feel a blush coming over my face; I need to push these thoughts aside for now.

Taking a deep breath, I walk over to Mikey. "Hey, slacker. How's your day been?"

Mikey gives me the biggest smile and pulls me in for a giant hug.

"Better now," he whispers into my hair.

I melt. I stay in his hold for a second longer than I should before pushing away.

"Everyone is ready for you to start sound check, and then when you're done, we have about an hour before the doors open," I tell him. "I have everything you need in your dressing room. I hope everything is to your liking."

God, I need to shut up. I ramble when I'm nervous, and ever since I started considering more with Mikey, I get nervous just thinking about him. Being in his presence, seeing him, smelling him, feeling him, is almost too much to take. I feel like I'm going to have a panic attack.

I take a deep breath and look up from my clipboard. Mikey is giving me his devilish smile, and for some reason, it calms me. I smile back, give him a quick wink, and walk away.

I hope I can get through this whole show without losing my shit. Maybe afterwards, Mikey and I can talk.

MIKEY

Tia looks amazing, and I can tell she's nervous. She gets this cute divot in her forehead and rambles on when she is. I'm not sure if she's nervous about the show or nervous to be around me.

We haven't spent a whole lot of time in person together, but we have gotten close over the phone. At least I think we have. I want to ask her out on a proper date. If she says no, then I'll finally give up. A guy can only take so much.

I've been feeling fantastic. Now that the drugs are out my system and I'm no longer going through withdrawals, everything is so much clearer. My music is coming along amazing now too. I feel like it's some of the best stuff I've ever written. And it's all thanks to Tia. If it wasn't for her, I wouldn't be turning my life around and this new music wouldn't be pouring out of my soul.

The sound check goes off without a hitch. Everything sounds and looks great. I get to my dressing room and notice that my favorite tea is already in a cup, ready for me to drink. There is a little note next to it.

Hope this makes your throat feel great.
Tia

That's so thoughtful of her. I think back to our game of twenty questions last night. She kept coming up with random questions that made me laugh, but I get it now. Instead of asking my friends, she came up with a clever way to figure out my favorite stuff. And we got to learn new things about each other. We didn't go super deep, but the things I learned about Tia made me smile.

Just as I'm about to get changed, there is a knock at the door. Thinking it's Tia, I tell her to come in. Amber walks in, wearing a tiny little dress and her hair down in ringlets.

"Um, hey, what are you doing here?" I ask, a little confused. Amber doesn't normally show up unannounced.

"I just wanted to see you before your big show, s-s-sexy." She slurs the last word.

"Have you been drinking?" I ask.

She is confusing the hell out of me. Yeah, we're friends, but we usually keep our friendship super casual, and mainly in the bedroom. She has been texting me a lot, but I've been ignoring her. I never wanted an actual relationship with her. Plus, I have my sights set on Tia now, so I need to get Amber out of my dressing room, stat.

"Maybe I have been?" Amber purrs, strutting closer to me. She reaches into her purse and pulls out a dime bag of coke. "Want to have some fun?"

I stare at the bag, remembering how amazing the feel of the high was. I close my eyes and take a deep breath. I need that out of here right now.

"I think you should leave, Amber, and I don't think we should see each other anymore. It was fun while it lasted, but I'm moving on," I say sternly.

That sounds harsh, but I don't think subtle is going to work on Amber.

Amber drops the baggie on a table before coming even closer to me. She grabs my arm and places her head on my shoulder.

"This can't be the end, Mikey. We are *sssssoooo* good together," she slurs.

Just as I'm about to pull away, she kisses me, and I hear my dressing room door open.

"Hey, Mikey, just checking to make sure everything is all good.... Oh, my God... I'm so sorry!" Tia stammers and leaves.

For fuck's sake!

"Get the fuck out, Amber!" I yell and push her away.

I need to go find Tia and explain. Damn, that looked bad. Just as things were getting good between us, something had to go and fuck it up. Or some*one*. Someone I want nothing to do with anymore. Just my fucking luck.

I spend the next half an hour trying to find Tia, but she is nowhere to be found. It's almost showtime and I'm a fucking wreck. Raking my fingers through my hair, I let out a frustrated sigh. I really want to punch a wall right now, but I still have to be able to play my guitar. I can't fuck this show up.

"Mikey, you're on in fifteen. Please be at the side of the stage in ten." Tia's eyes are slightly puffy and the light in them is gone. They're super blue, so I know she's upset.

I reach for her hand, but she pulls away. "Tia, that wasn't what it looked like. Please talk to me."

"It's fine, Mikey. You're allowed to have girlfriends. We're just *friends,* right?" She bites the word friends out, and it stabs me right in the heart. "I'll just remember to knock next time."

"She's not my girlfriend. Please let me explain," I beg.

Tia holds her hand up to cut me off. "We don't have time. Meet me at the stage shortly."

"After? Please, Tia. You're destroying me here."

She dips her head and takes a deep breath. "Fine. We can talk after."

Then she walks away. I grab the back of my neck. Fuck. I just want things to work out with Tia, but I can't worry about her right now. I need to put on a kick-ass show and give my fans what they want.

Jumping up and down to pump myself up, I chant a few words to one of my first songs: "They can't hold me down. I will rise." I've got this.

Just before I step onstage, I see one of the roadies who has been with me since the beginning. He's seen a lot of shit, so I know he's good at keeping his mouth shut. I walk over and pull him to the side.

"Hey, man, there is a bag of drugs in my dressing room," I whisper. "Can you dispose of it, please?"

He nods at me. "Sure, man."

I smile and turn back towards the stage. Clearing my head of everything else, I take a deep breath and walk out to the screaming fans. Yep, this is where I am meant to be. Fuck, it feels good.

TIA

Mikey is killing it, of course. His acoustic set is going off without a hitch. I sigh when he sings my favorite song of his, "Girl With the Hidden Smile." It reminds me of me as a child, the girl hiding from everyone, the one who gets kicked when she's down. I just wish my ending were the same as the girl's in the song. The love of her life picks her up and shows her how perfect she really is. But life isn't a love song; life is full of heartbreak and sorrow.

I'm looking over my clipboard, figuring out what all has to be done after the set is over, when I feel a tap on my shoulder.

I turn and see the redhead who was just kissing Mikey. The same girl who told me Mikey was hers. I want to punch her in her face.

"Can I help you?" I ask, not impressed that she is interrupting me.

"Yeah, next time can you knock when you enter my boyfriend's dressing room." Her words are dripping with venom.

I don't even know this woman, but I hate her.

"According to him, you aren't his girlfriend."

She wasn't expecting me to have that comeback. I can tell by the way her eyes go wide.

"Well, I am, so stay away from him," she bites out before walking away.

I should ask security to have her removed. She didn't have a pass and I'm pretty sure she isn't on any list I have.

My heart is still heavy and sad when Mikey finishes his set. The crowd loved it and that makes me happy, but I can't help replaying the scene of Mikey and that girl in my head. He says they aren't together, but she says something else, and so does that kiss. I want to scream and I want to cry, but I have a job to do.

Putting all thoughts aside, I go into work mode. I tell everyone where they need to be and what they need to be doing. Things are going awesome; the takedown is coming along a lot faster than I thought it would. I make notes of the staff that performed excellently so I can hire them again.

I'm talking to the photographer I hired when I see Mikey coming out of his dressing room. He walks towards me, but stops before getting too close. He is just staring at me. I see the same hurt in his eyes that I feel in my heart.

"Thank you so much for coming and taking awesome photos. I can't wait to see the finished pictures you send me." Smiling at the photographer, I give him my business card to make sure he has my email, then walk towards Mikey.

Mikey is standing with his hands in his pockets, looking a little timid. For such a large man, you wouldn't think he could look so scared. I want to know what is going on in his head, but I also just want to go home and cry.

"Hi," I finally blurt out, breaking the silence. I'm staring at my shoes because looking into his eyes is just too much for me.

"Hey." His voice sounds heavy with emotion.

I know I overreacted when I saw him with that girl, and I know he's been trying to talk to me, but I don't think my heart can take this.

"I know I said we could talk after the show, but I'm really tired, Mikey. I just want to go home," I half-lie.

I keep looking down. I can feel the tears bubbling in my eyes. I don't want him to see how he affects me and how hurt I was to see him kissing someone else.

"Please, Tia." He reaches forward and grabs my arm.

I want to pull away because his touch is too much, but I don't. I finally look into his eyes and my heart breaks more. He looks miserable.

"Let me explain," he continues.

"Mikey, it's fine that you have a girlfriend." I look away again, feeling the tears flowing down my cheeks.

He places his hand on my chin to lift my head. "But I don't have a girlfriend. At least not yet."

What is that supposed to mean? Are they just starting their relationship and keeping it a secret? Is that why she thinks they are together? I want to break down; I was trying to keep my heart guarded for this reason.

I pull away. "Mikey, I have to go. Great concert. I'll talk to you tomorrow."

Before Mikey can say anything, I run. I know I should be here for lockup, but I trust my team to do what needs to be done. I can't be around Mikey anymore without having a full-on breakdown.

The moment I get home, my phone starts blowing up.

Mikey: Please come back.

Mikey: Answer your fucking phone.

My phone won't stop ringing. Why can't he just leave me alone? I go into my kitchen for a bottle of wine, jumping when I hear a loud bang on my door.

"Answer the fucking door, Tia!" Mikey yells.

I freeze. I can't let him in. I don't want to see his face. He's with someone else. There is nothing I can do about it. I had my chance with him and I blew it. I slide down the cupboard, landing on the floor. Placing my head on my knees, I start to sob. Life is too fucking complicated.

The banging finally stops, but my phone starts buzzing in my pocket again.

Mikey: Let me in. I know you're there.

Mikey: Tia, seriously, open the fucking door.

Mikey: Fine. Suit yourself. Goodbye, Tia.

I'm lying in bed reading Mikey's messages over and over again. He spent half an hour banging on my door before giving up.

I've spent all morning in bed crying. Why did I have to be such an idiot? I can't do this with Mikey. Last night proved that more than anything. If I can't keep myself from overreacting to situations like that, how can I be in a relationship with a rock star? Of course he's going to have fans who want to kiss him. Of course there are going to be girls who are delusional and think that they're together. I'm way too insecure to deal with that.

I keep replaying last night in my head. He wasn't holding the woman. She was holding him, and he looked stiff. And that look of sorrow in his eyes afterwards when we were talking. He obviously wasn't into that woman, but I still lost it.

My heart is breaking from everything that happened. He doesn't need someone like me in his life. He needs a strong woman. Someone who can deal with crazy fans without losing her shit.

Me: Sorry about last night.

Mikey: We NEED to talk, Tia. Please let me come over.

Me: Fine.

I know Mikey isn't going to let this go; we need to have this conversation in person. Maybe I can finally get through to him.

I make myself a cup of tea and wait for him to show up.

"Thanks for letting me come over," Mikey mumbles as he walks into my apartment.

He looks like shit, and he has dark circles under his eyes. He clearly didn't sleep much last night. Well, that makes two of us.

I go to my living room, knowing that Mikey will follow. I choose to sit in my comfy chair and not on the couch so he can't get too close to me.

"You deserve a woman who isn't going to lose her shit over a crazy fan, Mikey, and I'm not that girl. I'm insecure and broken on the inside. I've replayed everything from last night over and over again in my head." I take a shaky breath, and the tears start. "I'm sorry I overreacted, but it just made it that much clearer to me that we can only be friends."

Mikey comes over to my chair and kneels in front of me. "I don't care about your insecurities. We can get through them together." He grabs my hand. "All I care about is that you trust *me*, and that you are willing to talk to me if things arise that make you uncomfortable."

I struggle to catch my breath. His eyes are pleading me to trust him, and I want to. So badly.

"I want to take you out on a real date and give this a try. Please let me. We could be so good together, baby. You just need to trust us," he says softly.

Before I realize what is happening, he is lifting me into his arms and placing the gentlest of kisses on my lips. I'm so taken aback, I don't even know what to do.

Everything in me is screaming to say yes, to give in, to let him love me, and to let myself love him back. Why can't we make this work? Why am I fighting this so hard? I should at least give this a chance. I'm already falling for him.

"I don't allow drugs in my life," I whisper.

"I've been clean for a few weeks," he tells me.

My eyes go wide. Even though I've thought about what I would do, what *we* would do, if he stopped using drugs, never in a million years would I have thought that he'd actually take the initiative to stop on his own.

"Why?" I stammer.

"You, Tia. I want to be a better man for you. I knew drugs were a deal-breaker, so I cut them out. I want you to be mine. Please say yes."

He's changing for me. How can I say no?

I place a soft, gentle kiss on his lips. "Yes."

Mikey growls, then deepens the kiss. I moan into his mouth. Damn, this man can kiss. I want him to take me to my bedroom and have his way with me, but I know we need to take this slow.

He slowly takes me over to the couch and pulls me onto his lap. I feel like he knows how I'm feeling and knows I need to take this slow, but he still doesn't want to break contact. Like he's afraid that if he lets go of me, I'll run.

We spend the next couple of hours just cuddling and watching TV.

I wake up on the couch and realize Mikey is gone. I guess I must have dozed off at some point. I feel sad and empty without him next to me, but then I see a note on my coffee table.

Sorry I had to leave, beautiful. I had studio time booked and my manager would have kicked my ass for missing it. But I want to take you out tonight. I'll be at your place to pick you up at 8 p.m. If that doesn't work for you, send me a text. Be ready, baby. I'm here to woo you.

Xoxo
Mikey

I giggle a little at the note. He *is* right. I hate wasting money, and missing studio time is a complete waste of money. I can't help but smile. He makes me so happy. I realize I haven't been truly happy in a very long time. Was I ever really this happy with Tom? I'm not sure. I thought I was, and maybe I was at first, but he made me change so much about myself I almost didn't even know who I was anymore.

Jay made comments about it all the time, and so did Leah. They warned me that losing myself for someone else wasn't healthy, but I didn't listen.

Mikey doesn't want me to change; he wants me for me, along with my insecurities and everything else. Tom only cared about himself, and what would make him look good. Mikey just wants us to be happy.

I glance at the clock and realize it's already 7 p.m. I rush to my room to take a shower. Before I hop in, I shoot off a quick text.

Me: Where are you taking me tonight? What should I wear?

Mikey: How about nothing? *waggles eyebrows*

I laugh and roll my eyes. Guys.

Me: Ha, ha… No, seriously, what is the plan?

Mikey: Hmmm… Are you sure being naked isn't an option?

Me: I guess it can be. You won't mind when other guys stare at me, right?

Mikey: Trust me. Where we're going, baby, it will only be you and me. No one will be able to hear your screams. ;-)

I gulp. Wow, that thought is hot.

Mikey: I'm taking you somewhere special. Wear something comfortable.

Mikey: I promised I was going to woo you, baby. Prepare to have your socks knocked off.

Where could he possibly be taking me? I don't know, but I'm excited.

I rush to get ready and decide to wear my comfy jeans and a cute long-sleeved shirt. I place loose ringlets in my hair and do a simple makeup look. I feel great and I can't wait to see where the night takes us.

MIKEY

I get to Tia's place just before eight p.m. and I'm nervous. I've never been nervous to pick a girl up before, but this is different. I've never had feelings like this before. I look in my backseat to make sure I have everything I need, and then I head up to Tia's apartment.

I knock on the door, and my breath is taken away the second I see Tia. Her snug-fitting shirt is showing off her curves perfectly, and those tits…man, I can't wait to get them in my face.

"You look amazing," I manage to choke out.

Her smile is breathtaking; I lean in to give her a quick kiss.

"So, where are you taking me?" she asks as we head towards my car.

"A place I never bring anyone, but I wanted to bring you." I hand my phone over to Tia. "Pick a playlist. It's a bit of a drive."

She gives me her best smile as she scrolls through my phone.

"Your taste in music doesn't surprise me at all," she giggles while putting on some classic rock.

"What do you mean? You say that like it's a bad thing. What's wrong with my taste in music?"

She lets out a big laugh. "Hmm." She puts her finger on her chin like she's thinking. "Nothing's *wrong* with it, but it's pretty much just rock, with a tiny bit of pop, and some metal. Where's the country? Or classical?"

I look at her, raising my eyebrow. "Country? Seriously? I don't want my ears to bleed."

Country is the worst. It all sounds the same. Your truck got stuck, you lost the girl, now you're drinking beer. If you've heard one country song, you've heard them all.

"What?" she shrieks. "Country is great!"

Wow. I have fallen in love with a girl who loves country music.

Wait. Did I say love? Can you love someone this fast? Maybe you can. I know I've never felt like this before, and it just feels right. I felt something close to this a long time ago, and this connection doesn't happen often. I don't want to let it go.

Tia makes me feel alive. After I left her place this morning, I almost felt high. I've been buzzing off that feeling all day. The feeling of her on my lips is burned in my memory.

"We are going to have to agree to disagree there, beautiful," I tell her.

My focus is back on the road, and I drive us to the place I always go to clear my head. We drive for about an hour out of the city and finally arrive to a remote tree line.

Tia looks around, obviously confused. "Is this where you murder me?"

I laugh. "Nope. Come on. We have a little bit of a hike to get to where I want to go." I grab the stuff out of my backseat and start walking into the trees. "Are you coming?"

"I guess so," she whispers, her eyes darting around. "I think if I stay here alone, I'm going to be eaten by a bear, so I'd better come with you."

I want to hold her hand, but my hands are full with the picnic basket and my guitar. We walk in comfortable silence until we finally get to where I want to be.

The lake looks perfect, as always. The sun is starting to set, but is still shining just enough through the trees to cast a perfect glow. The wildflowers are in full bloom and giving off a fantastic scent. I lead us over to the bench that my dad built years ago and set down the stuff.

"Wow. How do you know about this place?" she asks, taking in the view.

"This is my family's property; I grew up just down the road from here." I lay out a big warm blanket on the ground in front of the bench. "There's a quad trail just over there that leads to my parents' house." I point to our right. "We never wanted a road to here. This is our private getaway. We wanted it just for us."

"It's breathtaking," Tia admires, sitting down on the blanket. "How come I didn't know you came from the country? I always thought you were a city kid like me. Maybe you should be writing country music." She playfully elbows me in the ribs.

"I went to school in the city, but grew up out here. I'm really glad for it, actually. I come out here to write and commune with nature. I feel like it's grounded me." I pull out some sandwiches and give one to Tia. "I hope you like ham and cheese. I'm not much of a cook."

I shrug my shoulders with an awkward-feeling smile. That's an understatement. I suck at cooking. One time, I almost burned my house down. I decided then that I should stick to things that don't require a stove. I can make a pretty decent sandwich, and I wanted to impress her.

"I love sandwiches," she whispers, nervously biting her lip.

I sit down next to her and grab her hand. "Hey, are you okay?"

She's avoiding eye contact and just looks out at the lake. "I've never been treated like this before." She finally looks into my eyes. "You make me feel so special, and I just don't know how to react."

I lean over and caress her cheek with the back of my knuckles, feeling her shiver under my touch. "I care a lot about you, Tia. I want to make every day special for you."

I place my other hand on the back of her neck and pull her towards me, brushing my lips softly against hers. When I pull away, she looks deep into my eyes, as if she's trying to read if I'm lying or not. She doesn't say anything else, but leans in so her lips whisper on mine. I pull back, asking for permission with my eyes; she gives me the green light by pulling me back to her and deepening the kiss.

Her hands make their way into my hair, and I love the feel of her long nails on my scalp. My tongue passes over her lips and she opens, giving me access. As our tongues dance around each other, I feel myself starting to get hard. I start to roam my hands over her back, needing to feel her. I feel my erection growing and I know I need to stop this before I can't. I pull back, gasping for breath. Looking into her beautiful eyes, I see sadness.

"This has nothing to do with you." I place my hands on either side of her face, so she is forced to look into my eyes. "If you look down right now, you'll see how badly I want you, but I don't want to pressure you into anything. Let's take this slow." I kiss her gently.

"What if I don't want to take it slow anymore?" she asks with a little pout.

"How about we start a fire?" I suggest with a smile. "And then I want to play you a song."

She smiles. "Okay, that sounds nice."

Tia moves the blanket next to the small fire pit while I get the fire started. Once it's the size I want, I grab my guitar and sit down on the blanket facing Tia. I start to sing about a girl who's my world, about her perfect eyes and perfect soul. I look at Tia and see the tears filling in her eyes. I wrote this love song for her. I've never been with someone I've felt more connected to. The last time I had this strong of a connection with anyone was with a girl in junior high, and I never even talked to her. I finish the song and set my guitar down.

"Do you like it?" I ask, pulling Tia into my lap.

"It was amazing," she whispers. "It reminds me of 'Girl With the Hidden Smile.'"

I wrote that song about the girl from junior high. Although the song has a happy ending, our ending wasn't like that. I never had the courage to talk to her and should have stood up for her more. I hoped maybe she would hear it and know it was about her, but I don't know if she did. I still think about her sometimes, but I know things happen for a reason. Tia's eyes remind me of that girl, but she would have said something if that was her. Wouldn't she?

"That used to be my favorite song, but I think I have a new favorite now." She smiles at me.

This woman is perfect. I have no idea how I got this lucky to have her in my life.

"It's my new favorite too," I agree, and then kiss her cheek.

We stay silent for a long time just watching the lake and nature. It's starting to get dark, but I don't want to leave yet.

"Do you want to get going or would you like to make some s'mores?" I ask her. "I have all the supplies."

Her whole face lights up like a kid's on Christmas morning when I mention s'mores.

"Oh, my God, Mikey! I love s'mores!" she exclaims. "How did you know?"

"I didn't, but I know *I* love them, so I was just hoping." I give her a wink.

The more I get to know her, the more I realize we have in common.

Sixteen

TIA

I am so excited to be hanging with Mikey out in nature. I never would have known he was a country boy, and I still can't believe he *hates* country music. I *will* make him a country fan. He won't know what hit him.

I sit on the blanket watching Mikey get the s'mores ready. This has been the best date of my whole life. I've never had anyone take care of me like he does. It's like he knows me on a whole different level, yet in reality, we don't even know each other that well. I want to change that; I feel like I can be honest with Mikey about everything. But I'm still uncertain if I should tell him about who I used to be.

Will he look at me differently? Will he remember the ugly girl I used to be? I just don't know. It's hard to open up about being bullied to anyone, yet alone to someone who was there when it happened. I don't want people to think I'm weak. I've taken care of myself for my whole life. My past is in the past, and it made me the strong woman I am today.

"So, you said you're a city girl, born and raised. What high school did you go to?" Mikey asks, breaking me from my thoughts.

"I was homeschooled for most of junior and senior high. I was able to graduate early and start working towards what I wanted to do with my life." It's not a lie, but it's not the whole truth either.

He looks at me and smiles. "So, have you always wanted to work in the music industry?"

"Not really, but I'm so glad I started at Eaststreet. I loved working with the Broken Hearts. I wouldn't be who I am today without those guys. They're my family, and now that I know the music industry like I do, I love it so much." I pause for a moment. "The music industry wasn't my first choice. I was thinking maybe photography, but I needed a job and it's like the music industry chose me. What about you? Have you always wanted to be a musician?"

"Yeah. I played some sports in high school, but music was always my real love."

I smile; I can see in his eyes how much music means to him.

"What's something else you really love and are passionate about?" I ask.

I want to get into his head and really get to know him. I know I'm already falling for him; I just want to make sure it's going to be worth giving him my all.

"Well, I support this awesome charity, Hope For the Forgotten, so I guess that would be something," he tells me.

"That's right. I saw you have an event for them coming up next week." I bite my lip and look away. "What is the charity for? Sorry, I haven't had time to look them up yet."

Man, I feel stupid. My cheeks heat and I turn my head towards the fire, away from Mikey. As his manager, I should know what charities he supports and what they're for.

"It's okay. I don't expect you to know absolutely everything, Tia. You're already pretty perfect. If you add mind reader to your list of talents, then you would definitely be out of my league."

I giggle. Me, out of his league? Yeah, right. He takes a piece of hair that's hanging in my face and tucks it behind my ear, his hand lingering a moment too long, and I shiver.

"They help kids who have been bullied. I saw a lot of it in high school. I'll be the first to admit, I stood idly by while it happened and I feel like shit about it, but I want kids to know that's not okay, and that if they see that happening to someone, they should stand up and say something." He rakes his hand through his hair. "I was a chickenshit, and I didn't stand up to my friends. If I could go back in time, I would do things differently. There was this girl that I should have stood up for. I kick myself every day for not being her voice."

I take a deep breath. I never expected him to support an anti-bullying charity. It sounds like a great cause. I may have to talk to the leaders and see about making a donation or being a speaker. I've always wanted to talk to kids who are being bullied and let them know there is light at the end of the tunnel.

"That sounds like a great cause. I can't wait to hear more about it," I say quietly.

I stare into the fire, watching the flames crack and spark. I keep thinking I should tell Mikey my real name, who I am, or rather who I was, but I'm scared. Things are finally going great between us, and I don't want to wreck them again.

"You okay?" Mikey asks, reaching for my hand. The warmth of his skin on mine feels amazing.

"I'm fine. I was bullied as a kid, so it's great knowing that you're helping kids like me. That's all."

It's so easy to get lost in his eyes. I want to tell him he made a difference as a teen, even if he thinks he was a chickenshit, but I'm just not ready yet.

"I'm so sorry to hear that, sweetheart, but you turned out perfect, so you clearly had some people looking out for you," he says, smiling at me.

"I did." I smile back at him.

Everything about tonight is perfect. I'm so glad I gave this a chance.

I look up at Mikey and it's as if I see him in a new light. My decision is made. I sit up straight, place my hands on his face, and pull his mouth to mine. I can tell I took him by surprise, but he puts his hand on the back of my head and pulls me closer to him. I open my mouth for his tongue and moan as his hand moves to my side.

"I need you, Mikey," I whisper into his ear, then bite his neck.

"Are you sure?" He pulls back slightly, staring into my eyes for an answer.

I grab the hem of his shirt and start to pull it off. I hope he takes that as the "yes" I'm meaning it to be.

My breath catches when I see his hard chest and abs. This man clearly puts a lot of time in at the gym. Mikey rips off my shirt as if not seeing me naked is killing him. His eyes dilate when he sees my red lacey bra, and I know I made a good choice. He moans and covers my breast with his mouth.

I lean back and mewl when he bites my nipple through the lace of my bra. With lightning-fast fingers, he unhooks my bra and flings it into the darkness.

"You're perfect," he whispers against my skin, as he trails kisses and nips his way down my body. He stops at my belly button to undo my jeans and takes them off at the same time as my panties.

I am completely naked now and I should be cold, but I'm not. His hot breath is keeping me warm. He continues his trail of kisses until he lands right on my most sensitive area. I buck my hips when his tongue reaches out to part my folds.

"You like that?" he asks before going back for another lick.

Fuck, it feels so good.

"Yes, Mikey! Don't stop!" I cry out.

He inserts a finger and I let out another shriek. I'm thankful we are in the middle of nowhere, because there is no way I could be quiet right now. He slides another finger in and picks up the pace. I can feel my orgasm building up as he pulls my clit into his mouth.

"Oh. My. God. Yes!" I scream out as my orgasm washes over me.

I take a few moments to recover, but I'm nowhere close to satisfied. I need more.

"I need you inside me, Mikey. *Please*," I beg.

I see a sadness come over his face. "Baby, there is nothing I would want more, but I don't have any condoms."

I pull him up and kiss him like my life depends on it. I can taste myself on his lips, and it's actually a turn-on.

"I'm on the pill and I trust you. I need you."

"Are you sure, sweetheart? We can wait. I promise I'm okay with it."

I can tell he's being honest.

My hands go to his jeans and I start to pull them down. I want this so badly, and I can't wait any longer. When he started telling me his story about high school, I knew I wanted to give this to him. He helps me shuck his jeans and his body hovers over mine.

"I've never gone bare before, and I get tested regularly," he tells me while peppering kisses over my neck and shoulder. It feels so good.

"I trust you," I whisper.

Our mouths smash together like if we don't kiss this second, the world will end, and he slowly slides inside me.

"Fuck," he hisses out.

He is big, and I feel so full. He slowly moves his hips more and I love everything I am feeling right now. The coolness of the air, the heat of his body, even the roughness of the ground beneath the blanket. I am never going to forget tonight. He sucks my breast into his mouth, and I can feel that I am about to come again. He starts to move faster, and I know my orgasm is seconds away.

"Fuck, baby. I'm not going to be able to last," he grunts out.

"Don't stop!" I cry out. "That feels so fucking good. Come with me."

My climax hits me hard. I don't think I've ever had an orgasm this powerful before.

Mikey lets out another grunt and I feel him fill me up. I've always used condoms because, honestly, I didn't trust that Tom wasn't cheating on me. And it's a good thing I did, since I found out he actually *was* cheating on me the day we broke up. Tom was always so focused on himself in our relationship and I was always put on the back burner. But things feel so different with Mikey. I love that there are no barriers between us. After he pulls out, he grabs me and circles his arms around me.

"Sorry about that being so fast," he whispers into my hair.

"That was amazing. No one has ever made me feel like that before." My heart is beating so hard right now, I feel like it could come out of my chest.

I didn't realize at the time; I should have felt more cherished with Tom. Mikey makes me feel special, wanted, needed. Things I should have felt with Tom, but didn't.

He kisses my cheek and holds me. The world is silent besides the odd noises of nature and the crackling of the fire. Everything is just perfect right now. Not only did I just have the best sex of my life, but I feel honored to be in this special place with Mikey, a place he never brings anyone.

After laying down for a while, I start to shiver. I can feel Mikey's body heat, but now that the sun has set, it's not quite enough.

"Come on, let's get you dressed," Mikey says, sitting up and pulling me to my feet.

"You think we're going to be able to find my bra? You gave it a good throw," I chuckle.

"Damn thing was in my way." He winks at me.

If this is a hint at what life with Mikey is going to be like, I'm glad I said yes.

I'm meeting Mikey at the studio today to hear some of his new songs. I've been posting like crazy on his social media about his return to the studio and for his fans to expect new and exciting things this year. But I haven't heard the new stuff myself besides an acoustic version of the song he wrote for me.

When I enter, I see Mikey standing behind the microphone with his headphones on. He's wearing sweats that are hanging low on his hips and a sleeveless Metallica shirt. He is concentrating so hard on the lyrics that he doesn't notice me come in. His voice sends shivers down my spine; the way he hits those notes is almost orgasmic. This song is soulful and sexy. I'm really liking it.

He finishes up the part he is on, then looks my way. His mouth turns into the biggest smile I've ever seen, his dimple on full display. I can't help but smile back. Being with Mikey makes me so happy, and seeing him light up like this makes my heart flip. The way I am drawn to him is like nothing I have experienced before. I crave being with him. It's like he is my drug.

Mikey takes his headphones off and exits the recording booth.

"You made it!" he exclaims while picking me up and spinning me around.

I let out a loud joyful shriek before he sets me down and claims my lips with his. I melt into his touch; I'm addicted to the way he makes me feel.

"So, what do you think of the new song?" he asks.

I smile up at him. "Well, I only heard about three seconds of it, but it sounds super sexy."

He nips at my neck. "Good. That's the vibe I was going for."

I chuckle and push him away. "I'm here as your manager, so get back in that booth and show me what you've got."

"Come on, we could sneak away and have a quickie." He wiggles his eyebrows at me.

He's almost buzzing, and he seems like he's too happy.

I narrow my eyes at him. "Have you been using again?"

I want to trust him, but I know how hard it can be to stay away from drugs. Especially in this industry.

He throws his hands up. "No, I swear. I'm just happy with life right now. You make me like this."

My face softens and I smile. I believe him. So far, he's proven to be honest. I have to give him the benefit of the doubt.

"Okay," I concede. "Now, I mean it this time. Get back to work and show me what you've got."

He gives me one more lingering kiss before nodding and walking away.

My smile never leaves my lips the whole afternoon. Mikey gets a lot done, with plenty of breaks in between to give me kisses. He keeps telling me that he'll die if he doesn't stop to touch me. I giggle, but the feeling is mutual.

"So, give me all the details," Leah urges when she comes over for some much-needed girl time. "Is he as huge as the tabloids say?"

She wiggles her eyebrows at me. I blush and throw a pillow at her.

"Bigger," I admit, biting my lip.

Leah's jaw drops. "And he didn't split you in two?"

I let out a belly laugh at that comment. "No, but I was pleasantly sore the next day. Seriously, Leah, I don't think I've ever been happier."

Her face lights up. "I'm so glad to hear that. You deserve it!"

Sipping our wine, we sit in comfortable silence. "So, what about you? How have you been doing?"

Leah's face falls a little. "It's been better, but I'm getting there. I think I just need some time to heal." She looks out the window and plays with her hair. "It's easy to be angry. I just wish I would have seen through his lies."

I move closer on the couch and pull her into my arms and give her a tight squeeze. "I'm so sorry that you've had to deal with this, hon. I hope Chad dies a fiery death."

She giggles and squeezes me back.

"But seriously," I continue. "You deserve to be happy too. I know one day you'll find someone who makes you as happy as Mikey makes me."

She gives me a small smile. "You are the best friend a girl could ask for. Thanks for always being my anchor."

We spend the rest of the night drinking wine and watching reality TV.

The rest of the week goes by in a blur. Mikey and I talk every day and spend a couple of nights together. Everything seems so perfect. I don't want to hold my breath, though. Just when I think things are going awesome, something always seems to put a wrench in them.

Tonight is the gala for Hope For the Forgotten and Mikey asked me to be his date. This will be our first outing as a couple, and I'm a little nervous. I've never been huge in the public eye, since I'm just a manager. There have been the odd rumors about me dating the guys from the Broken Hearts, but other than that, the media typically leaves me alone. But once they get word that I'm dating Mikey Ecosta, I don't think I'll be so lucky.

I've spent the last hour getting ready with a hair and makeup artist. I never splurge on these kinds of things, but I want to look extra special for tonight. I know Mikey thinks I look beautiful all the time (he tells me so every chance he gets), but tonight feels special. Like the first big milestone in our relationship. Just thinking of him gets me giddy.

I look at my phone and realize it's eight p.m.; Mikey should be here any minute. I put on my sparkly six-inch heels that look killer with my bright red dress. It's a long dress, but the back is completely open, almost showing my ass. It's classy, but extra sexy. I take one last look in the mirror, loving the person looking back. I feel strong, beautiful, and powerful. The light in my eyes is back, and I finally feel like the woman I was before Travis passed away. The woman I was before I changed myself to be the woman Tom wanted me to be.

There is a knock at the door, snapping me out of my thoughts, and I smile brightly. I open the door and my breath is taken away. I've never seen Mikey in a tux before, but man, he pulls it off nicely. It's clearly been tailored to fit him, and the bright red tie matches my dress perfectly.

"How did you know I was going to be wearing a red dress? I just bought it today!" I exclaim.

Mikey gives me the cheekiest grin but doesn't say a word. Then I remember telling Leah about the dress earlier and connect the dots. This man is always one step ahead of me, and I think I love it.

I take Mikey's arm and he escorts me to the limo waiting for us. I'm used to limos and fancy events, but being Mikey's plus one, his date, feels different. It feels special, and it feels perfect.

As soon as we are in the limo, Mikey grabs my face and puts his lips on mine. I melt into him. I might have seen him yesterday, but I already crave being with him.

"God, I missed you," he whispers against my lips. "Is it wrong that I want to spend every minute with you?"

I giggle, because I feel the exact same way. "If it's wrong, I don't want to be right."

He resumes kissing me, moving to my neck and shoulders. "I know this gala is important, but I can't wait to get you out of this dress and bury myself deep inside you."

I blush; I never used to like dirty talk. It always seemed forced to me, but with Mikey it's so natural. It's perfect.

"We'll have plenty of time for that afterwards. I used the code you gave me and stopped by your place earlier to leave a bag, so I'm good for a sleepover," I tell him.

Mikey's eyes go wide. "God, woman, you're perfect. I'm never letting you go."

The confession leaves me speechless. Is he really going to want me forever? I'll eventually have to tell him my real name. Will he still want me then? I take a deep breath and push the thoughts away. Now is not the time. Maybe after the gala.

MIKEY

Entering the gala with Tia on my arm, I look around and smile. I've never been prouder. She looks absolutely amazing. I started sporting a chub the second I saw her, and these pants don't have a lot of room in the crotch area, so this might be an interesting night. I try to think of anything that will get this erection down, but every time my eyes land on Tia, my thoughts go straight to the gutter.

The gala is in full swing when we arrive, and everyone wants to get a picture of us. Tia is a natural and doesn't look nervous at all. That makes me happy. As much as I hate all the attention sometimes, it's part of the job, and I need someone in my life that isn't going to get upset about it.

As time moves on, I start to get nervous. I have to make a speech tonight and I absolutely hate it. I know I sing in front of thousands of people at a time, but public speaking is different. I've fucked up a lot of speeches because of nerves, and this one is really important. This is the biggest event the charity puts on, and the money is needed to get these kids help. They put it towards events for the kids, but also towards getting some of the kids the therapy they need.

As if reading my mind, Tia squeezes my hand and leans into me. "Are you okay?"

I squeeze her hand back and give her a kiss on the cheek. "I'm fine. Just hate having to give a speech."

Giving me the best smile, she presses a soft kiss to my lips. "You'll do great. I just know it."

Those words make me feel much better. Maybe tonight I won't fuck up. Maybe Tia is my lucky charm.

"Ladies and gentlemen if you would please take your seats, it's time for the speeches," the emcee announces.

I place my hand on the small of Tia's back and guide her to our table.

I'm the last one to speak tonight, to close out the Gala and thank everyone for coming. I have my speech in my pocket, but I'm really starting to sweat. For some reason, my anxiety is starting to spike. I wonder if it has something to do with Tia being here tonight. I want her to be proud of me, and everything I do, but I'm not proud of how I acted as a teen, so how could she be?

We listen to the speeches, from some people who have experienced bullying as kids, and I look at Tia and notice that she's crying.

"Are you okay?" I ask, placing my arm around her shoulder and pulling her into my side.

She looks up at me and her eyes are glossy. "I want to speak like those people, to help people who have been bullied, like I was. I want to tell my story one day."

She is such a strong woman; I am grateful to have her with me. And seeing how emotional she is right now gives me an idea.

The emcee calls me up. I stand, but I pull Tia up with me.

"What are you doing?" she whispers, glancing around.

"Giving you a chance to tell your story." I don't let go of her hand and start walking towards the front.

Tia follows behind me I glance back and see she is staring at the floor with wide eyes. Her hand is gripped in a fist. Maybe this wasn't the best idea. I probably should have run this by her first.

As we get to the front, I lean down and whisper into her ear. "Only if you are okay with that. I don't want to pressure you into anything, but I saw how moved you were by everyone else's stories, and I want to give you a chance to tell yours."

She stares into my eyes and nods hesitantly.

"Hello, everyone. Welcome to the gala. First of all, let's have a big round of applause for the previous speakers."

The crowd cheers and I glance at Tia to make sure this is okay. She gives me a small smile.

"I know I'm supposed to be giving you a speech and thanking you all for coming, but my girlfriend has an even better story to tell. Please put your hands together for Tia Marie."

The crowd applauds politely, but I see some people whispering. They weren't expecting this and are probably a little pissed. I step to the side to let Tia speak. She looks nervous, but she takes a deep breath and pulls her shoulders back, then looks at me.

You can do this, I mouth.

She smiles and nods.

"Hi, everyone. I'm Tia Marie, but that hasn't always been my name."

Her name isn't Tia? How did I not know this? What is her real name? Why hasn't she told me yet? It's seemed like we've been opening up to each other more lately, but apparently not as much as I thought.

"My birth name was Patricia Marie Daggen. I changed it after being bullied in school, for a long time."

Every last bit of air escapes from my lungs. Patricia? The girl with the hidden smile? The girl who I desperately wanted to help, but felt like I failed? She is Tia? I knew her eyes looked familiar. Why didn't she tell me the night I told her about where I went to school? She told me she was homeschooled. She knows who I am, but never said anything. I feel betrayed, lied to, and more than a little pissed off.

I try to calm myself down so I can listen to the rest of Tia's speech, but what I really want to do is just walk the fuck out. I hate being lied to. There is nothing that pisses me off more.

"Growing up, I was slightly larger, and just an awkward kid. Some kid thought it would be funny to call my Fatty Patty, and all his friends laughed at me, and would kick me when I was down. All except one." Tia looks at me and gives a timid smile before looking back at the audience. "There was one sweet boy who would always smile at me and make his friends move on. He never talked to me, but his kindness in other ways made me strong enough to leave school and homeschool myself. I thought about him for years and I never forgot that he was the one who made times in school bearable." She looks back at me again and this time holds eye contact while she continues. "He felt like he failed me, but he didn't. He felt like he should have done more, and maybe that's true, but to me, those smiles and him not joining in with the others was enough." She turns back to the audience. "I wanted to kill myself when I was young, but because Mikey smiled at me and didn't tease me, and didn't call me names, it gave me strength to keep on living. Michael William Ecosta is the reason I am alive today. He may think that he let me down because he didn't stand up to the bullies, but that couldn't be further from the truth. He was a hero, even if he didn't realize it."

Tia steps back and the room explodes into thunderous applause. She looks at me with tears in her eyes.

"I'm sorry I didn't tell you who I was earlier. I didn't want to ruin what we were starting. I didn't want you to take pity on me or think of the girl I used to be." She breaks down into sobs.

Pulling her into my arms, I kiss the top of her head. I was pissed that she didn't open up to me, but how can I stay angry when it clearly took a lot of strength for her to tell her story? I pull her face up to mine and kiss her.

"I love you," I whisper, and then turn to the audience.

"See, didn't I tell you this woman had a much better story to tell? She gave a much better speech then I ever would have been able to. I want to thank everyone for coming out and listening to all the stories that were told tonight."

Everyone cheers and the band begins playing soft music. I pull Tia to the side and kiss her one more time.

"Thank you for coming tonight and opening up. Now I know why I have such a strong connection to you. I've always wanted you, Tia, even in school. I hated myself for not standing up for you because even back then, I felt like we had a connection, but I was too chicken to talk to you."

Tia's face lights up. "I guess we were always meant to be together."

Just as I am about to take Tia back to my place, Amanda, the founder of the organization, stops us.

"Thank you so much for sharing, Tia! Your story was amazing!" She grabs Tia's hands and Tia beams at her. "I would really like it if you came to our teen event in September. We love letting kids know that bullying doesn't have to be the end. That people can grow up to be successful no matter what happened to them in the past."

"I would absolutely love to!" Tia's smile is as big as her face.

She just glows when she's happy like this. I hate that she was bullied as a kid, but I'm glad that she grew up to be a strong independent woman, and that she is mine. Reaching into her purse, she pulls out a card.

"Here is my number. Give me a call and I will definitely be there," she tells Amanda.

Amanda gives Tia a giant hug and walks away.

"You are amazing; I am incredibly lucky to call you my girl." I pull Tia into my arms and give her a soft kiss. I want to deepen it, but I know if I do, I won't be able to stop, and I want Tia in my bed tonight. "Let's get out of here. I want you to myself and naked." I wiggle my eyebrows at her.

Tia giggles and bites her lip. "Naked sounds fun. Let's go."

As soon as we get into the limo, I am on Tia, kissing her neck and running my hand up her thigh.

"I want you in my bed, but I don't think I can wait that long," I growl into her ear.

Giving her my best "fuck me" smile, I drop to my knees in front of her. I see her breath catch and her eyes dilate. Yeah, she wants this.

"I've always wanted to have fun in a limo. Are you ready to be my first?" I tease.

I wiggle my eyebrows at her and lift her dress. I run my cheek along her thigh and hear her moan.

"You smell so good, like strawberries and something that is strictly you," I murmur.

I move closer to her pussy and let my hot breath float over her. I feel her wiggle underneath me as I swipe a finger under her lacey thong.

"Are you always this wet or is it just for me?"

"Only you," she chokes out in a heavy breath.

Slowly, I slide her panties down towards her ankles and slip them off. I look up at her before I go down and trace a lick through her folds.

"Fuuuuccckkk," she hisses out.

I love watching her come undone like this.

She runs her fingers over my back and into my hair. After I give her another lick she tugs on my hair and I can't help but let out a moan.

"Keep going, baby. You feel so good," she whimpers.

Fuck, I love a woman who isn't afraid to tell me what she likes. I love to worship her body. I want to put her needs first. She is my queen; I'll do anything she wants me to.

Looking up, I see Tia rest her head back. I insert two fingers inside her and feel how fucking tight she is, and I love it.

"You taste fucking delicious. Come for me, baby. I know you're close," I say while holding eye contact with her.

Lowering my head again, I suck her bud into my mouth. I feel her contract around my fingers, but I don't let up.

"Oh, my God! *Yes!*" she screams.

I keep sucking and lapping at her juices, not wanting to miss a drop. I start to slow down, knowing that this could be almost too much for her. As her breathing starts to even out, I slide her dress down. I pull myself up and sit beside her, pulling her face towards me to give her a passionate kiss. I pour out all my love to her and hope she feels it.

Eighteen

TIA

Thinking back to Mikey telling me he loves me at the gala, I sigh. I was so taken aback that I didn't know what to say. We *just* started dating. Can you love someone that fast? I feel like we have always been connected, though. Like we were destined to be together. So maybe you can.

Resting my head on Mikey's shoulder, I look up at him. This night didn't go entirely how I thought it would, but it was still perfect. I was so afraid of losing Mikey, and when he told me to tell my story, I knew I was going to piss him off. I should have told him the night at the lake.

"Tonight was perfect, Mikey." I look into his perfectly blue eyes and feel like I'm staring up into the sky on a clear summer day. "I'm really sorry for not telling you sooner about who I am. I just was terrified."

He kisses my lips softly. "I get it, sweetheart. I admit, I was a little pissed off when you first started telling your story. I wish you would have told me sooner, but I get why you didn't. We've all had times in our lives where we lacked courage, but tonight, you showed so much strength. I'm proud of you, baby."

He pulls me into his lap to be able to look at me better. We sit there silently for a bit just staring at each other. It's a comfortable silence. I love that we can be so comfortable together. When things got quiet with any of my exes, it was always awkward, but it's not with Mikey.

"I love you, Mikey," I confess. "I feel like I've loved you since we were kids. Is that crazy?"

He chuckles and shakes his head. "Absolutely not. I have a confession to make. You know that song you love? 'Girl With the Hidden Smile'?"

I nod; it has always been my favorite. Well, second favorite, now that he has written that new love song for me.

"I wrote it for you. I know we didn't get our happily ever after back when we were kids, but I feel like we're getting it now."

Staring at him, I am at a loss for words. I always felt a strong connection to that song and now I know why. I can't believe he wrote it for me. He really did care for me back then. I can't help but wonder how life would have been different if he would have told me, but I'm a firm believer that everything happens for a reason. Our paths came back together like fate, and now we can be happy together.

Still coming up empty for words, I press my lips to his. I swipe my tongue across his lips, and he grants me access. Quickly, I deepen the kiss, his tongue meeting mine. Mikey glides his hands up and down my spine, and it sends tingles all over my body. I arch my back slightly. I can feel myself getting wet again, and I can feel his firm bulge against my thigh.

"Well, we crossed one sexual encounter off your bucket list. Why not go for two?" I ask as I throw my leg to the other side of him so I'm straddling him.

He moans, and just as I think we are about to have sex in the back of a limo, I feel us come to a stop.

"Fuck," Mikey curses. "Next time, baby. We're here." He kisses me and I let out a little pout. He chuckles. "You're cute when you pout."

Mikey comes up behind me and grabs my waist as I'm brushing my teeth.

"You're coming to my birthday party next weekend, right?" he mutters while kissing my neck.

I giggle and try to push him away with my butt.

"You make brushing my teeth difficult," I sputter before spitting out the toothpaste. I grab a towel and wipe my mouth. "What are you doing for your party again?"

Mikey's birthday is the 4th of July, so I'm assuming it's going to be a big party. I'm not sure how I feel about that. Yes, we just went to our first big event together, but a gala is way different than a private party with all his friends.

"We're doing a big bash in the backyard," he tells me. "Barbecue, drinks, and fireworks to end the night. Make sure to bring your bathing suit for the pool."

Giving him a devilish grin, I turn and trace my finger over his bare chest. "Did I say I was coming?"

His eyes darken as he picks me up, carrying me to the bed. I squeal and laugh as he throws me on the bed and starts peppering kisses over my shoulders and neck.

"You'd better be there; my birthday would suck if my girlfriend wasn't there," he says against my skin.

I smile so big it almost hurts. I love hearing him say *girlfriend*. I fought this so hard, and now I'm kicking myself for not giving in on day one. I'm just glad I gave in when I did. I can totally see a happily ever after with Mikey.

Today is the 4ᵗʰ of July, and I'm so excited to spend the day with Mikey. We have spent lots of time together this week, but we've been trying to be somewhat professional when we're working. Today, we get to just be a couple. I have butterflies in my stomach.

There have been a ton of articles about us since we were seen at the gala. Most of them are saying how we are a cute couple, and how Mikey looks happy again, but there a few telling mean lies. One said I am using him to further my career, and there was another saying how I'm just another notch on his bedpost. I know that I should know better than to read them, but still it's hurtful to see people talking about me like this. I'm used to the odd article, but everywhere I turn lately, I see our faces, and I don't know how to feel about it.

Looking in the mirror, I give a little twirl. This new bright red maxi dress is beautiful. I never used to wear a lot of red, but Mikey told me it was his favorite color on me. Since it's his birthday, I thought I'd surprise him. It's not super sexy, but my red, white, and blue bikini underneath it is, and I know he's going to love it.

My phone buzzes, pulling me from my thoughts. I know it's Leah here to pick me up. Leah agreed to come with me, since I don't have the happiest of memories of Mikey's house. And I'm not sure which friends will be there. I hope there aren't any drugs there. That would be a temptation Mikey doesn't need. Running my fingers through my hair one last time, I grab my sunglasses and overnight bag and head out.

"Thank you so much for coming," I tell Leah as I slide into her car.

I'm planning on spending the night, so I figured it would be easier for Leah to drive us and Mikey can just give me a ride home sometime tomorrow.

"Anytime. Maybe I'll meet my Prince Charming." She wiggles her eyebrows at me.

She isn't really looking for Mr. Forever, or even Mr. Right. But Mr. Right Now? She is definitely looking for him.

We get to Mikey's house and the party is already in full swing. Walking through the front door, I almost freeze. There are *a lot* of people here. Nobody looks familiar to me, and for some reason, I feel like I'm going to have a panic attack.

"I can't do this," I whisper to Leah.

Giving me her perfect smile, she pulls me through the people. "You've got this, girl. You've never been shy of crowds before."

"I know but I've never dated a rock star before either," I protest. "These are Mikey's friends. What if they hate me?"

"Then fuck them. You're dating Mikey, not them."

She has a point, but I'm suddenly very self-conscious.

After shoving my bag in the hall closet, we make our way to the backyard, and I light up when I see Mikey. He's in swim trunks, standing by the pool. He looks absolutely fantastic. His abs are on full display and his hair is slicked back; he must have just gotten out of the pool. I want to go over there and take a bite. I bite my lip; I can't wait until this party is over and I get him all to myself.

Leah and I start making our way over there when I see a very familiar redhead. I freeze. She's standing next to Mikey, her head tipped back like he told the funniest joke. She places her hand on his shoulder, and Mikey doesn't push her away.

"What's wrong?" Leah asks when she realizes I'm not moving.

How could he have invited her after the night of the concert? She clearly wants him, and he is with me. He must have known this would upset me. I don't even know what to do.

"Um, let's get a drink before we go see Mikey," I mumble, making my way back inside to the kitchen.

I grab a bottle of vodka and make an extra strong drink. I want to run away. If we are together, why would he invite a groupie, or an ex, or whatever the hell she is, to his party? And even if he didn't invite her, why wouldn't he tell her to get fucked the second she got here?

After a long pull of my drink, I finally turn to Leah. "Remember that redhead I was telling you about that kissed Mikey at his concert?"

"Yeah, the one who is delusional? You guys almost didn't end up together because of that skank," she says.

Taking another sip, I nod. "Yeah, well, she's here, and she was just throwing herself at Mikey. That's why I needed this drink."

Leah's mouth drops open and her eyes go wide. She's not speechless often, but this is one of those times. I'm trying to be calm. I promised Mikey that we would talk things through if I got upset, but I just don't understand why she is here. He can't be that clueless to think she wouldn't upset me.

After I finish my drink, I start to pour another. I'm almost done when I feel a pair of hands on my hips. I turn and see Mikey. His giant smile melts my heart, but I'm still upset. I try to force a smile, but it doesn't want to come.

He kisses me on the mouth, but I don't return it. His eyebrows pull together with a look of confusion.

"Is everything alright?" he asks.

I look up into his beautiful sky-blue eyes and shake my head. "No. Can we go somewhere to talk?"

I turn to Leah to make sure she is okay that I'm leaving her. She smiles and waves me off.

"I'll be fine. You two go talk. I'll find someone to spend some time with," she assures me.

Mikey grabs my hand and leads us to the bedroom. This room is filled with amazing memories, and now I'm concerned we won't be able to make any more. Sitting on the bed, I stare out the window. I know what I want to tell him, but somehow, I can't find the words to say it.

"Baby, please talk to me," Mikey pleads. "What is going on?"

I take a deep breath.

"Why is *she* here?" I manage to choke out.

Turning to Mikey, I see his confused face. "She, who?"

"The redhead from the concert, Mikey!" I shout, unable to keep the tears at bay anymore. "Why the fuck would you invite someone to your party that you knew I wouldn't want here?"

Staring out the window with tears streaming down my face, I avoid looking at Mikey. The laughter and music from the people at the party is so loud. Right now, I wish I was anywhere else.

"I didn't invite her, Tia. She just showed up." The bed sinks down as Mikey sits next to me. "We've been friends for a very long time. She knows I always have a party."

Biting my lip, I play with a piece of my hair. "I get that, but why didn't you send her away as soon as she got here? Did you think it would make me happy to walk outside and see you two laughing like best friends? Her hands were on you and you didn't push her away."

The tears are starting to slow down, but I'm not any less upset. I told him about my insecurities and about how this would never work. He promised me we could get through them. I'm not running, even though everything inside of me is telling me to. I'm talking to him like he asked. I just wish we didn't have to do this.

"I can ask her to leave if it would make you feel better," he says. "I just didn't want to cause a scene, so I thought it would be okay if she stayed."

I scoff. "Right. So now *I* have to be the one to cause a scene. Crazy girlfriend gets here and loses it over some bimbo."

Standing up, I start pacing. I feel like I'm crawling in my skin and I can't be still anymore. I shake my hands out, needing the movement.

Mikey stands and grabs my hand, stilling me. "Baby, I'm sorry. You're right. I should have thought about it more. Of course you're upset." He grabs my face and tilts it towards his. "Please let me make this right. I'll get someone to take Amber out of here and then we can go enjoy my party together." He leans down and kisses my lips softly.

I melt; this man can turn me to mush in a millisecond.

"Okay," I whisper.

He kisses me again and pulls me into his arms. His warmth makes me feel so much better. I'm glad I didn't run. He is proving to me that even though I have insecurities, we can work them out.

"Thank you for coming to me, baby," he murmurs. "I always want you to know you can talk to me about anything."

I go into the bathroom to freshen up before we head back to the party, hand-in-hand.

Nineteen

MIKEY

Never letting go of Tia's hand, I tell my buddy Craig to kick Amber out.

Why didn't I kick her out when she got here? I did think about it, but I didn't want her causing a scene. Instead, I upset my girlfriend and made an ass out of myself.

The second I saw Tia in the kitchen, I knew something was wrong. When I stared into her eyes, I saw a gloss over them, like she was on the verge of tears. And they were more blue than green. I've noticed this happens when she's upset. She didn't have to say anything for me to know something was wrong. When she didn't return my kiss, I knew it wasn't something minor. When we were in the bedroom, I knew she was ready to run.

I don't blame her. I was a fucking idiot for letting Amber stay, and now I'm going to have to make it up to Tia. I'm just glad she isn't running. Now I just need to make the rest of the day awesome, like I had planned from the beginning.

It's beautiful outside today. The sun is making it a hot day, and I can't wait to get Tia in the pool with me.

I look over at Tia and she still looks visibly upset. I stop us and grab her by the waist, planting a soft kiss on her mouth.

"Want to take that dress off and show me your bikini?" I wiggle my eyebrows at her.

She gives me the tiniest smile, but it doesn't reach her eyes. "Maybe later. Can we find Leah?"

She scans the yard for her friend, avoiding eye contact with me. I run my free hand over my face. Man, I really fucked up. I don't know how this day could get worse, but with my luck it probably will.

Taking Tia's hand again, we walk around looking for Leah. Finally, we find her inside getting a drink.

"Girl, you are not going to believe who I was just making out with!" Leah shrieks.

God, I can't even imagine. There are lots of people here today. I don't even know everyone here. That's kind of how my birthday turns out every year. It's always a big drink-fest and I don't typically care who shows up, but this year is different. This year I have Tia, and I don't care about all these people. I just want to make Tia happy and spend the day with her.

Tia puts on a smile and pretends to be interested. "Who? Please tell me it's someone famous!"

They both giggle. I see Tia returning slightly to normal, but I can still see the sadness beneath her eyes.

"I'll give you a hint. He's a baseball player." Leah is beaming with delight.

I freeze. Please, God, do not let Leah say Johnny. He was supposed to be out of town. I know it will send Tia over the edge if Johnny is here.

Tia bites her lip. "You know I don't watch sports. Just spill the beans. Who is it? Is he hot?"

Leah giggles. "Well, duh, he's hot. I wouldn't be making out with him if he wasn't." She looks over my shoulder and her eyes light up. "Girl, he's coming over right now. Be cool."

I feel a slap on my shoulder, and by looking at Tia's face, I know it's Johnny. The color completely drains from her face; it looks like she's stopped breathing.

"This is Johnny Crown," Leah beams, grabbing Johnny. "And Johnny, this is my best friend in the entire world, Tia."

Tia forces a smile, but it doesn't reach her eyes. "Nice to meet you."

Johnny stares at Tia for a second. "Do I know you from somewhere?"

Tia's whole posture stiffens. "I don't think so. Must just be a familiar-looking face."

"I didn't know you were going to be here," I mumble to Johnny, but my eyes are on Tia the whole time, pleading with her to believe me.

"I got back last night and knew I had to make your party, man." He grabs Leah by the waist and pulls her snug against him. "And damn, am I glad I did."

Leah giggles, and I see Tia tense up some more.

"I'm glad you made it, man, but if you'll excuse me, I want to spend some quality time with my girlfriend." I grab Tia's hand and walk away.

Knowing the theater room is most likely empty, I take Tia there. As soon as I close the door, I start apologizing.

"I swear to God, Tia, I didn't know he was going to be here today. I would never do that to you," I tell her.

Tia moves to the large recliner chairs and sits down, pulling her knees to her chest. She doesn't say anything, and I'm also at a loss for words.

After a few moments of silence, Tia pulls out her phone. She's refusing to look at me.

"I think I'm going to call an Uber and go home. I'm not feeling well, and I think I need some space," she mumbles.

This cannot be happening. Is she leaving me? I feel a panic attack coming on. I don't want to lose my girl before we even got a real chance at being an item. I don't want to push her into staying when she is clearly upset, but I feel like if I let her go, we might be over.

"Are you sure? I could drive you, or I could shut the party down. I just want to spend time with you," I say desperately.

She looks up at me and I see the tears falling. "Mikey, this is your birthday. Have fun with your friends. I'll be fine. I just need to rest."

I kneel down in front of her and kiss her hands. "Please, baby. I didn't mean to make you upset."

"I just need a little time to clear my head, Mikey. I'll call you tomorrow." She stands up, pulling me up with her, and kisses me passionately. Why does it feel like a goodbye kiss?

"Are we good?" I ask, searching her eyes for an answer.

She closes them and takes a deep breath. "I hope so, Mikey. Just give me some time, please."

With that, she walks out the door. I stand there, not knowing what to do. I know chasing after her isn't going to make a difference. It would probably make things worse, if anything.

I head to the kitchen and pour myself a stiff drink. Right now, I could use a hit, but then she'd really be done with me. I'm upset that my girlfriend walked out on my birthday, but I'm more upset that I'm the reason she left. For fuck's sake, why do I have to be such a fuck-up?

Heading to the pool, I see everyone having a great time. I need to just forget about everything right now and enjoy my party.

A few hours later, I'm drunk as fuck. Johnny comes up to me and sits down on the pool chair next to mine.

"Great party, man." He looks around like he's looking for someone. "Where's your girlfriend?"

"She left, so my new lover is this rum and Coke," I slur, holding my cup up.

"Dude, I didn't want to say anything, but I think I remember where I know her from." I stare at Johnny. His words are making no sense to me. "Remember the night you came out to All That Jazz with me? Well, I'm pretty sure your girl is the girl I fucked that night."

I see red.

"What the fuck did you just say?" I shout.

"Dude, calm down. I didn't know you and her were a thing. It was shortly after you left. I saw her dancing and I took her to the bathroom to fuck her. I didn't get her name and I haven't seen her since, but I'm sure it was her."

Tia was there that night, but why would she sleep with Johnny? She would remember him. He pretty much looks the same, and from her reaction tonight, she definitely knows who he is. Why would she sleep with someone she absolutely hates? I am so fucking confused.

"Are sure it was her? You were drunk. Maybe it was some other blonde."

"I mean, there is a possibility that it was someone else, but I really think it was her."

"FUCK!" I yell, and throw my patio chair into the pool.

Tons of people look my way, but I don't give a shit. This day is the worst day of my fucking life.

"Is Leah still here?" I ask, not really looking at Johnny. She would know if Tia slept with someone that night or not.

"Nah, man, she left a while ago. She got a text and had to leave. Something about a friend emergency. But I got her number." He winks at me, then slaps me on the back. "Sorry for the bad news, man, but I'm sure you'll figure it out. You can get all the pussy you want. Don't let this girl get you down."

I pull at the back of my neck. I don't know what the fuck is going on. I thought Tia left because she came face-to-face with the guy that made her life a living hell in junior high. Now I'm wondering if it's because she didn't want me to know she slept with him. Why the fuck would she sleep with Johnny? Was it some kind of way of getting back at him?

I make my way back to the kitchen. Fuck mixing drinks. I grab the bottle of tequila and take a shot. It fucking burns, but I take another. I should probably talk to Tia. I asked her to talk to me if something came up that upset her, so I know I should do the same. But here I am, drinking my problems away instead of dealing with them.

The fireworks are beautiful, as always, but I wish my girl was here. Before I head to bed, I call my housekeeper to come over first thing in the morning. I know there are drugs in the house, and I need them out of here ASAP. If I wake up in the morning and find anything here, I know I won't be able to stop myself. When I head to bed, the party is still going, but I know Betty will get everyone out when she gets here in the morning.

I can't stop thinking about Tia and Johnny, and it makes my blood boil. We weren't technically together when she slept with him, but her lying about it pisses me the fuck off.

I toss and turn all night, trying to forget everything I learned from Johnny. Getting out of bed, I groan. I shouldn't drink like I did last night. I'm not as young as I once was. I know I should call Tia and talk to her about last night, but every time I pick my phone up, I can't do it. Today is going to be a long day, I can already tell.

I'm exhausted as I head to the kitchen to make myself a pot of coffee. I'm thankful that Betty already showed up and everyone is gone. My house is exactly how I like it: clean and empty.

I lean against the counter and put my head back. I am such a fuck-up. I had the girl in my grasp and now she's gone.

My phone beeps, drawing my attention. A picture of the girl of my dreams pops up.

Tia: Can we talk? I'm sorry about yesterday.

I don't respond. I don't know what to say to her. Am I the reason she slept with Johnny? Was I pissing her off and she felt she needed to fuck me out of her system?

I don't know if a relationship between us is going to work. All I am ever going to think about now is her and Johnny together.

TIA

When I left the party, I came straight to my place and changed into some comfy pants. I cried pretty much the whole time until Leah showed up. She told me she didn't want me to be alone. I opened up to her about everything. Told her about how Johnny bullied me and how seeing him was just too much for me. She was so mad at herself for kissing him, but it wasn't her fault. She didn't know who he was because I never opened up to her.

I feel like I slightly overreacted by leaving the party, but it was all just too overwhelming. First Amber, and then Johnny? It's like everyone who has ever hurt me was there. Next to show up would probably have been my mother, but I don't even know what she looks like.

We spent the rest of the night watching chick flicks, eating ice cream, and drinking wine. I'm relieved Leah came over; I really needed my best friend. A small part of me wishes Mikey would have chased after me, but I told him not to, so I shouldn't be surprised.

After texting Mikey all morning, with no response, I'm starting to go crazy. I know he is probably hung over, but it's not like him to not return my calls.

"Did you see Mikey before you left the party?" I turn to Leah, who is lying in bed with me.

"I'm sorry, hon. As soon as I got your text, I gave Johnny my number and left." She grabs my hand, and I let out a small sigh. "I definitely won't be answering if he calls."

The next week goes by kind of slowly. Mikey starts returning my texts, but he's being so vague. He won't talk to me on the phone and any time I suggest us meeting up, he comes up with a lame excuse as to why he can't. He's been keeping everything about business, and it feels like our personal relationship is falling apart.

Finally, having had enough, I decide to drive to his house. I understand I ran away from him, but to stonewall me for a whole week over it seems a little ridiculous. Pulling up to the gates at his house, I have this uneasy feeling, like something bad is about to happen. I enter the code Mikey gave me, but it doesn't work. That's weird. I swear I'm entering it right. I try one more time, but it still doesn't work. I push the buzzer.

"May I help you?" his housekeeper, Betty, answers.

Weird. She isn't normally in on Saturdays.

"Um, yeah, I was just wondering if Mikey was home," I say nervously.

"Sorry. Mr. Ecosta is out of town for a few days."

I'm speechless. He never told me he was leaving town, and it's not in his schedule. I'm pissed off now. I get that he's upset, but to lock me out of his house and to not tell me he was leaving town is a little over the top.

On the drive home, I call Mikey, but of course he doesn't answer.

"Look I understand you're upset I ran away from your party. Seeing Johnny just brought up too many bad memories. Please call me back. I miss you," I say to his voicemail.

As soon as I pull into my parking spot, the tears start. I can't breathe. I feel like I'm going to throw up. Why does it feel like we're over before we ever really started? There has to be something going on, but I don't know what. All I know is my heart is breaking, and I wish he would just talk to me.

He told me to open up to him, to let him know when something was bothering me, and I did that. How come he isn't doing the same for me? Why won't he talk to me? What could I have possibly done wrong?

I decide to do some work to get my mind off my heartbreak, but since the bastard causing my pain is my client, my thoughts are constantly drifting back to when things were good. Getting a little done, I feel a tiny bit happier. I can still be a good manager, even if my client is the asshole who stole my heart and beat it into the ground.

This is why I didn't want to try a relationship. At least before we took it to the next level, I wouldn't have been this broken. But now I know how good it could have been, and I don't get my happily ever after.

A couple of hours later, I hear a beep from my computer. Checking the email, I see it's from Mikey's producer. When I open the link, I hear a new song. It's raw and angry.

You're a liar
You're a cheat
You didn't miss a beat
You're a bitch
You're a whore
I can't do this anymore.

My breath leaves my body. The words make no sense. Is he talking about me? I never cheated on him. He's the only guy I've had sex with since I broke up with Tom. Is he so resentful that I didn't tell him the truth about junior high earlier? Why is he doing this to us? He told me talk to him, and I did about Amber, but now he won't give me the same courtesy and talk to me?

Pulling out my phone with shaky fingers, I write the text that I really don't want an answer to.

Me: I just heard your new song. Wish you would talk to me about how you feel. Are we over?

His reply is almost instant.

Mikey: Yeah. You were right. This will never work.

My heart shatters. I felt like this was coming, but now that the words are out there, I'm utterly devastated. I take in a ragged breath and feel my whole body shaking. This can't be happening. This has to be a dream. I was so close to my happily ever after and now it's being ripped away from me. Am I not good enough for him? I want to beg him to give us another chance, but I also want to tell him to eat shit and die. I don't do either. I just text my girl. She'll make this better.

Me: Girl, can you bring me some vodka? I'm fresh out.

Leah: On my way.

I know Leah will always have my back. Tonight, I'm going to drink my sorrows away, and let out all the tears. Tomorrow, I'm going to be the strong, powerful badass I know I can be. He won't destroy me.

Life has started to go back to how it used to be. Leah and I have resumed our regular girls' nights, and I feel like I can breathe, sometimes. There are always memories that make me break down, but the tears have slowed down, and I'm not crying myself to sleep every night anymore.

Tonight, Leah and I are having a movie date. I'm excited to watch a stupid chick flick and just laugh. We picked out *Pitch Perfect* since it's a favorite for both of us.

"For fuck's sake," I hear Leah curse from the kitchen. Coming into the living room with a big bowl of popcorn, she looks pissed off. "Johnny won't stop texting me. I didn't tell him about your past, but I told him he was an asshole and that I hope he chokes on his own tongue and dies."

"That's a little extreme, isn't it?" I raise an eyebrow at her with a small smile.

"Don't tell me you haven't had dreams about his death in the past." Setting the popcorn down, she sits next to me.

"Totally have," I giggle. "What is he saying?"

You'd think he would get the hint and stop texting her, but he's been texting her non-stop since they met.

"Just stupid shit mainly. How he can't forget me, how the memory of my lips has ruined him for all other women." She laughs and rolls her eyes at the thought. "One of the weird messages I got though was an apology. I don't know what he has to be sorry for. He said something about doing it for a friend and he didn't realize it would upset me that much. Then he asked how you were doing, which is so weird. He met you for three seconds. Why would he care?"

"Doing what for a friend?" I wonder aloud. "And why is he asking about me? That is a weird thing to say."

Leah finishes her mouthful of popcorn. "Yeah, I don't know what he meant. I haven't responded to any of his messages. I think I'm going to have to change my number."

I laugh, but there is some weird feeling I have towards that message. What could he be apologizing for? And why is he asking about me? I don't think he remembers twelve-year-old Patricia, but something definitely seems off.

The next month goes by in a rush. Mikey and I seem to have a fine working relationship. We keep most of our conversations to texts or calls. Seeing each other face-to-face is still hard, but we do it when necessary. He keeps telling me I'm being too much of a hard-ass, but if he wants to get to the top, that's how it's got to be. I'm not going to coddle him. I'm not his mother and I'm not his partner anymore.

Today is my day off, and it's supposed to be a girl's day, but I can barely get out of bed this morning. I've been fighting this weird flu for a while now. I think it's just the stress of my life right now.

About one week after Mikey and I broke up, there were paparazzi pictures of him and Amber all over each other. I almost threw up, but I don't blame her for snagging him back, she clearly wanted him. I guess some girls get what they want in the end.

"Have fun last night?" I bite out at Mikey as I enter the studio.

"I did. Not that it's any of your business."

"Actually, it is my business. I'm your manager, and when your image starts to take a hit because you're hanging out with sluts, that affects me."

"Oh, please. You're not upset because my image is going down the toilet. You're pissed because it wasn't you I was fucking last night."

I move towards him and get into his face. Wrong move. His scent immediately fills my nose and I'm lost for words. I want to ream him out, tell him how my life is so much better now that we are no longer in a relationship, but I can't think of anything.

I stare into his face and see his nostrils flare. Do I affect him the same way he affects me?

"Why did you end it, Mikey?" I whisper.

I want to be strong, but when I'm this close to him, I just want him. I don't care that he broke my heart. I'll take him back. He is *my heart. Without him, what is the point of living?*

He leans down, and I think he's going to kiss me. I want him to kiss me.

Just kiss me, Mikey, and this will all be forgotten, *I silently plead.* We can move on. We can make this work.

He grabs my waist gently, his touch sending tingles through my whole body.

But instead of kissing me, he pulls back and leaves the room without another word.

Leah pulls the blankets off me, breaking me from my thoughts. I'm instantly freezing.

"Can we just stay in?" I grab the blankets, needing the warmth.

"I'm taking you to the doctor. This is ridiculous. You've been sick for weeks. That's not normal," she says sternly.

I sigh, but agree and let her help me up. She's right; this isn't normal. I've been throwing up a lot, and when that stops, I just have no energy. I honestly think I'm depressed. I just want so badly to be over what happened and move on, so I push all the feelings down.

A little while later, Leah takes me to a walk-in clinic.

"Do you want me to come in with you or stay in the waiting room?" Leah asks while holding my hand.

"I'll be fine. You just wait here," I whisper as the nurse calls my name to go in.

After giving a urine sample, I wait in the room for what feels like forever before the doctor walks in.

"Ms. Daggen?" the cute elderly doctor asks.

"That's me," I say, giving my fakest smile.

"Well, it seems congratulations are in order." She beams with a genuine smile that reaches her eyes.

"Um, I'm sorry. I don't understand."

"You're pregnant, dear."

My mouth drops open, and my eyes go wide. I feel like I'm going to pass out. This cannot be happening. How the hell is that possible? I was on birth control.

"Bu...but I'm on birth control," I manage to stammer out.

She looks at my chart and nods. "Yes, I see that, but I also see you had antibiotics a couple of months back. Did you use back up contraception?"

I shake my head. I completely forgot that antibiotics can make your birth control ineffective. How could I be so fucking stupid? I start to cry, and the doctor touches my hand.

"Would you like a pamphlet on your options, dear?"

I shake my head again. I know my options, and I'm keeping this baby. I'll tell Mikey and he can choose to do what he wants. I won't force him out of our child's life, but I won't make him be involved either. That's up to him to decide. I can take care of this baby on my own if I need to.

"I'm keeping it," I manage to choke out between sobs. "It's just a bit of a shock is all." I think back to all the alcohol I have consumed since the breakup. "I didn't know I was pregnant, and I've been drinking. A lot. Is the baby going to be okay?"

God, this child isn't even born yet, and I could already be fucking it up for life.

The doctor gives me a sympathetic smile. "It's still very early. The baby should be fine. But I do not recommend any more drinking, or smoking. I'll schedule you an ultrasound with an OBGYN so we can figure out how far along you are."

I nod. "Thank you."

The doctor leaves me alone and I call Mikey, but it goes to voicemail.

"Mikey, answer your fucking phone for once. I need to talk to you. It's urgent," I growl.

Sending a text message for good measure, in case he doesn't listen to his voicemail, I walk out of the office and fall into Leah's arms.

"Do you think I'm going to make a good mom?" I ask before breaking out into a full sob.

MIKEY

"What are you doing here, Amber?" I ask as she climbs into my lap.

The music is so loud here at the club, I'm not even sure she can hear me.

She grabs my face and smashes her lips to mine.

"I am so sorry to hear about your breakup. I thought I would come and make things better."

I'm not sure how she knows about the breakup. As far as I know, the tabloids haven't gotten a hold of that information.

She licks my neck. "Let me ease your pain."

I shouldn't do this. I know this will fucking wreck Tia, and I'm sure people are taking pictures, but I don't give a shit. I grab Amber's face and bring her lips back to mine. She tastes like a fucking bar mat. She's clearly been drinking a lot, and I almost gag.

"Let's get out of here." I say, standing and pulling her with me.

Her smile is so big. I'm definitely getting laid tonight. Maybe I can fuck Tia out of my head, because the alcohol isn't working.

Tia keeps giving me shit for drinking and partying so much. Says my fans aren't liking what they are seeing from the paparazzi. But I don't give a flying fuck. She's my manager and wants to get my career back on track, but I just want her to get off my fucking back.

I called my lawyer last week to see if there was any way to get out of the contract, but he said I would have to pretty much pay her every penny I have. Leah came up with an iron-clad contract, that's for sure. I don't want to leave Tia without a job, but seeing that we have to work so closely together, it's really fucking hard. I still love her, and I know I'm being an ass to her, but I can't let her back into my life.

Johnny texted me this morning and I responded for the first time since my birthday.

Johnny: Dude, can we talk? I know you're pissed at me, but I have something I have to tell you.

Me: I'm busy with interviews and have a concert in Vegas tomorrow. We can have beers when I get home.

Weird. I feel like I can forgive Johnny. How come I can't do the same for Tia? It's probably because I've been forgiving Johnny for our whole lives. His mom died when we were seven and it really fucked him up. His dad used to beat the shit out of him. That man was a real asshole and a man whore, and I think Johnny's just acting the only way he knows how. How can I stay mad at a guy who had such a shitty upbringing? He didn't even know Tia when they slept together. He never lied to me about it.

I have a few interviews I have to get to today, and tomorrow I fly out to Vegas to do a show with Jay. I look at my phone and see that I've missed several calls from Tia. I don't even listen to the voicemail. I just shoot her a quick text.

Me: I haven't forgotten the interviews. I don't need to be mothered.

Her response is instant.

Tia: IT'S URGENT! CALL ME NOW!

Nothing can be that fucking urgent. I don't want to talk to her right now.

Me: Later, Tia. I'm fucking busy right now.

I see the bubbles pop up like she's texting, but she doesn't respond. I know I'm treating her like shit. I feel bad about it, but I just don't know how else to act right now.

"So, Mikey, what happened with your relationship with your manager? We saw you guys looking so cute together, and then the next thing we know, you're making out with that redhead. Did you cheat on Tia?"

This reporter is starting to piss me off. I thought we were here to talk about my album, not my shit show of a personal life. I wish I could drink during interviews. At least that would make it easier.

"I like to keep my personal life personal. Can we talk about the album?"

The reporter smiles at me. "Of course, but first, do you think maybe you're getting a little old for all the partying we've seen you doing? Your fans have taken to social media saying how they don't like this version of you. Do you think it's going to affect your album sales?"

I am so fucking done with this interview. If it wouldn't look horrible, I would walk, but she is right. My fans are pissed at me, and they are who I need to buy this album. Walking would just make them even angrier.

"I've always been a party animal. I'm sure my fans know that. But I want them to know, I hear them and am planning on changing my life up a bit. I love my fans; they are why I am here today," I say, pasting on a fake smile.

That seems to satisfy the reporter and she finally starts talking about my music.

The rest of the interviews for the day pretty much go the same way. I am so excited when I finally get on the plane and can be alone.

The flight to Vegas is boring, as usual. I'm only here for one night and I'm trying really hard to stay out of the sight of the paparazzi, so I won't even be partying after the concert. I really want to get fucked up and forget everything, but after talking to all the reporters, I feel like they have a point. I am getting too old to be acting like this.

I get to the venue and I see Jay.

"Hey, man. Thanks for inviting me out for this show," I tell him. "It's going to really get my fans excited for my tour next fall."

Jay glares at me and I've never seen him look so pissed off.

"Have you talked to Tia yet?" he bites out.

Fuck. What's his problem? Just because we broke up doesn't mean everyone has to bite my head off.

"I sent her a text yesterday. I'll call her when I get home tomorrow," I snap back.

Jay shakes his head and walks away. "Whatever, man."

Tia was right all along. We never should have tried this dating thing. It's just made everything awkward, and possibly has fucked my career up.

Rehearsal goes awesome and now it's time for the big show. Jay is ignoring me, but his band seems pretty awesome. I do my regular hype routine and get ready for some guy to announce me. When I take the stage, the crowd is a lot smaller than I expected. I know I'm the opening act and more people will show up for Jay, but I've always had a large following in Vegas. I wonder if this has something to do with all the shit that's been happening in my life.

I give my all for the fans that did show up, and they eat it up. By the time I'm done, the crowd is starting to fill up. Jay will have a packed house. I'm happy for him; I just wish I had the same.

I'm pissed at myself that I let my life get away from me. I'm on a path of pure self-destruction. This is all my fucking fault. Tia was fucking right.

Me: I'm sorry about all the shit I've been doing. What can I do to get back in good graces with my fans?

I'm about to leave the venue when Pauly, Jay's guitar player, stops me.

"You fucking killed it, man, but is something wrong? You just seem down," he notes.

"Girl problems." I laugh it off like it's no big deal.

"I hear you, man. Women can be a headache sometimes." He slaps me on the back, then reaches into his back pocket and pulls out a bag of coke. "Snort a couple lines of this and you'll forget all about her."

I haven't touched drugs since I cleaned up my act for Tia. I've been drinking a lot, which probably isn't fucking smart either, but I needed something to numb the pain, and that isn't working anymore. I shouldn't, but I put the baggie in my pocket. Forgetting Tia wouldn't be a bad thing.

I'm pretty sure Tia isn't going to respond to my message, but as soon as I get to the hotel, I hear my phone go off.

Tia: Stop acting like an ass and listen to your manager. Then your fans will love you again.

I laugh. A real, genuine laugh. The kind of laugh I haven't had since my birthday. Tia makes me happy.

But then I'm instantly sad again. Why does this have to be so fucking hard? I wish I could get her out of my head. Maybe when I get home, we can have a good talk and get somewhere positive.

I grab the baggie out of my pocket and stare at it. Maybe I can finally get a good night's sleep and forget about Tia and all the heartache that brings.

I open the bag and dip my car key into the powder. Pulling it out, I stare at the coke. I close my eyes and bring it to my nose, snorting the bump. I take a deep breath as I start to feel the familiar high. Fuck, I've missed this.

Grabbing my stuff from the luggage area, I head towards the door, ready to call an Uber, when I see Johnny. He's leaning against a wall, staring at me. Does this seriously have to happen today?

"So, I guess you really wanted to talk?" I say, walking past him, knowing that he is now my ride.

"Yeah. Want to hit a bar or just go home?"

We start walking towards his truck. I'm dragging my feet, already regretting this.

"Home, man. I've got beer in the fridge. I'm super fucking tired from last night."

He examines my face. I start to fidget slightly. Does he know I got coked out last night?

"Yeah, you look like shit."

Thank God he doesn't know, or at least that he's not bringing it up. It's not like he is one to judge anyway. He's the one who first introduced me to cocaine. We continue the rest of the walk in silence.

Once we're in his truck, I expect him to start it, but he doesn't. He runs a hand over his face. He fidgets with his key, but doesn't put it in the ignition.

"Listen, man..."

I raise my hand, cutting him off. I do not have the energy for this conversation yet. At least let me get home and comfortable. And drunk.

"Not now. I need beer first."

He nods and starts the truck.

We are silent the entire drive. My head is fucking killing me. I wish I had more drugs to get rid of this headache, and also maybe make this conversation easier. I have no idea what he plans on saying, but there is no way it's going to be an easy conversation.

I grab my stuff and head into the house with Johnny right behind me. He has his hands in his pockets and is staring at the ground.

Heading for the fridge, I grab two beers. I'm opening mine when my phone starts ringing. Glancing at the caller ID, I see a face I don't want to see. Especially not when I'm with Johnny. If I could separate the two, maybe I could make my life go back to the way it was. But who am I kidding? Life is fucked now.

"Leave me the fuck alone," I mumble under my breath.

"Who is that?" Johnny asks, grabbing his beer from me.

"My girl. The one you fucked," I bite out.

Johnny places his beer down and rubs a hand over his face.

"Have you spoken to her?" he asks while peeling at the label on the bottle.

"No, and I don't want to be talking to you either. Thanks for the ride. I know I said we'd talk, but I can't fucking do this, man." I take a long pull of my beer.

"You need to take her call."

I shove Johnny. "I don't *need* to do anything."

Anger is bubbling inside of me. Who the fuck is he to tell me what I need to do? He's the one who fucked my whole life up.

"Calm down and take her fucking call, Mikey," he says evenly.

He doesn't push me back, and I'm surprised. We've fought in the past and he always pushes me back. He doesn't put up with my shit, and I don't put up with his.

"Get out of my house!" I yell at him.

The longer I'm in his presence, the more I realize why I've been keeping him at arm's length. He reminds me of better times. Of things I can no longer have.

"She's pregnant," Johnny says.

Wait. What? She's fucking pregnant? How the hell is that possible? Is it my baby? No, it's probably Johnny's baby. That's why he knows. Why else would she tell him?

"What the fuck did you just say?" I narrow my eyes at him. I'm going to fucking kill him.

Johnny puts his hands up and takes a step back, as I drop my beer to the floor and clench my hands into fists.

"You knocked up my fucking woman?" I yell.

I can't see straight. My vision is blurry, and I swear to God, Johnny is a dead man. This is my worst nightmare coming true. There is no coming back from this.

I swing at Johnny's face, but he's expecting it and moves out of the way.

"Listen, man, that's what I came here to explain," he says calmly.

I swing again, this time landing a perfect punch on his jaw.

He stumbles back, grabbing his face.

"There is no explaining. You're a piece of shit and you need to get out of here," I growl.

"Come on, Mikey. Just let me explain. It's all a misunderstanding," he insists.

I run at him and take him down to the ground, landing punch after punch. He's blocking the punches he can, but isn't punching back. He finally pushes me off of him and stands.

"Please let me tell you the truth," he says with blood running from his mouth.

"Get. The. Fuck. Out. Of. My. House!" I yell at the top of my lungs, taking a breath between each word.

His face falls. I can tell he doesn't want to leave, but tough shit.

"Get out of my fucking house or I'm calling the cops," I warn.

"At least talk to Tia," he says with defeat in his voice.

As the door closes my phone starts ringing again.

"You fucking bitch," I answer.

"Excuse me?" Tia says, and I can tell I've taken her by surprise.

"You heard me! I hope you and Johnny are happy together. You'll make a beautiful baby. Don't ever talk to me again."

I hang up, not letting her respond. I'm fucking done with those two.

Tia was my everything. Everything was better with her, and I only had her for a short amount of time. What if I could have spent my entire life with her? What an amazing life that would have been.

I bring up Pauly's number and make the call. "Hey, man. Do you want to set me up with more of that stuff you gave me last night?"

TIA

It's been three weeks since I've spoken to Mikey. We haven't communicated in any way, besides an email he sent, telling me he was taking a break from everything. He said I could sue him for everything and that he just didn't care anymore. Of course, I haven't. I'm just letting him have some space.

I'm still so confused as to why he thinks the baby is Johnny's. I wouldn't touch Johnny with a thirty-foot pole. I've tried calling, but he never answers.

And I'm really pissed at Leah for telling Johnny that I'm pregnant. I wanted to be the one to tell Mikey. Maybe then we could have worked this out. He wouldn't be stonewalling me, not giving me a chance to tell him my side.

No. Instead he thinks I'm with Johnny, and that Johnny and I are having a baby. Johnny, who mercilessly bullied me until I dropped out of school and started homeschooling myself. Perfect. Just fucking perfect.

I'm finally done with the first trimester of my pregnancy and feeling a lot better. I was around ten weeks pregnant when I found out. I feel like I'm starting to show, but Leah insists it's not noticeable at all.

Today is the day I have to talk to teens about bullying. I'm supposed to tell them how life can turn out amazing. How you can get through anything if you're strong enough. But I don't even know if I'm strong enough. My life is falling apart at the seams right now. What am I supposed to tell them?

I've been trying to work on a speech all week, but nothing seems to come out right. I don't have anything, but I can't bail on these kids. I make my way over to the community center, praying something will come to me before I have to speak.

Pulling up to the building, I feel a calmness rush over me. I wish I had something like this when I was young. Someone to tell me to not give up, that it does get better. I'm in a rough patch of my life right now, but I know it will get better. It has to.

Putting my hands on my belly, I look down.

"We've got this, Bubbles," I whisper to my unborn child.

When I first saw her on the ultrasound, the first thing I saw was bubbles, so the nickname stuck. I don't know the gender for sure yet, but I've been having weird dreams about baby girls, so I've started referring to her as a girl.

When I walk into the center, I see a bunch of happy kids. They have so much light in their eyes as they are laughing at the fun games the volunteers have put together for them. There is a group of girls taking selfies together and laughing. I don't have any memories like that from my childhood, but I know this is going to help these kids so much.

Looking around, I see a girl who looks to be about sixteen or seventeen and is very pregnant sitting by herself off to the side. I'm not due to talk for another half an hour, so I make my way over to her.

"Can I sit with you?" I ask.

She looks up with a half-smile and nods.

"I'm Tia. What's your name?" I say as I take the seat next to hers.

"Crystal," she replies, looking out at the crowd. "Are you one of the volunteers?"

I smile at her. "Kind of. I'm the guest speaker for today."

She doesn't smile back. "Oh, great. Another person to tell us that life doesn't suck, and everything turns out sunshine and roses."

I laugh. "Yeah, I guess that's what I'm supposed to say, but do you want to know a secret?"

She turns to me, finally making eye contact.

"I don't know what I'm going to say today, because to be honest, I don't know if life turns out sunshine and roses. It sure doesn't seem like that right now," I admit.

I feel the tears starting. Damn hormones. I try to blink them back, but I feel a few escape down my cheek.

She looks at me, searching my face. "Wow. Someone who is real, for once."

"If I would have given this speech two months ago, it would have been much different. Life seemed like it was going perfect, but now I'm not so sure."

I look across the room and see the volunteers chatting with the kids, laughing, making them feel like the world isn't such a shitty place.

"What's your story?" I ask turning my attention back to her.

She lets out a sigh. "I just wanted someone to love me. I come from a shitty household. My parents would rather spend money on drugs and booze than on me. I don't have the most stylish clothes and the girls at school love to tear me down." She pauses for a minute. "So, I went to a party one night and the most popular guy at my school asked me to go for a walk with him. I said yes. He was so sweet to me, and we started dating. Well, I guess it wasn't really dating. We never told anyone. Just hung out in private for a while." She stops for a minute, fidgeting with her hands, then takes a deep breath. "He told me he loved me, and I believed it, so when he asked me to sleep with him, I said yes. The next day, he stopped talking to me." I see a tear break from her eye and roll down her cheek. "I was a fucking idiot. When I found out I was pregnant, I was even more stupid, thinking maybe this would make him want to get back together. But he laughed when I told him. Said he never loved me and just wanted in my pants. I asked what he wanted to do with the baby and he told me to 'take care of it.' I couldn't do that, so now I guess I'm going to be a single mom."

More of my own tears roll down my cheeks. I pull her in for a hug. She stiffens at first, but then melts into my embrace and we just cry together for a few minutes.

Pulling away, she stares into my eyes. "How am I going to do this? I can't put her in the foster system. I've heard way too many horror stories. My house isn't really the most stable of environments either."

"You're having a girl?"

She nods. "Yeah, I found out at twenty weeks. I'm thirty-three weeks now, so it's not much longer before I meet her."

"You are going to be an amazing mother. I can already tell. The fact that you don't want her to suffer means you already love her with all your heart." I feel the same love for my unborn child. "You just gave me an idea. Please tell me you're going to be at the speech to listen to me."

Smiling, she nods again. "I wasn't going to, but now that I know it's you, I will definitely be there." She leans in and wraps her arms around me. "Thanks for listening to me and being real."

After giving Crystal one last squeeze, I make my way over to Amanda.

Amanda lights up when she sees me. "I am so glad you were able to make it today."

Giving her a quick hug, I smile. "Me too. Before I give my speech, I was wondering if I could ask you a few questions."

Our chat goes amazing. I am so happy, I'm practically beaming. I never would have thought about this if it wasn't for my shitty luck and talking to the very brave Crystal.

The volunteers have moved a bunch of chairs into a semi-circle with one chair placed at the front for me. Seeing all the kids waiting for me makes me a bit nervous, and my palms are sweating. I take a deep breath; I can do this.

"Hey, everyone. I'm Tia, and I guess I'm kind of like you guys," I start.

A bunch of kids are texting and not paying attention. They've heard these kinds of speeches before. But this one is going to be different.

"I was bullied so badly that I quit school and homeschooled myself. I wanted to take my own life, because I didn't see what good could come from this shitty world. I was supposed to get up here and tell you that it gets better, that if you work hard enough all of your dreams can come true. But, to be honest, I don't know if that's true."

The whole room goes silent. The volunteers' mouths are hanging open, and I have all the kid's attention now.

"I'm not going to lie to you and blow smoke up your ass. You're old enough to know that the world can be a bitch."

I hear Amanda clear her throat. Looking at her, I mouth "sorry." Sometimes my potty mouth runs away on me. I make a mental note to work on that.

"Everything isn't always going to be sunshine and roses, but what I do want to tell you is life's still worth living." I pause and look at my belly. Bubbles is already the best thing that has happened to me. "I've had everything I wanted get ripped out from under me, and I still know it's worth living. You will find one person who is your rock, and that's all you need. When the storms hit, and they will hit hard, just hold on to your rock and know that after every storm, there is a rainbow. The rainbow won't last forever, and there will always be more storms, some bigger than others, but there will always be another rainbow. That's what you need to remember."

Thinking about my rock, Leah, I smile. She has been by my side for everything, and I don't know what life would be like without her.

"I want to tell you all one more thing. I have been talking with Amanda and we are going to start a chapter for teen moms. You will be partnered with another mother and have unlimited support. This is our way of letting you know that you're not alone, and you have a rock to help support you." I look out and find Crystal sitting in the audience, smiling. "We are also going to be starting a bunch of weekly groups in different areas of the city, so you guys can connect more often. Maybe someone here will turn out to be your rock and lifelong friend."

The kids all cheer and smile. I'm ecstatic that I came today. Everyone starts standing up and putting the chairs away so they can start more games. I make my way over to Crystal and give her a big hug when I get there.

"Thanks for sticking around. I want to offer to be your mom support system, if you'll have me," I tell her.

She looks at me, obviously slightly confused. "You have kids?"

I smile and giggle. "Not yet, but I'm about thirteen weeks along, so I'll be popping out this baby shortly after you do."

Crystal snorts, then covers her face in horror. "Oh, my God. I hate that I'm a snorter."

Patting her on the shoulder, I grin. "Don't you worry about it. Some guy is going to find it endearing one day. So, what do you say? Want to be my mommy BFF?"

She gives me the biggest smile and nods. "I would really like that."

I give Crystal one last hug and we both have happy tears in our eyes. I put her phone number in my phone and head home. I thought today was going to be hell, but instead, it actually turned into a perfect day.

MIKEY

"You're so fucking sexy when you beg for my cock," Johnny says, pushing Tia to her knees.

She smiles at him, her plump lips parting. "You're so much bigger than Mikey. I love it."

She licks the tip of his cock and he moans. She opens wide and takes him fully in her mouth.

"Yeah, take my cock. Let me show you how a real man can rock your world."

He pulls her up and throws her on the bed. As he enters her, he bites down on her neck.

"I'm better than Mikey, aren't I?" he asks as he moves in and out of her.

"So much better," she moans. "I had to fake it every time with him. I never fake it with you."

I startle awake, sweat dripping down my whole body. These fucking nightmares are getting ridiculous. I just want to have one night where I don't think about Johnny and Tia. One night where I don't see them together when I close my eyes.

I stumble down the stairs in search of my phone to hit Pauly up when I hear my doorbell ring.

"Hey, dude. I come bearing gifts," Pauly says, waving a bag in front of my face.

I go to reach for it, but he pulls it away, walking past me to the living room.

"You still owe me from last time," he says placing the cocaine on my coffee table.

I grab a wad of cash and place it in his hand.

"I'd love to stay and partake, but I have other places to be," he says with an evil smile.

"See you next week," I mumble.

Pauly stops and turns around. "Don't you think you should slow down, man?"

"Mind your own fucking business," I snap. "I don't pay you for therapy."

He throws his hands up. "Whatever, dude."

Shortly after he leaves, my phone pings. It's always someone checking in. Why won't they just leave me the fuck alone? Can't they take my silence as a fucking clue? I don't want to talk to anyone. I just want to be numb.

I walk into the kitchen, needing some fucking rum, and check my phone.

Johnny: Are you okay?

Johnny: Just stay out of trouble, man. If you need me, I'm here.

Tia: Hey, I know you're taking a break, but can you just give me a call letting me know you're alright?

The last people on earth I want to hear from, and they seem to be messaging me the most.

Pissed off at their fucking names, I shut my phone off.

Grabbing the bottle, I stumble back into the living room, tripping over the pile of empty liquor bottles. I should call Betty, but she doesn't need to see me like this.

Sitting down, I grab the new bag of cocaine and dump the contents out onto the coffee table. I grab the razor blade and start cutting lines. Pulling a dollar bill from my wallet, I roll it up tightly, and begin the process of making myself numb again.

I close my eyes, letting the drugs numb the empty feeling inside me. My muscles start to relax as I lean back on the couch. I bring the bottle to my lips, letting the rum wash away the rest of the pain. The pain that comes with thoughts of Tia and Johnny, together, having a baby.

I chuckle to myself, but the sound has no humor in it. I take in a deep breath and let my mind wander to happier times with Tia, when she was mine.

"You smell so good," I whisper into Tia's hair.

She cuddles more into my body. "Shh, I'm sleeping."

I chuckle. She warned me she isn't a morning person.

"I want to wake up every morning with you in my arms." I caress her back gently with my fingertips. I feel her shiver before she hits me.

"I'm ticklish! Don't do that," she whines.

I kiss her forehead and see her tiny smile.

"You are the most beautiful girl I have ever been with," I murmur.

"And you are getting on my nerves. Let me sleep."

I smile and stare up at the ceiling. I have the girl of my dreams in my bed, in my arms. Life is perfect.

I scream as I come back to reality.

Life *was* fucking perfect. Then the universe had to laugh at me and say, "Not today, Mikey."

"Fuck!" I yell as I grab an empty bottle and throw it at the wall, glass shattering everywhere.

I sink down to my knees and put my head in my hands. Why did Tia have to sleep with Johnny? Why did the only woman who could take my breath away have to sleep with my best friend? Nothing makes sense.

I can't take this. I get up and stumble to my bathroom, remembering that Johnny had oxycodone for pain management when he got hurt playing baseball, and left the bottle here.

Life isn't fucking worth living. The drugs and alcohol only do so much. When the numbness wears off, I'm left with paralyzing pain. I want the pain to end forever.

I go into my kitchen and grab a pen and a piece of paper and I start to write my feelings. I get it all out. I write to Tia, telling her everything I feel. All the pain, the emotions, the hurt.

She was my life; without her, I can't breathe.

I grab the bottle of pills again and pour them into my hand.

I feel the smoothness of the pills. They look perfect. My life used to be perfect. I start popping them into my mouth, one by one, following every pill with a sip of alcohol. Soon, nothing will matter. I'll be free of the hurt. I'll finally be able to feel nothing.

TIA

The past few weeks, I have been putting all my effort into starting up the teen mother support group. I have gotten a ton of responses from mothers wanting to help these young teens who have gotten themselves into sticky situations. Some are single mothers, others not, but they all just want to give love and wisdom to these young soon-to-be mothers.

Today is Crystal's thirty-five-week checkup appointment, and I promised her I would tag along. I love listening to the heartbeat. The first time I heard Bubbles's heartbeat, I cried so hard.

Mikey has been strangely quiet. I hope everything is okay. There have been no sightings of him from the paparazzi as far as I have seen, so that's good. It's just weird that he has pretty much fallen off the face of the earth. I try to send him texts, just asking for him to check in, but he never replies. My paychecks still get directly deposited like clockwork, even though I haven't actually been doing any work for him. I've been keeping his social media running, saying that he's taking a break to get some writing done, but will be out performing again soon. I don't really know if that's true or not, but it's keeping the fans happy.

I look at my phone and realize that I'm running late. Grabbing my purse, I run to the door. I'm just about to turn the knob when my phone starts ringing. Looking, I see that it's Leah. We haven't really been talking much since she let my pregnancy secret slip to Johnny.

"Look, I can't talk right now. I'm late meeting Crystal for her doctor's appointment," I answer.

"I'm on my way to get you. Text Crystal and tell her you have to miss this one. We need to go to the hospital now." Leah sounds like she's in shock.

"What's going on? Why do we have to go to the hospital?" I ask.

Leah is silent for a second, and I hear her take a deep breath.

"It's Mikey. He overdosed and he's in the hospital. I'll be at your place in two minutes."

My phone slips from my hands as I collapse to the ground. This feels like déjà vu. Like the exact same conversation that I had with Jay when he found Travis dead on the floor in his hotel room, with a needle in his arm.

I knew Travis suffered from depression, but he told me he was getting better. When we found out he committed suicide, I was shocked. Why didn't he come to me? Why didn't he get help? I'll never know those answers. That's the thing about depression and demons. They don't discriminate.

This cannot be happening again. I can't lose another person in my life like this. I start to sob uncontrollably. I was okay with raising Bubbles by myself, but at least I knew she'd have her dad in the world. Now he might be gone forever, and I feel like this is all my fault.

I hear one knock on my door before it bursts open. I'm lying on the floor, sobbing uncontrollably. Looking up, I see Leah come rushing in. She bends down and helps me stand.

"We have to go, hon. You know you're going to want answers, and we have to be there for him," she says quietly.

I nod and walk out with Leah. She takes my phone and texts Crystal, telling her what's going on.

I'm a zombie the entire way to the hospital. I've stopped crying, but I feel numb.

We get to the front desk, and the nurse looks like she would rather be anywhere else.

"Can I help you?" she asks, like she's bored with the conversation already.

"Hi. I'm Leah Gulfson, Michael Ecosta's attorney, and this is his wife, Tia Marie Ecosta."

The nurse narrows her eyes at us. "I was under the impression that Mr. Ecosta was single."

"My clients eloped a couple of weeks ago and haven't informed the public yet. As you can see, Mrs. Ecosta here is pregnant, they were trying to keep to themselves for a small amount of time."

The nurse looks at my small baby bump and nods. Wow. I knew Leah was a fantastic liar, but now I'm wondering if she chose the wrong career path. She should clearly be an actress.

"I'll get the doctor. Please stay here," the nurse says.

As the nurse stands up to leave, a couple looking to be in their fifties comes rushing in with tears in their eyes. The woman is petite with beautiful blue eyes and sandy brown hair. The man is a giant, towering over her, with dark brown hair and hazel eyes. I remember their faces from pictures; these are Mikey's parents.

Fuck, we're about to be caught in a lie; I have to think fast.

"Hi, Mr. and Mrs. Ecosta, I'm Tia Marie, Mikey's manager," I say. "We told a small fib to the nurse, saying I was Mikey's wife, so we could get information. I'm really sorry. We are just very concerned for him."

Mrs. Ecosta looks me over, then pulls me in for a giant hug. "Oh, my God, it is so nice to meet you. Mikey has said the most wonderful things about you." She looks at my belly. "But he never said I was going to be a grandmother."

I'm about to tell her that Mikey doesn't know that the baby is his, about all the shit we've been through, when the doctor comes out.

"Mrs. Ecosta?"

Mikey's mom steps forward. "I'm Mikey's mother, and this is my lovely daughter-in-law. Please tell us how Mikey is doing."

With tears in my eyes I mouth, "Thank you."

The doctor looks at all of us and nods. "Please come with me." He takes us to a small empty waiting area. "Mr. Ecosta was found by his housekeeper, unconscious with an empty bottle of pills next to him. There were also remnants of other drugs, and many empty liquor bottles. We're not sure how long he was unconscious for when he was brought in. We pumped his stomach to get everything out. His vitals are all normal, but he still has not woken up. The housekeeper found a note on the coffee table. I'm sorry to inform you that this was an attempted suicide."

Mikey's mom breaks out into wails and her husband holds her. The tears have started flowing down my face again, and Leah holds on to me to prevent me from falling.

"Once the police officers are done with the investigation, we will be able to provide you with the note," the doctor continues.

Mikey's father nods.

"I wish I could tell you more, but until Mikey wakes up, this is all I have. You may go in to see him two at a time."

My vision starts to blur, and I lose all feeling in my limbs. I hear Leah shriek as everything around me goes black.

TIA

The lights are bright as I wake up in a hospital bed. Leah and Crystal are on either side of me.

"What's going on?" I ask groggily.

Suddenly I'm hit with all the memories of why I was at the hospital in the first place. I sit up suddenly, feeling my heart rate spike.

"Mikey!" I yell. "I need to get to him, now!"

Leah pushes me back down. "Calm down. He still hasn't woken up. We need to worry about you right now."

Laying down, I take a few deep breaths. After I calm down, I hear the whoosh, whoosh of Bubbles's heartbeat. Oh, my God. Is she okay?

"The baby?" I choke out at Leah with pure panic.

Please, God, let Bubbles be okay. I can't lose everything all at once like this.

"The baby is fine. They just hooked you up to a fetal doppler to keep an eye on it. The heartbeat has been steady this whole time. You just need to calm down so you don't pass out again."

She's right.

I turn my attention to Crystal. "What are you doing here? You are supposed to be in school. This is your last year. You can't be skipping classes."

Smiling at me, she grabs my hand. "I don't have afternoon classes on Friday, remember? And as soon I was done with my appointment, I came right over. That's when I found out you passed out, so I stayed. We are supposed to support each other, right?"

I smile back. She is so mature for her age.

"Thank you for coming," I sigh.

I put my hands on my belly and breathe. I'm staring at the ceiling when my OBGYN walks into the room.

"I was delivering a baby when I heard about your fainting spell." She looks at my chart, then looks back at me. "How are you feeling now?"

"I'm feeling okay. Just got some shocking news, is all." I return to staring at the ceiling. Every time I think about Mikey, I want to break down and cry.

"You need to keep your stress level down, but everything looks fine. I am releasing you if you feel up to it."

I smile and nod. "Yes. I would like to go see my husband, please."

She gives me a knowing look, but just nods. "Let me get your release papers."

I'm getting my stuff together when I hear a knock on my door.

"What the fuck are you doing here?" Leah yells.

"Please, I need to talk to Tia. I made a big mistake. I fucked up. I'm sorry," Johnny mutters, grabbing the back of his neck.

I was *not* expecting him to show up. What the fuck could he possibly want to say to me?

"You don't get to talk to her, and you don't get to talk to me. Just leave!" Leah shouts, pushing him back.

"Stop," I blurt out. It's not loud, but everyone stops and turns to me. "It's fine, Leah. Let him say what he came here to say."

Johnny slowly walks into the room staring at the floor. "Tia, I fucked up, and I feel like I'm responsible for what happened to Mikey."

Not saying anything I wait for him to go on.

"The night of Mikey's birthday, Amber came up to me. She asked me to figure out a way to break you and Mikey up. I told her to fuck off at first, but then she pulled up a very bad photo of me. She was fucking blackmailing me." He stops and runs a hand over his face. "After talking to Leah, I figured out you and I were at a bar at the same time. I told him I fucked you, knowing that would make him so mad that he wouldn't want to be with you anymore. I'm sorry, Tia. I don't know you, but now I know you mean a lot to Mikey. I shouldn't have fucking done that. Amber is probably going to share those photos now, but I don't care. My best friend tried to kill himself because I lied to him."

I sit down on the bed, shocked. I feel numb. That's why Mikey accused me of sleeping with Johnny. Amber was such a bitch that she was blackmailing someone so she could have a chance with Mikey. She never had a chance with him anyway. He doesn't love her. I think back to everything that has happened and it all makes sense now. Finally, I feel like I can breathe, but I break out into full sobs.

Johnny puts his hand on my shoulder. "I'm going to tell Mikey the truth as soon as he wakes up. I'm sorry, Tia."

I don't say anything. I just continue to cry. Damn pregnancy hormones.

"You should leave now," I hear Leah demand in a strict tone.

"Can I call you later? I want to talk to you and apologize for everything."

I look up and see Leah freeze. Her eyes dart to me. I give her a shrug. This Johnny isn't like the one I remember, or even the one I saw at the party. I don't know who this Johnny is. Leah is a big girl. She can make decisions for herself.

Leah lets out a sigh. "I'll think about it, Johnny, but now is not the time or the place."

Johnny nods, then leaves.

"I'm ready to see Mikey now," I whisper to Leah.

She nods. I need to see Mikey now. He needs to wake up.

Stepping into Mikey's room, I feel nauseous. He looks peaceful. His hair is swept to the side, like his mom was brushing it out of his eyes. Leaning over, I press a simple kiss to his forehead.

Sitting on the side of the bed, I reach out and grab his hand. "I don't know if you and I have a future together, Mikey, but there is a tiny person growing in my belly that really needs a daddy. Please wake up."

The tears pour down my face again, as I think of Bubbles growing up without a daddy. With the amount of crying I've done today, I'm surprised I have any tears left.

I sit with Mikey in silence for a while, just holding his hand. I think back to the couple weeks we had together that were perfect. To our first time at the lake. I love those memories and will hold on to them forever.

I'm lost in daydreams when there is a knock at the door. Looking up, I see Mikey's mom; she gives me a small smile and walks over to me.

"I never got to properly introduce myself. I'm Carol." She sits down in the empty chair by the bed. "The police were just here and gave us this note." She places the paper in my hands. "It's addressed to you, but I hope you don't mind that we already read it."

I nod. "Of course, I don't know what is said in that letter, or what Mikey has told you. I just want you to know, I never cheated on Mikey. I love him so much." I pause to take a shaky breath. "I don't know if we can repair what has been broken, but I want him in our child's life."

"Johnny came and told us everything," she empathizes, taking my hand. "Mikey only told us good things about you. He said he felt like he was finally complete. I can't tell you what to do. I don't even know what I would do in your situation. Just listen to your heart, honey. It will tell you what to do."

I nod, but don't say anything.

She squeezes my shoulder before walking out. "I'll leave you alone to read the note."

I sit still for a long time, not knowing what to do. Finally, I move from the bed to the chair and get comfortable. I take a deep breath and open the note.

My Dearest Tia,

I am sorry that you are reading this note, but I couldn't take this pain in my heart anymore. I loved you the moment I met you, when we were kids at school. The first day I saw you, you had a purple butterfly clip and bright pink shoes. I think it was your first day of first grade. You were younger than me, but I remember thinking you were the most beautiful girl I had ever seen. Every day that I saw you, I wanted to talk to you, but I was scared.

I don't remember what year it was, but it was picture day. You came to school in this purple dress with butterflies all over it. Your hair was done in two cute braids, and you had the biggest smile on your face. I remember wishing there was a way I could keep that smile on your face forever. It made me excited to see you so happy.

As the years went on, my affection for you grew, but for some reason, Johnny didn't see you like that. You were always so smart, and I think that intimidated him. When you skipped a grade and joined our class, that pissed him off. Johnny had a hard life growing up, and I think it made him feel better to bring other people down. I'm sorry I didn't stand up for you. I'm so fucking sorry. I wish I had done things differently back then. I really do. I'm sorry you had to go through that much shit.

When I met you again as an adult, I felt an immediate connection. Like, even though you weren't mine yet, I was whole just being in your presence. The memories we had together are some of the best memories of my life. I guess they will always be the best of my life, since I won't be making any more.

I'm sorry to leave you, Tia. I hope you raise a strong child. I hope Johnny loves it with all his heart.

Every time I close my eyes, I see you and Johnny together. I just can't take it anymore. I want the pain to stop. I wish I could take you back. I wish we could be happy together. I wish everything was different. But I just need the hurt to end.

Please don't blame yourself. Just know I always have and always will love you.

Xoxoxo

Mikey

I hold the note in my shaking hands. He remembered everything. Who would remember that I had bright pink shoes in the first grade? He cared more than I ever imagined. I'm so sorry he believed that lie Johnny told him. I am so fucking pissed at Johnny, I want to punch him. But my anger towards Amber is like none I've ever felt before. How could anyone do this to another person? I hate that he had to deal with so much hurt by himself.

I lean over to Mikey with tears streaming down my face and grab his hand. "I am so sorry, baby. Please come back to me. Please don't leave our child. We need you. *I* need you."

I look up at the ceiling. If there is a God, he won't let our child grow up without a father. I close my eyes and just breathe. I feel fingers twitch in my hand and my eyes snap open.

"Mikey?" I ask.

His fingers twitch again. Oh, my God. He's waking up.

"Nurse? Anyone? Please come! He's waking up!" I yell.

Two nurses come in.

"His fingers were twitching in mine. I think he's trying to wake up."

They move to check his vitals, but don't say anything.

"Please, baby. You've got this. Just wake up. Wake up for your child, wake up for your parents, wake up for me," I plead with him; he *has* to wake up.

His eyes start to flutter. One nurse pages for the doctor to come in.

"That's it, baby. Open your eyes. You can do this. Come back to me." My free hand covers my mouth.

Please open your eyes, I silently beg. *Please.*

As if hearing my unspoken words, Mikey's eyes finally open. I see the bluest eyes. Eyes I haven't seen in months. Eyes that make my heart melt.

His voice is coarse, but he manages to mutter, "Tia."

I cry so hard. He's back. He's awake. I don't know what to say. I'm about to speak when the doctor comes in.

"Ma'am, I'm going to have to ask you to leave for a moment so I can go over Mr. Ecosta's vitals," he says.

I want to protest. I can't leave him. He just woke up. But the doctor gives me a stern look. I stand and place a quick kiss on Mikey's forehead before leaving.

"I'll be right back, baby. Be good for the doctors."

It feels like forever that I am in the waiting room with Mikey's parents. I've been pacing the floor back and forth so much, I'm surprised I haven't made a hole. Leah took Crystal home a while ago, since I needed some time alone with Mikey.

Finally, the doctor comes in, smiling at us. "Mikey is doing very well. You may go in and see him now if you like."

We all stand, but the doctor stops me.

"Um, I'm sorry, but Mikey has requested that only his parents be allowed in right now."

"Excuse me?" I am so taken aback that I don't even know what to do.

"I'm sorry, ma'am, but those were his wishes."

I look at Carol, pleading for her to change the doctor's mind.

"I'll talk to him, honey," she promises, taking my hand. "But maybe it's best if you go home for now. I can call you later when he's ready to talk."

I nod. I gave her my number earlier so we could stay in touch. She is such a kind woman, and she really has been amazing to me.

I sit back down as Carol and Henry leave to go see their son. Pulling my phone from my purse, I text Leah, asking her to pick me up. I don't say much, and she doesn't pry. She just tells me she is on her way.

Walking out of the hospital, I feel empty again. Mikey didn't want to see me. After everything he has put me through, he still hates me. I know he doesn't know the truth yet, but will knowing the truth change anything? Is our relationship beyond repair?

"Come on, Bubbles. Let's go home and take a nap," I whisper, rubbing my tummy.

At least she still has a father.

MIKEY

When I woke up, I saw the most beautiful pair of eyes. I could tell they were sad because they were the bluest I have ever seen them. The green was almost gone entirely. I wasn't even sure they were her eyes at first, but when I saw that petite nose and those full beautiful lips, I knew it was her.

"Tia," I managed to choke out.

When she kissed my forehead, it was like fire on ice. It burned me, leaving a mark. I wanted to grab her, hold her, and never let her go, but I'm fucking weak.

After she leaves, the doctor goes over everything that happened to me after I took the pills.

"You're very lucky, Mr. Ecosta," he says. "As per legal protocol, we will keep you overnight, but tomorrow, you will be transported to a mental health facility for two weeks. After that, you will have to see a therapist every week for one year, possibly longer, if deemed necessary by your therapist. The police have also opened an investigation, but they will inform you about that after you leave the mental health facility."

I blink. Why the fuck am I still here in this shitty fucking life? Taking those pills was supposed to end the misery, get rid of all the pain. Instead, it's only caused more pain. I nod at the doctor. It's mandatory, so I don't really have a choice. I make a mental note to call my lawyer. I've had a couple of run-ins with the cops. Hopefully I can get out with just some community service.

"I will go and get your parents and wife," the doctor tells me.

Wife? Tia isn't my wife. Why did he have that idea? I'm thinking maybe they didn't want to give her information, so she lied. That's smart thinking on Tia's part. I would have done the same thing. Not wanting to get Tia into trouble, I don't correct the doctor.

"Please just send my parents in. I don't want to see my wife right now," I tell him.

The doctor gives me a confused look.

"Actually, can you please make sure no one but my parents is allowed into my room?"

The doctor doesn't say anything. He just nods and leaves the room.

My parents enter the room, and I hate how they look. My mom's eyes have no light in them; she looks as if her world has been ripped apart. My dad looks pissed. I don't think I've ever seen him look this angry. Running, my mom wraps her arms around me.

"I thought we'd lost you forever. How could you do that to me?" she asks while crying.

Her tears pool on my neck and shoulder. I can't believe I did this to her.

"I'm sorry, Mom," I mutter. "I just wanted the pain to end."

Pulling back, she stares at me. "I get that, son, but don't you think talking to someone would have been the better route, rather than trying to take your own life?"

I nod. "I'm sorry, Mom. I feel like my heart has been ripped from my chest and I don't know what to do." For the first time in a long time, I start to cry.

My dad's eyes are glassy, "Don't you ever do that again, son."

I don't reply. I just give him a nod. It was stupid, and it didn't work at all. Instead of taking away the pain, I just passed on extra pain to the ones I care about.

Mom sits on the edge of my bed and holds my hand. "Why didn't you want to see Tia? She's very concerned about you."

I look at the ceiling. I don't want to make eye contact with her right now. "It's a long story, Mom, but we broke up."

"Yes, I heard that. It sounds like everything was just a misunderstanding, though."

A misunderstanding? How was Tia sleeping with my best friend, who she hates because he bullied her so badly, a misunderstanding?

"I don't think it was, Mom."

Mom pulls her phone out of her pocket. Tapping away, she makes a call.

"You need to talk to Johnny," she demands, then hands me the phone.

The last person I want to talk to right now is Johnny, but I know better than to argue with my mom.

The phone rings a couple times, then Johnny picks up.

"My mom says you and I need to talk. What's up?" I mutter.

"I'm so fucking sorry, man," he says, his voice breaking.

I'm silent as he explains everything to me. My blood pressure rises. How the fuck could he have done this to me?

"What the fuck kind of pictures could she possibly have of you that would make you betray me like this?" I yell into the phone.

"Remember that party last year at the lake house? I think it was Amber's birthday? Well, I guess Amber took pictures of me doing coke. If those got out, man, my career is fucking ruined."

I'm seeing fucking red. Yes, I remember the party. I remember how fucked up we all were. Did she take pictures of me too? I understand how bad those pictures would be to get leaked, but is that more important than our friendship? Than me?

"You cared more about yourself than you did about me. We're supposed to be brothers, man. After everything I have done for you, after everything I have put up with, this is the last fucking straw, Johnny," I spit out.

"Don't cut me out of your life. I'd be fucking dead if it wasn't for you."

His voice sounds scared, and he should be. I can't deal with him anymore.

"Maybe you should have thought about that before you went and destroyed my life. Goodbye, John." I end the call and hand the phone back to my mom.

I stare up at the ceiling. I have ruined everything in my life, because I believed someone who I should have cut out of my life a long time ago. What the fuck do I do now?

"So, tell me about the day you overdosed."

I've been at the mental health facility for one week now. The sessions are all the same. Why did you want to kill yourself? Are you going to attempt to kill yourself again? Do you think you will be able to stay clean? And then there's the one that hurts more than anything. Do you think you will be a suitable role model for your child?

Tia hasn't spoken to me since I left the hospital. She didn't reply to any of my texts and won't answer my calls. I destroyed her, and now she doesn't want me in her life at all.

I hate these sessions. They're so fucking pointless. Especially when they keep asking me the same fucking questions over and over again, like they expect my answers to change.

"I thought the love of my life had slept with my best friend and was having his baby, and I couldn't get the thoughts out of my head," I sigh. "I got into a dark place. I felt like I was drowning. Every day was a fight to get out of bed. When I closed my eyes at night, all I saw was Tia and Johnny sleeping together, and it really fucked with my head. The weight of it all was suffocating and so painful, and I just couldn't take it anymore. I thought it would be easier and better for everyone if I just wasn't here anymore."

The doctor nods. "Yes. So what is to stop you from attempting suicide again? Life isn't always fantastic, Mikey. You are going to have to learn ways to deal with stressful and potentially hurtful situations."

I think about the question. At the time I thought it was the right decision, but looking back, I know it was a mistake.

"When I first woke up, I was pissed I was still here," I answer honestly. I take a deep breath before continuing. "But now I'm happy I'm still here. I don't ever want to do something that stupid again."

It's the truth. Attempting suicide was the dumbest thing I have ever done. Even if Tia and I never get back together, I'll never try to take my life again. I need to be a good role model for my unborn child. I will not let him or her down.

The doctor smiles at me. She's pretty. She has short brown hair and big hazel eyes, but I'm not attracted to her, I don't know if I'll ever be attracted to anyone other than Tia again.

"You are making great progress, Mikey," she says. "I'm proud of you. Depression isn't easy to deal with, but I am certain that with the skills we are going to teach you, you'll be able to deal with any situation life throws you." She stands and walks to the door. "I'll see you tomorrow."

I have to see Dr. Anette every day while I'm here, along with group sessions three times a week, and family sessions twice a week.

I talked to my lawyer. The cops wanted to nail me with a lot of drug charges, but he's talked them down and I'm getting away almost scot free. Because I have "mental issues," the charges are being dropped as long as I stay clean and see therapists for a year.

I've asked for Tia to come to the family sessions, but only my parents show up. Mom tells me that Tia just needs time, but I don't know about that. After everything I did to her, how could she ever forgive me? I couldn't forgive her for something that was minor in comparison to what I did to her. And the truth is, she didn't even do anything. I was just too stubborn to hear that.

I should have talked to Tia. I should have heard her out. But I didn't believe anything she said. I was fucking angry. I didn't care about anyone but me. I should have known that Tia would never sleep with Johnny. That isn't who she is. But no. I was a fucking idiot and believed Johnny over Tia. Johnny, who's notorious for lying and manipulating people. I should have seen through the lies. Or at least I should have questioned it more.

And then there's Amber. Every time I think of her, I want to explode, to punch something. I have no idea what was going through her head. She was sick. I will never talk to her again. I fucking despise her.

I head to my room and shut the door. There isn't a whole lot to do around here. I'm not allowed my cell phone or access to the Internet. We can watch movies, but we have no live TV. I've been hitting the gym a lot. I spend the majority of my free time there. Working out gives me some clarity and helps me work out my frustrations in a healthy manner. My mom brought me some books, but I've never really been a reader. I know she means well, but sometimes she can be smothering.

I lay down on my bed and look up at the ceiling. My thoughts always drift to Tia, to the baby. I'm going to be a dad. I'm going to be a fucking dad. I close my eyes and see Tia's beautiful face. The way her eyes go brighter green when she's happy. The way her whole face lights up when she is excited. Will our kid have her eyes or mine? Will it be musically inclined like me, or smart like Tia? Is it going to be a boy or girl? I don't even care, as long as it's healthy. I am going to be a part of their lives as much as I can. As much as Tia will allow.

Today is our last family session. I'm praying Tia will show up. Mom told me she would talk to her and ask her to come, but she's said that every time, and Tia still hasn't shown. My mom and dad walk in, but Tia is nowhere to be seen.

"Is she coming?" I ask my mom.

Mom smiles, but it doesn't reach her eyes. "She said she would think about it. I'm sorry, honey. I tried my best."

I feel my heart break even more. I really want to see her face. I want to apologize. I just want her to know I still love her.

Dr. Anette enters the room and greets me and my parents with handshakes. "Thank you so much for joini—"

She is interrupted by a knock on the door. Looking up, I see the most beautiful woman. Tia came. She's here.

"I'm sorry for being late," she says. "My car was having some issues this morning."

My eyes are immediately drawn to her growing belly. That's my baby in there. I can't believe I thought it was Johnny's. I'm such a fucking idiot.

Giving me a small smile, she sits beside my mom.

Dr. Anette shakes Tia's hand, smiling widely. "Thank you for joining us today. You must be Tia."

"Yes. I decided to listen to you after you told me it would be beneficial for Mikey for me to be here. Again, I'm sorry I'm late," Tia says.

"No, it's fine. We were just beginning. Since this is your first session with us, I would like to give you the floor. Is there anything you would like to say?"

Tia looks to the floor and bites her lip. "Um, I can't think of anything."

"Be honest, Tia. Tell us how you felt when you heard about Mikey's attempted suicide."

Tia's eyes go wide. I know the drill by now. My parents have both opened up and been extremely honest. It hurt at first, but I'm glad they told me how they felt. It really hit home for me about how selfish I was being by trying to take my own life.

"I was hurt, and scared. I've dealt with one person in my life committing suicide. I didn't want to have to go through that again. I don't want our child to grow up without a parent. I grew up with only my father. My mother left me when I was a baby. I didn't want the same for our child," Tia explains.

I didn't know Tia only had her father. She always had a woman picking her up from school. Maybe it was a babysitter or an aunt.

"Go on," Dr. Anette encourages.

"When you love someone, you don't want to see them hurting. Mikey refused to talk to me or open up about his feelings before he OD'd. We've been broken up for a while now, but of course, there is still love there. I'm growing our child right now." A single tear escapes Tia's eye.

She still loves me. Maybe there is hope for us after all.

Tia turns to me and takes a deep breath. "Dr. Anette and I spoke on the phone before I came here today. She explained what I should say to you. Mikey, I love you, but you need to know, there can't be an us anymore. You will be in my life as a parent to our child and nothing else. I have Leah drawing up the paperwork to cancel our working agreement. It would be best for both of us. If you sign the paperwork, I will not be taking any more money from you for work. If you would like to pay bills for the baby, that can be worked out in the future in a custody agreement."

The air in my lung escapes. I can't breathe. Why is she doing this? If she loves me, she'd give us another chance. Wouldn't she?

"Thank you for sharing, Tia. Now, Mikey, what would you like to say to Tia?"

I pause for a moment, reflecting like Dr. Anette has taught me. "Tia, I need to apologize for so many things. First, for scaring you like I did. Second, for how I've treated you these past months. I was an asshole, there is no excuse for my actions. Thank you for sharing your feelings today."

I want to beg her to forgive me, to give us one more try, but I can't. Tia and

I must not be destined to be together like I thought.

The tears are flowing down Tia's face now. She nods and stands.

"I am so sorry. I completely forgot that I have another appointment today. I have to go." She gives me one last look, then leaves.

TIA

Going to see Mikey was the hardest thing I have ever done. I wasn't sure I was going to go today. I'm still not sure why I even went. Seeing Mikey's face drop when I told him we couldn't be together anymore made me nauseous.

I was half-expecting Mikey to beg me to take him back. From the way his mom has been talking, I'm shocked that he let me go so easy, but I'm grateful. This is the hardest decision I have ever made. I so badly want to forgive him and let him love me. But how can I be with someone who so quickly threw us away? He could do it again, and I don't know if I could survive something like that.

And now I have to think about our child. She is the most important thing in the world now. She needs to come first in everything I do.

While Mikey has been at the mental health facility, I've been working with a PR company to make sure news about his suicide attempt didn't get out. All the tabloids have released speculations of what they think happened, but the official report is he was hospitalized due to an illness and is being taken care of at home by a private team. So many people are writing "get better" messages on his social media. His fans still believe in him. That's good. His new manager won't have much cleaning up to do; I've done it all for them.

It's been a month since I've seen Mikey. He sends me texts sometimes, asking how the baby is, asking if I want to hang out. I always give the same reply: baby's fine and I'm busy. But today is the day I find out the gender of our baby. I promised Mikey he could come along. He was mad at first that I want to find out, saying that it would be better if it was a surprise. I lost my shit and told him it was my body. I may have also brought up the fact that he denied the baby was his at first, so he lost voting rights. Not my proudest moment, but it shut him up.

Me: The appointment is at 1 p.m. Please meet me at the doctor's office.

Mikey: Are you sure you don't want me to pick you up?

Me: I have other running around to do today, and I have to be able to get to the hospital fast if Crystal goes into labor. I need my own wheels.

Crystal is already a week overdue; they are talking about possibly inducing her if the baby doesn't come soon.

Mikey: Okay, I understand. See you this afternoon.

Mikey has been understanding for the most part. He doesn't push me. He lets me have my space. But it's so awkward at times. How am I supposed to be friends with a man who ripped my heart out? Who I still love deeply? I keep reminding myself it's the best thing for Bubbles.

I find myself putting extra care into getting ready today. I tell myself that it's because it makes me feel better and it has nothing to do with seeing Mikey. I pick out my favorite red shirt. It's almost too tight on my growing belly, but since the material is stretchy, it still fits for now. Mikey likes me in red.

Ugh! I need to get these thoughts out of my head. I can't be thinking like that. He treated me like shit. He can't be trusted with my heart again.

Running a brush through my hair, I take a deep breath. "We've got this, Bubbles. Now, let's go see your daddy."

When I show up for my appointment, Mikey is already there. He looks good. Of course. He stands and wraps me in a warm hug. The smell of pine and peppermint fills my nose. I forgot how his scent could make me go lightheaded. I hold on for a moment too long and then step back.

"I need to check in. I'll be right back," I say quietly.

I take a few deep breaths as I walk away. Our connection is still as strong as it has ever been. I guess a connection like ours doesn't just go away overnight.

Even though I wish so much that it would.

After checking in, I sit next to Mikey and pull out my phone. I know I should talk to him, but what is there to say?

"So, Amanda told me about your awesome work with Hope For the Forgotten. I'm proud of you, Tia." Mikey has a genuine smile on his face, one I haven't seen in months.

I smile back at him, but it doesn't reach my eyes. I'm so nervous around Mikey. I need to keep my heart as guarded as possible.

"I'm really happy to be helping. We already have a waiting list of mothers wanting to mentor more teens. We're also going to be doing girls' nights where we have a doctor come in and talk about safe sex. Our education system isn't doing it, so someone has to. If more girls have access to this information, maybe we'd have fewer teen pregnancies. We are also trying to teach the girls to stand up for themselves and build their self-esteem," I say, figuring sticking to talking about the charity is safe.

Mikey grabs my hand. "That's amazing, Tia. I'm happy that you're doing something meaningful to help those girls."

His touch burns me and sends tingles straight to my heart. I still remember how that touch feels all over my body. I pull my hand back and see Mikey's face drop.

Thankfully, the nurse calls us to go into the room. After a short wait in awkward silence, my OBGYN comes in.

"How are you today, Tia?" she asks before realizing Mikey is sitting in the chair next to the bed. "And you must be the father. I'm glad you were able to join us today."

She asks me to slide my pants down slightly and squirts some cold jelly on my belly. She moves the camera around, and I see Bubbles. She has gotten so much bigger than the first time I saw her.

"Wow," I hear Mikey say with awe. "That's our baby?"

Dr. Amelia nods. "Yes. Now, let's see if we can find out the gender today."

Bubbles is doing lots of flips and not staying still. It looks like she is dancing in there. Finally, she slows down.

"There." Dr. Amelia points and takes a picture. "Now, I need to ask if you are certain you want to know the gender."

I smile. "Yes. Please tell me if Bubbles is a boy or girl."

I need to know if my intuition is right. Is Bubbles a girl?

"Bubbles?" Mikey asks.

"Um, yeah, that's what I call the baby right now," I tell him.

"Okay, Tia, I am very happy to inform you that you are having a baby girl," Dr. Amelia announces.

I was right; she is a girl. Happy tears stream down my face.

"A girl?" Mikey asks.

I look and see his wide eyes.

I smile at him. "She's going to be perfect."

The doctor takes some more photos of Bubbles, then hands me a towel to clean my stomach off.

"Everything looks amazing, Tia. I will see you back next month, unless you have complications, or questions. Then please come back and see me sooner," she says.

She leaves the room, and I am once again left alone with Mikey.

"I'll let you know when I book the next appointment. You can come with if you'd like." I don't look in Mikey's eyes. This already feels too intimate.

"I would really like that." Mikey stairs at the floor and twiddles his fingers. "I was wondering if maybe I could take you out for dinner tonight."

He looks up and his eyes meet mine. They are pleading me to let him, but I can't.

"I don't think that's a good idea, Mikey. We need to keep some distance between us right now."

I stand up and grab my purse from the hook, but before I can turn the handle on the door, Mikey grabs my arm.

"Please, Tia. I'm fucking broken without you. Can't you give us one more try?"

I don't turn and look at him.

"I'm sorry, Mikey," I say while taking a ragged breath.

I grab the handle and leave the room. I don't know what else to say. He's broken? Well, he fucking destroyed me. He would have stayed mad at me if Johnny had never told him the truth. He wouldn't even give me the chance to tell him the truth. He wasn't willing to forgive me for an offense I didn't even commit. So why should I even try with him?

I get in my car and all the tears release. Pounding on the steering wheel in frustration, I let out a scream. My heart belongs to Mikey, but it's in eight million pieces right now. How will I ever be whole again?

"Bubbles, I need you to be my strength right now, because I don't have very much left," I sniffle.

My phone rings, breaking me out of my sad thoughts. I look at the screen and see Crystal's face.

"Hey, girl," I answer. "The ultrasound went great. I'm having a girl too."

"That's great, Tia, but my water just broke. I need to get to the hospital." I hear the panic in her voice.

"My doctor's office is just around the corner from your house. I'll be there in five minutes," I tell her.

I start the car and rush to get Crystal. Her parents are never home, so I knew

I would be the one getting her to the hospital when the time came.

"I'm so scared, Tia. How am I going to be a mother?" Crystal asks on the drive to the hospital with tears in her eyes.

Reaching over, I grab her hand. "I've got you. We are in this together."

Crystal ends up having a surprisingly fast labor. Because the baby came out so fast, she is going to need some extra time to recover. I'm wracking my brain trying to figure out what to do for Crystal. Her parents aren't going to help her. They don't give a shit about anyone but themselves.

I look down in the tiny plastic bassinet at the perfect angel sleeping there. Olivia Dawn Barrett. She was the perfect size baby at seven pounds, four ounces. She has a head full of hair already. Looks like it's thick and brown just like her mama's. Her eyes are sky blue. Crystal says she gets them from her daddy.

Crystal is sleeping, recovering from the exhausting labor. I kiss her forehead and sit down in the chair next to the bed. We've been at the hospital for twelve hours now. Crystal should be able to go home this evening, but is home really the best place for them?

I answer my own question as soon as I think of it. No, home is the worst possible place for them. Crystal needs to be in an environment where she's loved and supported, and she needs a leg up in the world so she can be the mother Olivia deserves. I take a leap of faith and call Crystal's mom.

"Hi. Esther?" I ask.

"Yes, and who is this?" She sounds like she's taking a drag from a smoke.

"Hi. I'm Tia, Crystal's mentor from Hope For the Forgotten. I'm not sure if you got her text message, but she had her baby today."

"Yeah, I got her message. Another fucking mouth to feed. Lucky me." The sarcasm is dripping off her tongue.

I close my eyes. How could anyone be that cold to their child?

"Yeah, about that. Crystal is going to need extra care at home because the baby came too fast, causing injuries to Crystal's body," I inform her.

"I can't just quit my job! She got herself into this situation, so she can fucking take care of herself!" Esther yells into the phone.

"I understand that taking care of a newborn and a mother who needs some extra care is a lot to take on, so I was hoping you would allow Crystal to move in with me. I have the time and money to take care of both of them."

There is a pause on the line. I really hope she agrees to this. It would be best for Crystal and Olivia.

"I don't give a shit, but don't call asking for any money. We don't have any," she finally replies.

"Oh, no, I would never ask for anything. I'll swing by tomorrow to gather Crystal's things. Thank you so much for agreeing to this."

"Whatever." She hangs up.

Olivia starts to fuss. I pick her up and inhale that perfect newborn scent.

"I've got you, baby girl. No one will love you more than your mother and I do," I promise.

I rock her for a little bit, and she settles into silent bliss.

"You look good holding her," Crystal says with a smile.

"I can't wait to meet my own little one," I agree, handing Olivia over to Crystal so she can feed her. "You're a great mom. I hope you know that."

"I don't know how I'm going to do this, Tia," she mumbles with tears in her eyes.

"With my help, of course," I tell her with a smile. "I talked to your mom while you were asleep. She's agreed to let you move in with me. It's not going to be a free ride, but I'm going to help you as much as I can."

Crystal's eyes go wide, and she starts crying. "What did I do to deserve someone like you in my life?"

Sitting on the edge of her bed, I put my hand on her shoulder. "Honey, this is what unconditional love is like. You should have had it from the moment you were born. It's what you already feel towards your daughter. I am so sorry you grew up in such a hateful household, but you will never feel that way again, and neither will Olivia."

We sit together crying for a little bit while Olivia nurses.

After a talk with Crystal's doctor, I leave the hospital so I can go get some baby essentials. I'm hoping that Olivia grows out of some of the things I buy so we can use it for Bubbles afterwards.

While I'm at the store my phone rings. I don't recognize the number, but I answer anyway.

"Tia Marie speaking."

"Hi, Tia. My name is Dustin. Jay Coldheart gave me your number. Said you might be looking for a new client," comes the voice of a guy who can't be more than twenty.

I *could* use a job. I just don't know if I want to be working with another guy, to be honest. But he does sound really young.

"Um, possibly. How old are you?" I ask.

I'm not in my usual business mindset, so I could be coming across rude, but I don't really care.

I hear a chuckle on the other end of the phone. "I turn eighteen next month. I'm just starting out my career, but I know what you did for the Broken Hearts and I could use somebody like you in my corner."

Hmm. An eighteen-year-old isn't going to be able to pay very much, but it could be something.

"Let me get back to you, Dustin. I'll check my schedule and see if we can arrange a time to meet up and discuss details. You are in luck, though. I don't currently have a client," I tell him.

"Thanks, Tia!" he says excitedly. "This is the best number to get in touch with me, so call or text anytime."

"Talk to you soon, Dustin. Goodbye."

So weird. I'm going to have to talk to Jay later. It's great that he is looking out for me, but I don't even know if I want to manage anymore. There is an empty spot inside of me where my love of music and managing used to be.

On my way back to the hospital, I call Leah.

"Did she push that watermelon out of her vagina already?"

I let out a full belly laugh to that one. "Yep. Early this morning. She gets to go home tonight. That's why I'm calling. Can you meet me at my place this evening to help set up all the baby stuff? Crystal is moving in with me. Also, I might need help getting her stuff tomorrow."

"Yeah, no problem. I don't have plans tonight, and I could use a girl talk anyway. Are you sure this is a good idea, though? Crystal is still a kid herself, with a kid, and you're about to pop out your own vagina watermelon soon."

"I know, but what other option is there? Her parents don't love her, and I do. I already told her this isn't a free ride. I am going to set her up to succeed instead of fail."

Crystal is like a little sister to me. She needs help, and I can afford to help her. This is what you do for the people you love.

"You know you have a heart of gold, right?" Leah says.

I giggle. "Hardly. I've pictured Mikey's fiery death a few times. I don't think that counts as a heart of gold."

I hear Leah sigh on the other end of the phone. "Are you ever going to give him a second chance?"

We've had this conversation before, and I am *so* not in the mood right now.

"We'll talk about it later. I have to go. See you soon," I sigh.

I hang up and head into the hospital. Getting to Crystal's room, I see her and Olivia all dressed and looking ready to go.

"I bought a car seat for Olivia, and a few other things she will need," I tell her.

"Thank you so much. I really want to pay you back as soon as I can." Crystal gives me a giant hug, and we just hold each other for a few minutes.

"Of course. The doctor told me you need to heal for a few weeks, but you'll still be able to do your schoolwork from home. When you go back to school, we will look for a part time job for you. Like I said before, this isn't a free ride. You eventually need to be able to support Olivia all on your own, but I am going to give you all the tools you need to succeed. I'm not just throwing you to the wolves."

"Thanks again, Tia. I won't let you down," she promises.

We give each other one more hug, then put Olivia in her car seat. She looks so little; it makes me think of Bubbles. I can't wait to meet my perfect baby girl.

Crystal is tending to Olivia, while Leah and I set up the bassinet and baby swing.

"So, Johnny has been texting me a lot," Leah states while holding up two pieces for the baby swing.

Johnny fucking Crown, the bane of my existence. Every time I hear his name, my blood boils.

"Oh. Have you been responding?" I ask, trying not to show how pissed off I am. Leah is a big girl. If she wants to play with the devil, that is her prerogative.

Leah fiddles with the pieces, not really trying to put them together, more like just trying to keep herself busy.

"A little," she admits. "He told me the whole story, about how he's made a lot of mistakes in his past, and he's realizing now how stupid he has been."

"Are you fucking kidding me?" I scoff. "He's just realizing now? Sounds like a line to me."

"Don't shoot the messenger, Tia. People can change." She goes back to putting the swing together.

I don't respond. If I do, I know I'll just end up hurting my friend. I won't tell her who she can and can't talk to. I just don't want to see her get hurt.

We've been home for a month now, and everyone is doing awesome. Olivia is growing like a bad weed, and Crystal is back in school. She has a great part-time job at Future Foods. Her shifts right now are three weekdays from five until eleven and weekends from nine until six. She has complained a few times about being tired, but for the most part has kept the whining to a minimum.

I watch Olivia while Crystal is working or at school. Crystal wanted to breastfeed but wasn't able to pump consistently, so her milk supply depleted fast. Thankfully, Olivia takes a bottle like a champ and loves her formula. Crystal pays for formula, diapers, groceries, and public transit right now, and is putting the rest of the money into savings. She was walking to work, but now that it is the beginning of December it's a bit too cold to walk. We discussed that after she graduates, she should find a place for her and Olivia. I'll still be more than happy to watch Olivia while Crystal works, but this was always temporary.

Today, Leah is watching Olivia, and I am heading to my doctor's appointment. Mikey said he will be there, and I'm nervous to see him. He's been sending me a lot of texts, but I don't respond to most of them. I didn't want to tell him about this appointment, but I also didn't want to lie, and I promised he could come.

When I walk into the doctor's office, Mikey is already there. I don't acknowledge him at first; I just head to the front desk to check in. Taking a few deep breaths, I wander over to where Mikey is sitting. I quickly sit down, before Mikey has the chance to give me a hug. I don't want to feel his body on mine. Looking at him, I see the disappointment on his face.

"How have you been?" I ask, breaking the silence.

"Not bad. My therapy has been going well," he responds, fidgeting in his chair.

"I'm glad to hear," I tell him.

I really am. Mikey has been going through a lot, and I'm happy that he's getting the help he needs.

"Tia Daggen," the nurse calls out.

"Well, that's us," I comment as I stand.

I reach for my purse, but Mikey grabs it for me.

"Let me get that for you. It's the least I can do since you won't let me do anything else."

I feel a pain in my heart, but try and push it aside. I don't reply. I just follow the nurse to the exam room.

"The doctor will be in shortly," the nurse informs us, then leaves us in an awkward silence.

"I'm happy that you are doing so well, Mikey," I confess.

"Whatever," Mikey scoffs.

I frown. He hasn't been this hostile with me since he's gotten out of the hospital.

"Is something wrong?" I inquire while fidgeting with the paper on the exam table.

"Yeah! The love of my life, who is carrying *my* baby, won't give me the time of day unless it's to come to a doctor's appointment, and I'm pretty sure you only do that because you promised and would feel guilty to not invite me," he snaps.

Wow. He hit the nail right on the head with that statement.

"I've been busy, Mikey, and we agreed that it would be best if we are just friends and keep our distance for right now."

"No!" he shouts. "*You* decided that. I never fucking agreed to anything. I want you in my life, but you won't fucking forgive me."

I see red. I've been trying to handle him with kid gloves because of his mental state, but I'm done holding my tongue.

"*I* can't forgive *you*?" I scream. "You believed the stupidest lie of all time and refused to forgive me for it or even fucking *listen* to me. You never would have forgiven me if you didn't learn the truth. You tried to fucking *kill yourself*, Mikey. So, excuse me if I have a hard time forgiving someone who ripped my heart from my chest and stomped all over it."

Just then, Dr. Amelia enters the room.

"Am I interrupting something?" she asks with a concerned look on her face.

I take a deep breath and try to force a smile.

"It's fine," I insist.

Dr. Amelia nods. "Okay, then. Let's hear the baby's heartbeat."

The rest of the appointment is fine, but awkward. Mikey and I refuse to look at each other, and Dr. Amelia looks concerned.

"I'll see you in another four weeks. Remember, stress isn't good for the baby, so try to keep calm. Continue with those prenatal classes we talked about." She gives Mikey a stern look, then walks out.

"What prenatal classes?" Mikey asks, with a bitter tone.

"Leah has been coming with me. It's none of your concern," I bite out at him, grabbing for my purse. "I'll let you know when the next appointment is."

Mikey grabs my arm hard, not letting me get very far.

"Please let me go," I whimper.

Mikey has never touched me like this before, and I'm kind of scared. I wonder if he's back on drugs and that's why he's acting like this.

"Let me in, Tia," he snarls at me.

"Not until you learn to act like a man instead of a beast," I spit out and pull my arm out of his grasp. "Don't *ever* touch me like that again." I blink back the tears in my eyes. "Like I said, I'll let you know when the next appointment is. Goodbye, Mikey."

I bolt out of the office as fast as I can. I'm still in shock at Mikey's behavior. I think about sending his mom a text, but stop. She'll just worry about him. I'm sure he's fine. He wouldn't be stupid enough to start drugs again, would he?

Tonight, Crystal is off, so I am relaxing on the couch with a tea, watching some reality TV.

"You're lucky Olivia is such a good baby," I tell Crystal while getting up to grab a box of cookies. Bubbles love chocolate mint cookies.

"Yeah, I got pretty lucky with this girl. I just hate that I miss so much of her. She is changing so much every day." Olivia lets out a shriek of joy as Crystal tickles her.

In the kitchen, I hear my phone ping. Thinking it must be Leah, I ignore it. But then it pings again, and again. Weird. Leah doesn't normally send that many text messages.

"Crystal, can you grab my phone for me?" I holler from the kitchen.

As Crystal is bringing me my phone, it starts ringing,

"It's Mikey," she states while looking at the screen.

"Hello?" I answer.

Mikey doesn't call often, and usually I ignore it, but with all the missed messages, I'm assuming it's something important.

"I'm *sooo* f-fucking s-s-sorry Tia," Mikey slurs into the phone.

Oh, my God. He does *not* sound good.

"Mikey, have you been drinking?" I ask.

He is supposed to stay sober with his therapy. Why is he drinking? He said he wants to get better, to be better for Bubbles. This is ruining his progress.

"Just a l-little," he stammers.

"Mikey, you know you're supposed to stay sober. Why are you doing this?" I let out a sigh.

His whole life has been fucked up. I don't know if he will ever get back to normal.

"I need you, Tia. I'm lost without you," he says, his voice breaking.

I let out a little cry. I so badly want to forgive him, to move on, to just be us again. But so much has changed since when we were happy. My heart is broken, and my head is confused.

"You should call your mom. You shouldn't be alone like this," I tell him.

"No," he cries out. "Please don't call my mom. She can't know about this. It will break her even more."

I know this might not be a smart idea, but I cave. "I'll be over in a bit."

I hang up the phone and go to my room to change.

"I'll be home before you have to go to work tomorrow, but you and Olivia are on your own tonight. Mikey needs me," I tell Crystal while grabbing my purse.

"We'll be fine. I'll call Leah if there's an emergency. Mikey obviously needs you a lot more than we do right now," she assures me.

I give Olivia a kiss on the forehead, and Crystal a hug.

"I'm sorry to be leaving you," I whisper with tears in my eyes.

"We're fine, Tia. Go!" she insists.

I grab my winter coat as I walk out the door, feeling so unsure as to what to do. Why the hell does this have to happen to me? I have a sinking feeling I'm going to regret going over there tonight.

Pulling up to Mikey's house, I fight back the tears. He texted me a code after I hung up with him; thank God it worked.

"Mikey!" I call out as I enter. "Where are you?"

I hear Mikey running down the stairs.

"You came!" he exclaims, and kisses me on the lips.

I don't return the kiss. He tastes like alcohol. It almost makes me want to vomit.

"Stop it, Mikey!" I shout, pushing him away.

Walking past him, I see at least half a dozen empty liquor bottles.

"How much have you had to drink?" I ask, picking up the empties.

Mikey saunters up behind me, grabbing my waist and kissing my neck. "Not enough to forget you. Believe me, I've been trying."

He reeks of alcohol; I'm definitely regretting coming here.

"Please, Mikey, stop," I beg. "I'm here to help you, but you need to stop touching me like that."

"Like what?" he whispers in my ear, moving his one hand from my hip to my breast. "Like this?"

I whimper and lean into his touch. He slides his other hand down to my thigh, trying to slip it between my legs.

Regaining my self-control, I push Mikey away.

"I said stop it," I bite out. "I'm here to help you. Now, go take a shower and brush your fucking teeth. Touch me again and I'm gone!"

The look on Mikey's face is heartbreaking. He looks completely hopeless. I want to give him hope, to tell him that we can work this out, but I just can't. He doesn't say another word. He just walks up the stairs and slams his bedroom door.

I clean up the mess and grab a bottle of water and some aspirin. Knocking on Mikey's door, I wait for him to answer, but he doesn't. I open the door.

"Mikey?" I call out.

There is no response, but I hear water running. Making my way to the bathroom, I knock on that door and open it slightly.

"Mikey are you okay?"

Again, no response, so I go in.

What I find makes me break out in sobs. Mikey is huddled in the corner of his shower covered in vomit and barely conscious.

"For fuck's sake, Mikey!" I cry out.

I drop the water, and pain pills to the floor and open the shower door, grabbing Mikey.

"You need to help me," I whisper to him. "Come on, Mikey. Let's get you cleaned up and into bed."

He doesn't say anything, but gives me some help. I clean Mikey up, then hobble him over to his bed. I don't dress him because I want to avoid as much contact as possible. Before I head downstairs I grab a t-shirt and a pair of sweats so I can change. My clothes are completely drenched, and I feel emotionally drained. Why is he destroying his life like this?

I sit on the couch and decide it's time to call in the cavalry. He needs help. The kind of help I can't give him.

MIKEY

The light through my bedroom window wakes me up. My head is throbbing, and I feel like I'm about to puke. I'm trying to put the pieces together of last night. I remember Tia coming over, and then I remember her helping me in the shower.

Fuck! I was such a piece of shit to her last night. That's not how I'm going to get her back. Frankly, I don't know if she will ever be mine again. I don't fucking blame her, but I need her in my life. Life doesn't even feel like it's worth living without her.

I lay in bed for a while, thinking of ways to apologize, when the smell of bacon drives me to get out of bed.

"Hey, look, I'm sorry about everything that happened last night," I begin, before realizing that it's not Tia standing in my kitchen.

It's Chris.

"Save your apologies, fuckwad. She's gone, and you'll be lucky if she ever comes back," Chris states, flipping the bacon.

Tia must have called him last night. This is bad. Really bad. My therapist told me time and time again not to push her, not to test the boundaries, and what did I do? I pushed her so fucking hard. I couldn't just let her heal. No, I had to drink so fucking much that I ended up passing out in the shower, puking all over myself and waking up to Tia crying while helping me shower.

I just keep hurting everyone I care about. Self-destruction is my middle name right now.

"What do I do, man?" I ask, staring out the window into my backyard.

Chris shuts off the pan and plates the bacon. "That's up to you to decide. You can continue down the path you're on and lose everyone, or you can clean your act up and be a fucking man." He reaches down and grabs a clean pan for the eggs. "I should be home with my sick wife right now, but instead I'm here babysitting your pathetic ass. I think it's time to grow the fuck up, man."

I scrub a hand over my face. He's right and I know it. But how the fuck do I do that? Every time I see Tia, I lose it. I know what I should do, but the caveman in me comes out and tries to stake his claim on her. I just need her so desperately.

After Chris finishes cooking breakfast, he shoves a plate at me.

"Eat," he demands, and I do as I'm told.

We eat in silence. I don't know what to say, and I can tell Chris is pissed. I take our plates to the sink after we finish and start washing them. Once I'm done, I turn around and see Chris standing there with his arms folded, holding some papers.

"Look, man, I know you're trying, but clearly doing it on your own isn't working. I found a place that I think you should go to. It's a self-care center. Once you sign up, you agree to stay the three months, and you're not allowed out once you go in. You will have no access to TV, internet, or your cell phone. It's intense, man. Lots of meditation and therapy sessions, but their track record is impeccable." He hands me the papers and steps back.

"Three months? But isn't that close to Tia's due date?" I can't miss the birth of my daughter. "And what about Christmas? I have never spent a Christmas away from my family before."

"She isn't due for three and a half months. You should be out just in time. Your daughter deserves someone to look up to, and right now that's not you."

Wow. He's always been honest, but he isn't holding anything back today.

"I can't force you to go. You have to sign yourself in. I know spending the holidays away from your family is going to be hard, but I really think it's your best option. You're allowed to bring your guitar. Maybe you could write while you're in there," he says.

I have had no inspiration to write, but it's not a bad idea to bring my guitar just in case.

"And do they have openings?" I ask.

Chris smiles. "Yeah, man. You go in today. Now pack your shit and let's hit the road."

Well, I guess that's settled. I don't want to miss Tia's pregnancy, but Chris is right. If I don't change something now, I won't deserve to be in my daughter's life.

I call my mom while I'm packing.

"Hi, honey," she answers.

"Hey, Mom," I sigh, mustering the strength to tell her the truth. "Um, I messed up last night. I drank, and almost did drugs. I need more help. Chris has gotten me into a self-care center, but I'll be there for three months and I'll miss Christmas."

I hear my mom sob on the other end of the line.

"I need to get better for everyone and myself, Mom. I'll be able to call you, but I can't see you until my treatment is over," I tell her.

I hear her take a deep breath. "I'm glad you are trying to better yourself. I'll call you as often as you're allowed. I'll miss you, but I agree this sounds like it's the best thing for you."

"Thanks, Mom. We'll talk soon."

"Take care, son."

We hang up and I finish packing.

The drive to the self-care center is long. It takes us four hours to get there, and it's in the middle of Butt Fuck, Nowhere. We enter through large gates. Chris is allowed to check me in, but he has to leave immediately after.

"Thanks for helping me out, man," I tell Chris as I give him a hug.

I see tears in Chris's eyes. "You're my brother. I'd do anything for you. Just get better, okay?"

I nod. "You got it, man."

Chris leaves, and it all sinks in. I'm stuck here for three months. I hope this fucking works.

This place is utter bullshit. Do they really think that meditating and talking about our feelings is going to make everything better? I've been here for a month, and it's been hell.

The psychiatrist has been running tests on me, but I don't even know what they're for. I'm a drug addict with depression. Just fucking fix me.

I've spoken to Tia once. She told me she hopes I get better, but not to call her again until I'm out. I guess she has decided to see her own therapist and thinks it's best if we cut off contact for the time being. It fucking gutted me to hear that. Doesn't she understand that she's my everything? My shrink says it's a good idea, but what the fuck does he know?

Yesterday was Christmas. They don't do anything special at this center, so it was just like any other day. It was my first time ever being away from my family for the holidays, and it felt like the world was collapsing around me. I called my mom and she cried. I thought I was going to die at the sound.

The fitness center is my favorite place here. At least there is a place where I can forget about everything. If I stop and think, my thoughts go straight to Tia. At first, I miss her, but then I get pissed off that she keeps pushing me away.

Therapy sessions are driving me crazy. I don't want to talk about my feelings, because I don't want to think about the shit storm that is my life. The doctor says that's normal at first, but I just want him to shut up. I keep telling him to fuck off, but he literally laughs at me and says he won't give up on me.

I don't want to go to my session today. I'm sick of talking about my feelings, but I do want to get better for my daughter, and for Tia. Walking into the office, I see Dr. Hannen at his desk.

"'Sup, Doc?" I mumble while I sit on the sofa.

"How are you today?" he asks.

"How the fuck do you think I am?" I shout. "I'm crawling out of my goddamn skin. I've fucked my entire life up, and if I don't get my shit together, I may not be allowed in my daughter's life."

He nods and writes some notes. I lose my shit.

"And what the fuck could you possibly be writing? That I'm a basket case? I already know that. I wish I wouldn't have failed at my fucking suicide. Everyone would be better off without me in their lives."

That's the first time I've admitted that out loud. I regretted the attempt at first, but now I just regret that it didn't work.

"Now we are getting somewhere," Dr. Hannen says, looking into my eyes. "Tell me more about that."

"I'm a fucking idiot. I believed a story I shouldn't have. Why did I listen to a person who has used and abused our relationship since the moment we first became friends, over the woman I have loved since I was a fucking child? I didn't give her a chance to talk to me, and now she hates me because I'm an asshole. I fucking manhandled her in a doctor's office. You should have seen her face. She was terrified." I scrub a hand over my face. "I just need her, Doc. I can't imagine a life without her."

My life is in a downward spiral, and there is no one to blame but myself.

"That is a lot of self-hate, Mikey," he says calmly.

"Well, no shit, Doc," I spit out.

"Are you mad at Johnny?"

I pause for a minute. I should be. I've cut him out of my life, but am I angry with him? Not entirely. Yes, he lied to me and is the cause of the majority of this hurt, but he was just protecting his image. I get it, to an extent. He didn't realize at the time how much hurt he would be causing, and I'm used to just ignoring the stupid shit he does, so it's easy to not be mad at him.

I look up at the doctor. "What good is it being mad at him? He didn't make me cut Tia out, or say the hurtful shit I did. That's all on me."

He smiles and nods. "You are right. Now that we have you finally admitting to your feelings, we will be able to deal with them."

This therapy shit is confusing as fuck, but I actually feel like he is listening. Maybe we will get somewhere eventually. We still have two months to go.

"We need to turn your negative thoughts into something else. We need to break down your feelings and pinpoint exactly why you are feeling that way. You say you're a 'complete fuck-up,' but look at everything you've accomplished over the years. That statement isn't true. You say you've let everyone down, but your mom is happy that you're alive. You have also paid off their mortgage so that they can travel. That doesn't sound like letting them down to me. Do you see where I'm going with this, Mikey?"

I nod. "But what about Tia? I hurt her so bad, Doc. I need her. She is like my air. How can I live without air?" I blink back the tears.

"We'll work on it, Mikey. I'm going to suggest that you start writing a journal. Every night, write a letter to Tia, or your daughter. Get your thoughts out, all of them, and then when we are done here, you can choose to keep it to yourself or share it with them."

I think about that for a minute. That's actually a great idea.

I stand and shake Dr. Hannen's hand. "Thanks, Doc. I'll see you tomorrow."

Walking out of the room, I actually feel better. Maybe there is something to this therapy shit after all.

I write my first journal entry to Tia and Bubbles before I go to bed.

Dear Tia,

I'm supposed to write to you every night, so here I go.

I wanted to apologize, again. I have issues, and I'm working on them, for real this time. I promise that when I get out of here, I'm going to be the man that deserves to be in Bubbles's life.

Love,

Mikey

Dear baby girl,

Your daddy isn't perfect. He has made lots of mistakes. But I love you very much. I want you to look up to me, to be proud that I am your daddy. I'm working on that. I won't let you down.

Love,

Daddy

I'm really connecting with Dr. Hannen and starting to understand his techniques. That's making the second month here a lot more bearable.

He has diagnosed me as bipolar. It's not the first time someone has brought this up to me. When you do as many drugs as I have, you do a few stints in rehab. I've always thought those quacks were full of shit. There is no way I could be bipolar. Even when Dr. Hannen brought it up, I thought he was crazy at first. But he is someone I trust, so I thought more on it. And the more I thought about it, the more I thought he was right. It actually makes a lot of sense. I always thought my symptoms were just from the drug use. I've been using for so long that it's hard to know what I'm really like without them. But even after I stopped the drugs for Tia, I still had crazy highs and crazy lows.

He's also said that I have an addictive personality, which is accurate. I've been doing drugs and abusing alcohol since I was seventeen. I guess the combination of having an addictive personality and being bipolar is especially brutal.

Tia turned into another addiction for me. I felt high when I was around her and craved her in an unhealthy way. I believed that she lied to me, and it sent me into a downward spiral. Even when I pushed her away, I still craved her. I turned back to drugs to try and fill the void, but it didn't work.

Dr. Hannen has put me on a medication to help with the bipolar symptoms. I was nervous about taking another drug since I'm an addict, but he promised me this would work. These drugs don't make me high. They just make me…normal. They help my brain function like it should. I can still have some mood swings with them, but they are less severe.

"How has your writing been going?" Dr. Hannen asks in my next therapy session.

"Really good, actually. Ever since you got me opening up, the words have just been flowing. I've written five songs, and a bunch of hooks. I've never been this in tune with my music before," I tell him.

He nods and writes a few things down. "That's good to hear. And what about your journaling?"

My face falls a little. I've continued to write my journal entries every single night, but it still hurts not being able to talk to Tia.

"Okay," I reply.

"You're still really affected by Tia, aren't you?"

I nod. "I believed that I was destined to be with her, but I also see now that the addiction to her wasn't healthy. I messed up badly, because I thought I *needed* her. My delusions fucked with me. I understand why she wouldn't want to be with me. I do still want her in my life, but I know now that it has to be on her terms." I run a hand over my face and let out a sigh. "The medication is really helping. I hope I can be the man and the father she needs me to be."

"Your progress is coming along nicely, Mikey. You're right. It is up to Tia to take you back. Obviously, she will have a role in your life as the mother of your daughter, but if you want her to take you back as more, you will have to build trust. Show her how you have changed. She may still not take you back, and you'll have to learn to be okay with it if that happens."

I nod at him.

"But with everything I have seen, I believe you are a suitable person to be in your daughter's life. And I hope the best for your future," he says.

Dr. Hannen understands me and he has made these therapy sessions life changing. The other doctors couldn't get me to open up like he does. They couldn't read through my bullshit.

"Doc, when I'm out of here, what do I do? My other therapists were shit compared to you," I sigh.

He lets out a laugh. "I'm sure they weren't shit. You just didn't connect with them. But I do have one opening in my private practice. If you want to see me, I would be more than happy to continue our sessions."

"I would really appreciate that. These sessions are really helping me."

He nods. "I'm glad these sessions are helping you, Mikey. You have already come a long way. I see a very promising and bright future for you if you keep practicing the techniques I've taught you. And continue to take your medication. You may feel better, but don't stop taking the pills."

I nod and stand up. "Thanks again, Doc. I'll see you tomorrow."

Walking out, I head down the hall to the call center. I want to talk to Tia, to see how she and Bubbles are doing, but I need to respect her wish for space, so instead I call my mom.

"Hello?" she answers.

"Hey, Mom, it's me."

"Oh, Mikey! I wasn't expecting your call today. I'm so happy to hear from you! How is everything going?" she asks.

"Good! Have you heard from Tia?" I can't help but ask.

I know my mom stays in contact with her. I just want to make sure she's okay.

"She's doing well. She wanted me to tell you her therapy sessions are going really well, and that the baby is doing awesome."

I smile. I'm glad her sessions are going well. I wish I could see her, but I know we are apart for a reason.

"How about you? How are your sessions going?" she inquires.

"Really good, Mom. Only one month left. I can't wait to see everyone," I tell her.

"Just focus on getting better. I'm looking forward to giving you a hug when you get home."

"Thanks, Mom. Talk to you soon."

I hang up and head to my room. Time for a little journaling.

Dear Tia,

I just talked to my mom, and she says you're doing well. I'm really glad to hear that. I feel like I'm really getting somewhere with Dr. Hannen. He is helping me understand myself more than I ever have. I really hope we can have a real conversation when I get out of here, just as co-parents.

I still love you, Tia, but I know we can't have that kind of relationship anymore. I want to respect you in every way. I want us to raise our daughter in a happy, healthy way. She is my everything now, and I know you feel the same way.

When I get out of here, we will figure everything out. Just let me know what you want from me, and I'll do it.

Love,
Mikey

Dear baby girl,

I think about you every day. I know you are growing so fast. I can't wait for the day I meet you. You already own my heart. I will do everything to protect you and keep you safe. You will forever be my little girl, even when you are fully grown.

Love you forever,
Daddy

Today is the day. I get to go home! My parents are coming to pick me up, and I'm excited to finally sleep in my own bed. I'm happy that all the rooms here are private, but the beds were still shit. Dr. Hannen is waiting with me to sign me out. I'm really happy now that I came here. I learned things about myself I never knew before. My mom's face lights up, when she sees me.

"Mikey!" she cries, running towards me.

I drop my bag and wrap my arms around her. She's so tiny; I always feel like I'm going to crush her.

"It's good to see you, Mom." Holding her, I give her a quick kiss on the top of her head. "I want you to meet Dr. Hannen. He's helped me a lot. I finally feel like my old self, but honestly, an even better version."

My mom looks at Dr. Hannen with a huge smile. "Thank you so much for bringing my son back to me!"

She gives him a big hug, and I can't help but chuckle.

My dad comes up behind my mom and gives me a nod. "Son."

He has never been very affectionate, but I always knew he loved me. Surprising us both, I give him a tight hug. He freezes at first, but then returns the hug.

"I'm glad you're back to your old self. I can see it in your eyes," he tells me.

I nod. "I'm doing really great, Dad. I feel like I finally deserve to be in my daughter's life."

He smiles at me and pats me on the back. "Let's get you home."

TIA

"Yessss," I hiss out as Mikey's tongue laps at my clit.

I feel his hot breath on my sex, and I buck my hips into his face. I can feel him chuckle as he places a hand on my stomach, holding me down.

"Damn, girl. You taste so good," he says before taking my clit between his teeth.

"Fuck!" I yell as he inserts two fingers inside me.

He curls them just right, hitting me in the perfect spot.

"I need more, baby. Please," I pant.

He slowly removes his fingers and pulls himself up to hover over me.

"Your wish is my command," he whispers against my lips, before pushing his tongue into my mouth. I love tasting myself on his lips. It's dirty, but so good.

Slowly, he pushes into me, and I feel so full. There is nothing I crave more than this feeling. Mikey starts to pick up speed and I can feel myself getting ready to go over the edge.

"Yes, Mikey! Don't stop!" I scream at the top of my lungs as I reach my high.

I grab my belly as my eyes snap open. My breathing is heavy, and I feel sweaty. Why do I keep having these dreams? Must be the hormones.

Rolling around, I try to get out of bed. It takes a couple of tries, but finally I am sitting. Looking down, I can't even see my feet. This damn belly keeps getting in the way of everything. I don't know what I would do lately without Crystal. She has been a lot of help around the house. When she isn't working, she's cleaning and taking care of me. I was supposed to be the one taking care of her, but she doesn't complain. She keeps reminding me that we're in this together. I helped her when she needed it, now she is returning the favor. Olivia is getting so big. I can't believe she is almost five months old. And in three short weeks, Bubbles will be here. It feels like she has already dropped. I get the feeling she may be coming early.

The holidays were crazy. My dad came over for Christmas, along with Leah and her brother Mason. I feel bad for not seeing my dad more often, but he moved a couple of years ago for a better job. I know six hours isn't super far, but it's far enough that we really only see each other on holidays. This year, he was able to take time off work and stayed until the new year to celebrate my birthday. Having a holiday birthday was kind of crappy as a kid, because everyone was gone. It's kind of awesome as an adult, because there is always a party! I was only three hours away from being a New Year's Day baby.

Overall, the past three months have just been odd. I've been seeing a therapist; I just couldn't cope with my emotions anymore. I was sad all the time. Some of the feelings were because of hormones, but others were because of issues I never dealt with.

I never realized how much my mother leaving me really affected me. I didn't keep people at arm's length because I was used to doing things for myself. I did it because I was terrified that if I let someone in, they would just leave me. My own mother didn't want me, so why would anyone else? I know now that she had her own issues, and I can't take ownership for them. The people in my life are there for a reason. I will let them in. I am stronger when I do so.

My issues with Mikey were more confusing to deal with. There was so much anger and resentment there. I wanted to forgive him, but I also wanted to hold on to my independence. I thought that if I forgave Mikey, that would make me weak. And I also didn't want to forgive him out of spite. If he couldn't forgive me, why should I forgive him?

With help from my therapist, I've learned to deal with my past. I've forgiven my mom and Mikey. There is no way we can raise our baby together if I harbor so much animosity towards him.

Staring at the ceiling, I decide it would be best to shoot Mikey a text and invite him to my next appointment.

Me: Hey. Long time, no talk... I wanted to let you know I see the doctor

in six days. I would really like it if you came with. :-)

Mikey doesn't respond for a while, and I start to think he isn't going to reply. Maybe his therapist told him it would be best if we have as little contact as possible. But how is that feasible when we are going to have a daughter together?

Just as I'm beginning to lose hope, my phone pings.

Mikey: What time? I would love to be there.

My heart lights up. I'm happy he will be there. We can start to rebuild a friendship and be amazing co-parents.

Me: 10 a.m. I hope that's not too early.

Mikey: Not at all. Mind if I pick you up?

Hmm. I'm not sure if this is a good idea, but I do want to be friends.

Me: Okay, pick me up at 9 a.m. I like to be early.

Mikey: See you in a couple of days, Tia.

Is it wrong that I miss him calling me beautiful or sweetheart? I know part of me will always love Mikey. My therapist said that's normal. I'm just happy that we can be involved in each other's lives again, without hate.

Today, I'm meeting with Dustin Maxx. Apparently, he's a YouTube superstar. Crystal lost her mind when she found out I could possibly be managing him. I told Dustin that I was pregnant, and things would have to revolve around my daughter at first, but that we could get together and discuss what direction he wants to take his career in.

I'm excited to be getting back into what I love to do. I thought my love for music was gone forever, but once I started fixing the sad parts in my life, the happy parts fell back into place.

I pull up to Dustin's parents' house shortly after noon. I would have been on time, but I had to pee right before I left the house. Bubbles loves to kick my bladder now. It's like it's her own personal punching bag. Looking out my window, I take in the view. The house is cute. It's in a good neighborhood. Not too fancy, but not the slums either. Knocking on the door, I take a deep breath. Time to get back into this. I know I can do it.

A lady looking to be in her mid to late thirties opens the door. "You must be Tia!"

I smile and reach out my hand. "Yes, and you must be Dustin's mom."

"Grace," she corrects me. "I'm so happy you were able to join us today. Dustin is very excited to meet you."

"I'm sorry I'm late. This little girl likes to kick my internal organs," I laugh, patting my belly.

"Oh, I remember those days. Come in. Lunch is almost ready." She ushers me in, and the house is even prettier on the inside. It really feels like a home.

Entering the dining room, I see Dustin and his father. They both stand to greet me.

"I'm Al." Dustin's dad extends his hand to me; I shake it with a smile.

"I'm Tia." I turn. "And you must be Dustin."

"Yes, ma'am." He nods his head very fast. "I'm happy you're here."

I giggle a little. "Please don't call me 'ma'am.' That makes me feel old."

A blush spreads over his face and he grabs the back of his neck. "Sorry."

I smile and sit down on one of the chairs. "I'm happy to be here, Dustin. I've seen your work on YouTube. You're very talented. I have no doubt that you'll be able to do great things."

He gives me the biggest smile and his eyes light up with pride. He definitely has a very charismatic charm. I can see him being a heartbreaker in the future.

"I met Jay when I was going for an interview at Broken Ax Records. He told me I was perfect for their label, but that if I wanted to get big, I would need an amazing manager. That was when he gave me your number."

I smile. I love that Jay is doing well for himself. His label is doing amazing, and his most recent single is topping all the rock charts.

"Thank you for considering me. I've had a little bit of a career backslide lately, but am really excited to get back in the game." I rest my hands on my stomach. "Like I said on the phone, I am due right away. That might slow me down slightly at first, but thankfully, I'm able to do the majority of my work from home. I think what you need to do is open for someone who will be headlining a tour sometime this year."

Dustin nods. "That's a great idea! What about Mikey Ecosta? You know him, right?"

My heart drops. I don't even know if Mikey will still be doing a tour. He still needs to find a new manager, and I honestly don't know much about what is going on in his life right now.

"Um, yes, I do, but he's taken a step back from his career to focus on his health. I'm not entirely sure if he will still be doing a tour or not."

"Yeah, I read about that. If he does tour, I want to be on it! Our music fits well together."

I nod. Dustin is right. He would be a perfect opening act for Mikey, but would I be able to deal with that?

"I'm actually meeting with Mikey in a couple of days. I'll let you know what his plans are," I concede.

Dustin starts beaming. His age really shows when he is excited. "That would be great! Thanks so much."

Grace comes in with a pot of amazing-smelling spaghetti. "I hope you're ready to eat."

I smile. "Yes please. I love carbs."

Grace giggles and sets down the pot. "I was the same way when I was pregnant. Let me go grab the garlic toast."

The rest of the afternoon is very pleasant. We discuss the legal stuff and I recommend a lawyer to Dustin. He can't use the same firm I use, but Leah's brother is also a lawyer and works for a different company, so it should work out very well. If Dustin doesn't want to use Mason, I know he will recommend someone just as good.

"Thank you for having me over this afternoon," I say while struggling to get my coat on. Everything is an obstacle when you're as big as a house. "I'm glad I got to meet you, Dustin, and I'm excited to join you on your journey."

Dustin leans in and gives me a hug. I smile. I can already see him turning into my little brother.

"Thanks, Tia. I'm really glad we clicked so well. Jay was right. You're kick-ass."

"Language," Grace warns.

"Sorry, Mom," he mumbles, and runs a hand through his hair.

I giggle. You have to love parent-child interactions.

I give Grace a hug goodbye and leave.

The rest of my day is spent at home cleaning. I've been having this overwhelming urge to make sure everything is perfect. I remember hearing about this in prenatal classes. It's called "nesting." I honestly thought it was a joke, but here I am cleaning my tub, making sure there are no soap spots. I've always been a clean freak, but this is a new level even for me.

Finally, I feel like the house is clean enough and lay down on the couch. Just as I'm about to close my eyes for a second, Olivia wakes up. This little lady is getting me good and prepared for when Bubbles arrives.

Today is Crystal's birthday, and I have everything planned out. I'm exhausted from being super pregnant, but I can make it through a dinner just fine. As I finish texting Leah, making sure she is coming tonight, I hear Olivia's little shriek of joy as Crystal comes into the living room carrying her.

"Happy birthday, girl!" I say, trying to get up from the couch.

Crystal laughs. "Don't bother standing, I'll just come over there." She places Olivia in my lap, then wraps her arms around me for a hug. "Thank you for everything."

I smile. "Don't thank me yet. Your birthday dinner is going to be amazing! Are you sure you don't want to invite anyone else beside me and Leah?"

"I'm sure. You guys are my family, and that's all I need."

I sigh. I hate that she is keeping to herself so much lately. She needs friends her own age.

I finally get enough momentum to stand up, and an idea pops into my head.

"I'm going to go take a shower," I tell her, walking out of the living room.

Now, hopefully, I can put the plan into motion.

Pulling my phone out, I start sending off texts. I know one person Crystal's age. I just hope he's free tonight.

When we get to the restaurant, I help Crystal get Olivia out of the car. She looks extra cute in her party dress.

"I can't get over how adorable she is," I say, giving Olivia a kiss.

Crystal giggles. "I know. That dress was worth every penny."

Once we are in the restaurant, I see Leah and our special guest already sitting at the table, with a giant *Happy Birthday* balloon. We are almost at the table when Crystal freezes.

"What is Dustin Maxx doing here?" she whispers.

"I thought it would be nice to have someone your own age here," I tell her.

"Tia, this is a bad idea. We should go home," she says nervously.

"Oh, come on. It's fine. He's a really nice guy. And look, he even brought you a gift." I point to the box in front of Dustin.

She sighs, but follows me to the table.

Leah stands up and gives Crystal a giant hug. "Happy birthday, sweetheart. Officially an adult now." She picks up the gift off the table and hands it to Crystal. "I hope you like it."

"Thank you. You know you didn't have to get my anything." Crystal places the gift back on the table, then turns to Dustin.

"Crystal, this is Dustin," I introduce them.

Dustin is staring at Crystal, but not saying anything.

"Thanks for coming, but you really didn't have to get me anything. You don't even know me." Crystal finally breaks the silence between them.

"I can't show up empty-handed. What kind of guy would that make me?"

Dustin gives her a show stopping smile, but Crystal rolls her eyes.

"And who is this gorgeous princess?" Dustin asks, grabbing Olivia's tiny hand.

"This is my daughter, Olivia," she tells him.

Olivia babbles at Dustin and reaches out for him.

"Can I?" he asks.

Crystal nods and passes Olivia to Dustin.

"I've always loved kids," he tells her. "I'm the oldest of my cousins, so I babysat a lot before I started doing music full-time."

Crystal gives Dustin the once-over, clearly checking him out, but he isn't paying attention. I try to hold back a chuckle, but it breaks out a little. Everyone turns to look at me and I turn fifty shades of red.

"I'm fine. I just choke on air sometimes. Don't pay any attention to me," I say, not smoothly at all. "Let's sit down so the waitress will come and get our order."

The dinner goes smoothly. I think I pick up on slight flirting between Crystal and Dustin, but I'm not too sure. I'll have to ask Leah about that later.

Speaking of Leah, she has been texting a lot. It's not like her to have her phone out during get-togethers. I can tell she's trying to be discreet, but whoever she's messaging is making her smile. I'll have to ask about that too.

Olivia starts to fuss, and I think it's time to go.

"Are you tired, little girl?" I ask her, like she can actually answer me.

"It's way past her bedtime. It's probably best if we head home," Crystal says picking Olivia up.

She cuddles into her mommy's shoulder and I almost tear up. Damn hormones. I take Olivia from Crystal so she can say her goodbyes.

"It was really nice to meet you," Dustin says, then grabs the back of his neck. "Do you mind if I get your number?"

Crystal blushes. "Um, sure, but I'm really busy, so don't get offended if I don't respond right away."

"Noted." He gives her that smile again, and I swear I see her melt.

I'm going to have to keep a close eye on those two, I think.

I'm seeing Mikey today. I'm extremely nervous. I've forgiven him for everything, but how do we move on? How do we make this work? I want to distance myself from him, but we are having a child. I can't keep him out of her life. That wouldn't be fair to either of them.

I wonder what version of Mikey I will see today. I found out he was diagnosed as bipolar while he was in the self-care center. It actually makes a lot of sense. His mom says he's doing really well. The medication he is on is helping him a lot. She has never seen him this full of life before. But over the past ten months, I have seen so many different versions of Mikey, I feel like it could be anyone I'm meeting today. I hope it's this new, full-of-life version, because I need positivity in my life right now. Any more negativity, and I think I'll drown.

I start to get ready, but I am exhausted. I didn't sleep at all last night and my back hurts so bad. It's been spasming all morning, and it's a crippling pain. I knew back pain was a thing with pregnancy, but this is ridiculous. I make a mental note to book a massage for later.

Looking at the clock, I realize Mikey will be here any moment to pick me up, and I'm nowhere near ready.

"Fuck," I huff out.

I quickly brush my hair and try to quickly pull up my pants, but I fall over. This day is turning out to be a fucking shit show.

As I lay on the floor crying, because that's what I do all the time now, I hear a knock at the door. Fuck! I would love to go and answer it, but my pants are stuck around my ankles and I can't really move.

I let out a whine and yell, "It's open! Come in!"

"Tia?" I hear Mikey call out.

Oh, my God. How embarrassing is this? The first time I've seen him in months, and he's about to catch me with my pants down, literally. If I could crawl into a hole and die right now I would, but I need help, so I guess this is happening.

"Help, please," I whimper from my room. At first, I'm not sure if he heard me, but then I hear his feet coming down the hall.

"Tia. Oh, my God. Are you okay?" I can hear the panic in his voice.

I pout. "I'm fine. I was just trying to get my pants on, but I'm as big as a fucking hippopotamus and I lost my balance and fell down. Now I'm lying on the floor crying because these hormones make me cry over everything. I was watching a video of a puppy last night on Facebook, and so many tears."

Mikey's face turns from panic to a heartbreakingly cute smile.

"Don't give me that perfect smile! Get down here and fucking help me!" I bark.

Mikey lets out a little chuckle, but doesn't say a word. I can't help but smile as he helps me to my feet and pulls my pants up. His fingertips graze my skin and it takes all of my power to not let out a whimper. I haven't been touched in so long, and I crave it. As soon as my pants are up, he backs away. No lingering touch. No kiss on my check. Just distance.

I look down at my feet. Well, at the floor. I can't actually see my feet anymore.

"Sorry you had to see me like that. I don't do the best impersonation of a turtle," I mumble.

I turn my focus to Mikey and see his dimple. My heart melts a little. I bend over as another back-spasm hits.

"Fuck!" I yell.

Mikey is right by my side. "What was that? Are you okay?"

The look of panic is back on his face.

I straighten up and sit on my bed. "It's just back spasms. I've been getting them all day. I'm going to book a massage for tomorrow. I'll be fine."

I rub my back a little until I feel the bed sink next to me and Mikey is pushing my hands out of the way. His fingers press deep into my back, and the pain melts away.

"How does that feel?" he asks as his fingers continue to work magic.

I let out a little moan. "Amazing!"

I glance at the clock beside my bed and realize we have to leave.

I let out a sigh. "Time to go. I don't want to be late."

I stand and make my way to the door.

"Do you have your hospital bag?" Mikey asks.

How does he know about hospital bags? And why would I need it? The baby isn't due for another few weeks.

"Um, I don't think I need it," I reply.

Mikey's eyes soften. "Please get it, just to be on the safe side."

I pout, and that makes him chuckle.

"Fine," I mutter.

I waddle back to my room to get the bag, and my pillow. As I bend over to grab the bag, I see a large hand picking it up.

"You don't have to do that," I tell Mikey as I go to grab my pillow.

He smiles and grabs my pillow from me. "I know. I just want to feel helpful. Okay?"

I smile back and nod. It *is* nice to have the help. I've gotten a lot better at accepting help lately. It was another thing I worked on in therapy.

Mikey throws the bag and pillow into the backseat of an SUV, then helps me in. I breathe in the new car smell.

"When did you get this car?" I ask, looking around.

"Yesterday." He pauses for a moment, then turns to me. "I was actually hoping I could gift it to you. It's number one on the market for safety, so you and Bubbles will be in good hands when you have to drive her around."

I smile. "Mikey, that's super sweet, but I don't think I can accept it."

His smile drops for a moment. "That's okay. I guess it would be good for me to have a safe vehicle as well, for when I have Bubbles."

I feel my heart stop. I mean, of course Mikey is going to have Bubbles sometimes. That's what co-parenting is all about. But at the same time, I can't see her ever being away from me. I've been growing her for nine months. Her heart is my heart. How can I ever let her out of my sight? I feel the tears start falling down my face.

Mikey reaches out and grabs my hand. "I'm not taking her away from you, Tia. We can make arrangements later. I know how much you are already attached to her. We'll make this work."

I nod. His touch is comforting.

He starts the car and takes us to my doctor. I am so uncomfortable, and these back-spasms are happening a lot more often as well. I see Mikey checking on me occasionally; he can tell I'm in pain. I don't know why, but I'm craving contact, so I reach over and grab his hand. At first, he freezes and looks concerned, but his face softens and he envelopes my hand in his.

We get to the doctor's office and check in. Thankfully, we don't have to wait long before we go into a room. Mikey keeps massaging my back, trying to relieve some of the pressure. The spasms are starting to become unbearable, and I don't know what to do.

We hear a knock at the door, and Dr. Amelia smiles at us both. Mikey starts to get up, but I glare at him.

"Don't you dare stop," I almost growl.

Both Mikey and Dr. Amelia chuckle.

"Well this looks promising," she says with a smile.

"Promising how? These back spasms are driving me nuts," I whine.

"Dear, by the looks of it, I think you're in labor."

"How is that possible? I haven't had any contractions, just back spasms."

"Lay down and I will examine you." She puts on gloves and squirts some lube on her fingers while I lay down. "I believe you are experiencing back labor. Sometimes when the baby is positioned funny, they can put pressure on your back, causing the contractions to be felt there instead of your stomach."

I let out a whine. "I don't want to have a baby if it feels like this."

She lets out another giggle and begins the exam. "Yes, just as I thought. You are about six centimeters dilated."

My face gets hot and I think I'm about to pass out. "What? But my water hasn't broken yet."

"Sometimes the water doesn't naturally break on its own," she explains. "I'm going to encourage you to go up to the hospital and get admitted. I know you are wanting an epidural; you can get that at any time now."

"Oh, thank God." I let out a huff, then turn my gaze to Mikey. "What are you waiting for? Let's get this vagina watermelon out of me."

They both laugh, but Mikey helps me get up.

"I can't wait to meet our daughter," he says, with another of those damn smiles.

MIKEY

"Where the fuck is the anesthesiologist?" Tia screams.

I continue to rub her back, but she is getting more and more aggravated.

"I'm sure he'll get here soon. Just take deep breaths," I encourage her.

"Don't talk to me about deep breaths! You don't have a baby clawing at your spine!"

I can't help but smile at her. I've missed how feisty she can be.

Finally, the doctor walks in.

"'Bout fucking time," Tia hisses. "Do you enjoy seeing women in pain? Are you some sort of sadist?"

He doesn't say anything. He just prepares his station. I see a giant needle and my eyes bug out. That needle seems a bit excessive. I swear it's going to come out of her chest.

"What is it?" Tia asks.

I try to calm my face. "Nothing. It's going to be fine."

The doctor gets Tia to hunch over a table while sitting on the bed.

"How the fuck am I supposed to bend anymore? I have a beach ball for a stomach," she growls.

I grab her hand. "You've got this. Just breathe."

She looks up into my eyes. Her eyes are green, so I know she's not sad, but she still has tears in them.

"Thank you so much for being here," she sniffles.

The doctor finishes inserting the needle, and has Tia lay back. "The drugs will start working shortly."

He doesn't say anything else. He just leaves. Smart man. I'm pretty sure Tia wanted to castrate him.

She looks exhausted.

"How are you feeling?" I ask.

"Better now. Drugs are good." She gives me that smile that used to drive me crazy. Hell, it still drives me crazy. "I think I'm going to try and rest now, I'm exhausted."

I smile at her and nod. "Good idea. I've heard the delivery itself can be very grueling sometimes."

She looks at me, studying my face. "Have you been reading baby books?"

I feel my cheeks heat. "Maybe a few. I wanted to be prepared."

Her smile grows wide. "You're too much, Mikey."

Her eyes slowly close, as she begins to drift off. I sit next to the bed, just staring at her for a while. She's fucking perfect. I hope our daughter takes after her. Not only is she beautiful, but she's kind and forgiving. I wasn't sure how she was going to react to me today, but I'm glad she's letting me be here.

I decide to go the cafeteria to get a cup of coffee. I don't want to miss anything once Bubbles decides it's time to come out.

I'm waiting in line when I feel a hand on my shoulder. Turning, I see fiery red hair.

"Get the fuck away from me," I hiss at Amber.

Her face falls, but I don't give a shit.

"I'm sorry Mikey," she says. "I made mistakes. I was in love with you. I just wished you loved me back."

"That's not love, Amber. That's manipulation. All you and I ever were, was fuck buddies. I never had any feelings toward you, and now all I feel towards you is disgust," I snap.

"I understand that. I just wanted to tell you I'm pregnant."

I freeze. "There is no fucking way that is my baby. We always used protection, and most times I even pulled out and came on your ass, tits, or face."

"It's not yours, but the baby has changed me, Mikey. I'm going to be a better person. I'm moving back to Colorado to be with my family. I just really wanted to tell you I'm sorry. I'm glad I saw you today."

She walks away and is finally out of my life. I hope she is changing and has a good life, but I also never want to see her fucking face again.

I pay for my coffee and head back up to see Tia. When I walk in, she is awake and playing on her phone.

"Hey," I say, giving her a small smile.

It's been killing me not to call her beautiful or sweetheart, but I don't know how she would feel about that. I don't ever want to push her or hurt her again, so I'm taking a step back and just being there for her in any way she needs me.

"Hi." She beams at me.

Her face looks a lot more alive. I'm assuming it was a good nap.

"How are you feeling?" I sit down next to her on a chair.

"Better. They woke me up and broke my water while you were gone, and I think it's almost time." She looks uncomfortable for a moment, then presses the call button.

A pretty young nurse comes in and gives me a flirty smile. I roll my eyes. Seriously? This could be my wife, for all she knows.

"May I help you?" she asks.

"Yes. First of all, if you could stop making fuck-me eyes at my boyfriend, that would be great. Second, can you get my doctor? I'm ready to push," Tia snaps.

"Are you sure?" the nurse asks timidly.

"Yes, I'm fucking sure! I feel like I have to poop, and in prenatal classes they told us that means it's time to push. So, if you would kindly go and get my fucking doctor or deliver this baby by yourself. I don't give a shit, but I am going to be pushing soon, so hurry the fuck up."

The nurse rushes out of the room, and I can't help but chuckle.

"Boyfriend, huh?" I ask.

Tia rolls her eyes. "I had to come up with something. She was about to make me vomit."

About five minutes later, Dr. Amelia walks in. "I hear we're ready to have a baby."

"Yes!" Tia nods enthusiastically. "Please get this monster out of me."

Dr. Amelia laughs and does an examination. "Yes, my dear, you are fully dilated, and I can feel the baby's head. Now, what you need to do is breathe and push with your contractions. If you can't feel the contractions because of the epidural, just push when you feel the time is right."

Tia nods her head with a look of pure determination on her face.

"And as for you, Dad, I need you to help me and hold her leg up," the doctor says.

What the fuck? I don't say anything. I just do as the doctor instructs. Tia starts screaming as she pushes. This is the craziest thing I have ever witnessed, and I've seen some fucking weird shit.

Before I know what's happening, our baby girl is out, and showing off her amazing lungs. The doctor asks if I want to cut the cord. I nod with tears in my eyes. As soon as I cut the cord, she is placed on Tia's chest.

"Have you come up with a name?" Dr. Amelia asks.

I look at Tia and see her radiant smile. "Yes. Cecelia Lively Ecosta."

I smile too. A perfect name. I look at our baby and see she has already latched on to Tia's breast and is trying to eat.

"She's perfect," I whisper.

Tia nods. "She really is."

We didn't bring the car seat when we came to the hospital, so Tia gave me a key to go and get it from her apartment. After I grab it, I decide to stop by a baby store. As I'm looking through the teeny tiny clothes, I see the perfect outfit. A little onesie with a frilly skirt around the waist but it has an electric guitar printed on it and says, "My dad rocks." Before heading back to the hospital, I grab some candy from a convenience store, for Tia.

"How is everyone?" I ask in a quiet voice, not sure if CeCe is sleeping or not.

"Really good," Tia replies sleepily.

"You look exhausted. I thought you were supposed to be resting."

She gives me a shy smile. "Cecelia really likes to eat, and I don't want to discourage her, so she has been on my boobs a lot."

I look in the tiny plastic baby bed and CeCe is sleeping like the angel she is.

"Can I hold her?" I ask Tia.

She nods. "Of course. You *are* her daddy."

I pick her up, and she is the tiniest thing I have ever seen. I feel like I could break her.

"Daddy loves you, CeCe," I whisper to her.

"It's Cecelia." Tia says in a deadpan voice.

I have no idea if she is joking or not, but then she starts laughing.

"Oh, my God. You should have seen your face." She can barely breathe from laughing so hard.

"Are you okay?" Leah asks, walking in and seeing the tears rolling down Tia's face.

"I'm. Fine," she says between breaths. "I. Just. Made. The. Best. Joke."

"I think she's high," I tell Leah.

She laughs. "Yeah there is no way any joke is that funny."

Leah walks over and gives Tia a hug, and she is finally breathing normally. She wipes the tears from her eyes.

"You, my friend, did not see Mikey's face. It was priceless," she says.

"May I?" Leah asks, reaching out her hands and flexing her fingers, not giving me the option of saying no.

I place CeCe in her hands.

"I am your super amazing Auntie Leah. I will love you for forever. If you ever want anything and Mommy and Daddy say no, just come to me," Leah says.

I look over at Tia, who is rolling her eyes.

This might not be the most traditional of families, but it's kind of perfect. As long as my daughter is in my life, that's all that matters now.

CeCe is one week old today. So far, I've seen her every single day. Tia told me that as long as I text her in advance, I'm more than welcome to see her. I plan on going over later, after my meeting with Dr. Hannen. He warned me before I left the self-care center that any event that causes a lot of emotions, good or bad, could hinder my progress. I've been feeling fine, but I know these appointments are going to be necessary. It's not going to be forever that I get to see CeCe and Tia every day. Life is going to start to go back to normal. I have to start working again, and Tia has things she needs to do.

"Hi, Mikey. Good to see you. Please take a seat," Dr. Hannen greets me. "How's everything going?"

"Hey, Doc. It's going amazing, actually. Tia had the baby. She named her Cecelia." I'm pretty sure I'm grinning like the Cheshire Cat, but I can't help it.

Tia told me she named the baby after her great-grandmother, and honestly, the name suits her perfectly. She may only be a week old, but she already has me wrapped around her tiny finger.

"That's fantastic. And how are you feeling about things?"

"Well right now, it's fantastic. Tia is letting me see CeCe every day, but I know that won't last forever. I don't know how I am going to react when that changes." I run my hand over my face.

That little girl is my world. It already sucks that I only get to spend a few hours a day with her. How am I supposed to go more than twenty-four hours without seeing her?

"It will be challenging for sure, but we can discuss coping mechanisms to help. Now, she is a little young, so a phone call won't work, but maybe Tia can agree to send pictures throughout the day when, for whatever reason, you have to be apart."

I nod. That's actually a really good idea.

"I could maybe even ask for a video," I suggest.

Dr. Hannen smiles. "See? You're getting the idea. Life isn't always easy, but for the most part, if there is open communication, the majority of issues can be avoided."

"What if she forgets me?" I ask, voicing my biggest fear aloud.

"That's highly unlikely, Mikey. While it isn't practical that you will get to see her every day, I can't see Tia keeping her away from you for more than a day or two. But if it is something that causes you anxiety, you could always record your voice in a bear and leave it there."

"That's a fantastic idea!"

I feel less worried already. I use the breathing techniques Dr. Hannen taught me a lot. It helps to calm me down when I feel like everything is too overwhelming.

"That's why you pay me the big bucks," he jokes.

"I saw Amber when Tia was having CeCe," I sigh.

He writes a few notes. "Interesting. How did that go?"

"It was weird. She told me she was pregnant." I fidget with my foot a little. "Of course, I thought she was trying to get something from me. I knew there was no way it was my baby, but I wouldn't put it past her to try anyway. She admitted it was someone else's baby and told me she's moving out of state. She apologized, but I don't know how I feel about it."

"That's understandable, Mikey. She wronged you, and even an apology doesn't erase what she did."

I nod. "I was really happy that she was moving. I'm happy for her that she is getting her life together, but I'm happier that I'll never have to see her again. I came to terms with what she did and forgave her, but I'll never forget."

"You've come a long way, Mikey. I'm proud of you. Let's touch base again in two weeks."

"Sounds good, Doc. Thanks again." I shake his hand and leave. Time to go see my baby.

TIA

My perfect angel is three weeks old today. I don't think I'm ever going to have another child; this has got to be a trick. I bet it's some sort of way the universe repopulates; it makes you think, "Wow, kids are easy," and then, BAM! Your second child is a monster!

Mikey is coming over today, like he has every day, but he said he has something he wants to ask me and I'm nervous. What if he wants to start splitting our time with CeCe? I mean, I get that it's not reality to have him coming over every day, but I also don't want to give up any time with her. Maybe when she's older, I'll feel differently, and of course I want him to have time with her, but I'm so attached to her that it's causing me anxiety to think of not being with her twenty-four-seven.

I pick up my little princess and walk around the living room.

"I love you more than life itself, my little angel," I whisper to her.

She starts to fuss a little, so I sing her a lullaby. I've learned she loves music. Already taking after her daddy.

I'm lost in the moment when I'm startled by a voice. "I never knew you could sing that well."

CeCe starts cooing when she hears her daddy's voice.

I smile. "Thanks. I'm not that good, but our baby girl sure loves music."

Mikey snatches CeCe from my arms and gives her kisses. "I missed you so much, CeCe."

She makes some noises and I know she feels the same way. I hate that the three of us can't spend all day, every day together, but that's not reality for us.

"Would you like coffee, water, juice?" I ask, walking to the kitchen.

"A water would be great."

After I grab two bottles of water, I join Mikey on the couch. "She really loves you."

He smiles at me and, with his free hand, grabs my hand. "And she is loved so much."

"So, what did you want to talk about?" I feel like I should treat this like a Band-Aid and just tear it off.

He takes the now-sleeping CeCe to her swing and gently places her down. He grabs the back of his neck, and I don't know how to feel.

"I really want to get my career back on track, and I just can't imagine doing it with anyone else but you."

I take a deep breath. "Mikey, I think it's better if we don't work together. It's just too hard. Plus, I already have a new client."

"Manage us both," he blurts out.

"I don't know if I can do that. You know how hands-on I like to be, and with CeCe, I just don't think I have enough energy to manage two clients. And besides, my new client is just starting out and he needs my full attention."

His face turns red.

"Are you fucking him?" he yells.

I'm taken aback. How dare he talk to me like that?

"Excuse me? First of all, no. Second of all, it's none of your goddamn business if I am. We aren't together, Mikey. And you need to watch what you say next, or you can leave."

He runs a hand over his face and sits in the big comfy chair. I can see him shaking, but I don't say anything. I just let him calm down. I hear him counting to four between deep breaths.

"I'm sorry," he finally says. "You're right. You don't deserve to be spoken to like that, and you can see whoever you want. Who are you managing anyway?"

"Dustin Maxx," I reply.

I see Mikey's face change; he obviously knows who he is.

"Fuck. I'm an idiot," he sighs.

I raise an eyebrow at him and nod. A small smile starts spreading across my face.

"Yeah, I'm not into cradle robbing," I joke. "But I have been told on the Internet that I'm a MILF."

Mikey breaks out into a full belly laugh and I can't help but join. It's so contagious.

"I'm sorry, Tia. I'm still working on myself. I still really care about you and I just want what's best for you."

I nod. "I feel the same way, Mikey. How about I make you a deal?"

He gives me a look saying to continue.

"I'll help you out for a while, but you still look for a new manager. This can't be permanent. I'll do as much as I can, but Dustin takes first priority. And you agree that he is your opener for your tour this fall."

Mikey's smile grows. "Deal!"

I hope I don't regret this, but working with Mikey will probably benefit CeCe, since she will be able to continue to see him a lot. He's already stuck in my life. I might as well help him out for the time being.

"Okay. Do you think we need a contract? Or how do you want to do this?" I ask.

Mikey gives me a smile that drips of sex. Fuck, I'm getting wet and he's not even touching me. Goddamn feelings. I wish they would hit the fucking road.

"Well, I can think of some arrangements I would like." He wags his eyebrows at me.

I can't help but laugh. "You never change, do you?"

He smiles. "Nope. Would you want me to?"

I shake my head. "Definitely not."

"I've got popcorn, chips, and all the *Broken Lizard* movies. Let the marathon commence," Mikey says, carrying a large bag of goodies.

"I made punch earlier," I tell him. "It's kiwi watermelon. So yummy."

Mikey takes the groceries and unloads.

"You still like dill pickle dip?" he asks, shaking the container.

"Is the sky blue?" I joke.

I never thought I would be able to be friends with Mikey, but things are so easy with him. He's over every day visiting and helping with CeCe, and when he suggested a movie marathon, I jumped at the chance.

"Please tell me you brought the cheddar popcorn shaker." Crystal says, walking into the kitchen.

"Of course I did. Do you think I'm some sort of monster?" he chuckles.

Our dysfunctional family is all here. Well, except Leah. It seems like she's kind of been avoiding me. Or maybe it's just that she still doesn't have kids and can go out whenever she likes. Our lives are different now. I know she's still there if I need her. I just wish I saw her more often.

"Are the kids both bathed?" I ask Crystal.

"Yup. Liv is already in bed and CeCe is ready for the boob."

"Okay. You two start the popcorn and I'll put her down."

CeCe is great when it comes to bedtime, so in no time, I'm out and ready to watch the movies.

When I enter the living room, I see Mikey and Crystal joking around like siblings. I love having them both in my life. It might not have been how I envisioned life, but it's still pretty special.

"So, which one are we starting with?" I ask, letting them know I'm back.

We agree on *Slammin' Salmon*, and there isn't a moment we aren't crying from laughing so hard. I know we're going to be quoting these movies for weeks. After the movie is over, Crystal is texting someone and has this giddy smile on her face.

"Well, I think I'm going to head to bed. You two have fun." She giggles and leaves.

"Who do you think she was texting?" Mikey asks me.

"Dustin." I wiggle my eyebrows at him.

Crystal and Dustin have been non-stop texting since they met at her birthday. She tells me they're just friends, but I think something more could be brewing.

"*Club Dread*?" I ask Mikey seeing if he's still up for our movie marathon.

"Damn right." He gives me his perfect smile and my heart does a flip.

My friendship with Mikey has been amazing since CeCe was born. We joke lots, talk all the time, and see each other every day, since he can't go more than twenty-four hours without seeing CeCe. It's easy being around him again, but every once in a while, I feel my feelings coming back. He'll accidently graze my arm and I'll melt, or he'll tell me how beautiful I am, and I just want to kiss him. It takes a lot of energy to keep myself in check, but I feel like I'm doing good, for the most part. I just have to remind myself that we won't work in a relationship.

I laugh so much my face hurts. Sitting on the couch, I snuggle up against Mikey. I didn't think this was something friends could do, but it feels so natural and right. Before I know it, I'm drifting off to sleep.

I wake up and the TV is playing the beginning part of the DVD over and over again. I feel warm arms wrapped around me and I snuggle in. I let out a little moan before I realize whose arms they are.

"Fuck," I mumble, and pull away.

Mikey grumbles and wakes up. "Shit. I didn't realize I fell asleep."

I stand up, grabbing the empty popcorn bowl and cups. "It's fine, but maybe you should go home."

I avoid eye contact the entire time. How could I do that? We are supposed to be just friends. Yet here I was wrapped in his arms and moaning at his embrace. I'm an idiot. I need to put more distance between us.

"His studio time was booked over a month ago! What do you mean he is getting bumped last minute?" I yell into my phone.

"I'm sorry. The person who did your booking was new and didn't last. I'm doing my best to rearrange everyone, but Mr. Maxx is going to have to wait until next week," the lady says on the other end of the phone, sounding frazzled.

I take a deep breath. "Fine, but I want the cost to be half the price we originally talked about. This is setting my client behind."

"That shouldn't be a problem, Ms. Daggen."

I hang up and run my hands over my face. I've been working with Dustin for around three months now, and we have been hit with so many issues, it isn't even funny. First, it was a record label claiming Dustin had made a verbal agreement to sign with them. They were threatening to sue him for everything. Thankfully, it was shut down fast, considering that he would have only been seventeen at the time of the alleged agreement and wouldn't have been allowed to make any legal decisions without parental consent. Then, it was someone claiming Dustin had stolen all of his work and didn't write any of his own songs. But Dustin had phone recordings of all the stuff he has ever written and the time frames that the person suing Dustin gave didn't match with the physical proof.

After all those setbacks, we were finally hoping to get him into the studio to finish recording so we could get the album out in the next couple of months before the tour starts this fall. But, of course, now we have to wait *another* week. I don't know what could possibly happen next.

I could really use a drink, but I don't think that's acceptable at nine in the morning. CeCe starts squawking, pulling me out of my bad mood.

"How's Mommy's little angel?" I ask her, blowing raspberries on her tummy.

She lets out a joyous shriek.

"We need to tell Uncle Jay that it's about time he opens a recording studio for his new label, because other people are idiots," I say in my happy baby voice.

She smiles at me; I love this little girl more than I have loved anyone else.

I hear a knock at the door. Glancing at my phone, I realize I lost track of time.

"I'm so sorry. I completely forgot to make lunch," I say, opening the door. "People at S.B.R. are stupid, and I think I need to find Dustin a new place to record."

Mikey laughs as he enters, but as soon as he takes his shoes off, he makes a beeline for CeCe.

"How's Daddy's little princess?" he asks her, and she coos back at him.

She may only be just shy of four months, but she has so much personality already.

This year has gone by so fast. It's almost Mikey's birthday again, and I don't know how I feel about it. He brought it up last week. He said he wants to do something small, just family, but I keep having flashbacks to last year.

"So, what do you want me to order? Chinese or pizza?" I ask Mikey while he plays with CeCe.

"Pizza's fine. Do you want to use my recording time this week at A.J.'s place? My songs for the album are already done. We were just working on a couple of new ones to maybe release as singles."

I think about it for a minute. If I could keep Dustin in the studio, I wouldn't have to worry about the release date for his debut album.

"Are you sure? I know you were really excited about your new songs. I still can't wait to hear them, by the way."

"I'm sure," he insists. "Dustin is my boy now. I want the best for him, and missing studio time is not going to be good for the album."

I nod. "Thank you so much. I'll text him right now."

I text Dustin the address, then order the pizza. I sit down on the couch and feel like I can finally take a breath. I see CeCe making a sucking face, and know she is hungry.

"Can you pass me the princess so I can feed her, please?" I ask.

Mikey smiles and gives me the angel.

I used to feel weird breastfeeding in front of Mikey, but it's become like second nature now. CeCe hates a blanket over her head, but it's not like Mikey hasn't seen my breasts before. Hell, he used to be the one sucking on them.

"How's apartment hunting going for Crystal?" Mikey asks.

"Really good. We think she'll be able to move into one next month. We're just waiting for them to run my credit check." I agreed to co-sign for Crystal since she doesn't have much credit yet. "This place is going to feel so empty without them."

"Yeah, it will be a lot quieter for sure," he jokes.

It definitely gets loud when everyone is in the house. The girls feed off each other's energy and sometimes go crazy. It's kind of nice that Crystal and Olivia are at the park right now. I like the quiet for a bit, but I know I'm going to miss them when they're gone.

"It's okay to miss them," Mikey states, almost like he is reading my mind.

I smile. "I know. It's going to be hard at first, but it's best for everyone."

The plan was always for Crystal to do this on her own, eventually, but I feel like a mom saying goodbye to her child. Crystal is my family now; it's hard to see her leave, but I'm proud to watch her spread her wings.

The apartment that she is hoping to get is a small two-bedroom, and it's only two blocks away, so Crystal can easily walk Olivia over here before she goes to work. I'm not at home as much as I used to be, but when I can't watch Olivia, Leah usually can. We have turned into one big family and I love it.

"I was talking to my mom, and she said it would be great if you and CeCe came over for a barbecue on my birthday."

I smile. I love Mikey's mom. She has been so amazing since CeCe was born. She comes over once a week for special "Grandma bonding." It's great to see our child being loved so much. My dad has only been able to come down once, but I get that it's hard with his work schedule.

"Just family?" I ask.

The last thing I need is to see any of his friends.

"Yes, just family. I was thinking of inviting Leah and Crystal too, since they're your family."

Why does he have to be so sweet sometimes?

"That sounds great. I know Crystal won't have plans, but I don't know about Leah."

I make a mental note to touch base with her tonight. It's been too long; we need girl time.

CeCe finishes eating, and I put her down for a nap. That's pretty much all she does still: eat, sleep, and poop. She is getting livelier, though, and I can't wait until she's crawling around and wreaking havoc.

As I'm walking out of her room, I see Mikey paying for the pizza. The teenage delivery guy looks star struck.

"Would you like me to take a picture of you guys?" I ask.

"Would that be okay?" the delivery guy asks eyes wide.

Mikey smiles. "Of course. Do you mind if I put it on my social media?"

"Really? That would be awesome!" He is shaking, he is so excited. "I've been a fan of yours since I was a kid."

I giggle. I bet Mikey is feeling old. I take a couple pictures, then grab a sharpie from the kitchen so Mikey can sign the guy's hat.

"Thanks for being a fan, I hope to see you at a concert this fall," he says to the kid.

"I already have my alarm set on my phone to get online for tickets next week."

The guy walks off and his smile is so big. Mikey just made his day, maybe even his week.

"You're so sweet to your fans," I tell him, taking the pizzas to the kitchen.

"They deserve it. I wouldn't be where I am today without them."

I give him a piece of pizza and take mine to the living room.

"Do you have the list finalized for the tour yet?" he asks, sitting next to me.

I swallow my bite and nod. "The last venue just confirmed this morning. It's all set! You start in October with very little breaks until December, then you return in the middle of January, finishing the tour around May." I pull out my phone to look at a couple of notes. "And if things go according to plan, we may have you signed up for a world tour in July, co-headlining with Five Finger Death Punch."

Mikey's jaw drops. I was planning on surprising him for his birthday, but this felt as good of an opportunity as any.

"Are you serious?" he asks.

I nod with a grin. "Happy birthday! Their manager reached out to me last week. It would be amazing for your career. You're already doing amazing, but this would put you over the top."

Mikey places his plate on the coffee table and leans over to give me a hug. His scent of peppermint and pine invade my senses, and I feel lightheaded. We have avoided long contact since we have been back in each other's lives, so my body is feeling overwhelmed. I take a deep breath and break the hug.

"I'm so proud of you, Mikey. This year has been full of crazy rollercoasters, but you have risen above every obstacle thrown at you and come out the other side shining," I tell him.

I feel the tears rising in my eyes. He almost ended his life, and none of this would have happened.

"I wouldn't be where I am today if it wasn't for you." He takes my hand in his. "You are the best manager and co-parent a guy could ask for. I wanted to ask you if you would consider staying on as my manager. Since Dustin and I are touring together, you'd be on tour anyways. Please say yes. I can't do this without you."

I look into his sky-blue eyes. I could get lost in those eyes. It's happened before. I've actually been thinking about this a lot. I wasn't sure how it would be managing Mikey again, after everything we went through, but it's been fine. Better than fine. CeCe gets to see her daddy every day, Mikey has been a great role model for Dustin, and things haven't been awkward. It's been easier than I thought to manage two people as well.

I bite my lip and I see Mikey's eyes go to them, as he stares a moment too long.

"Okay," I whisper.

So much for creating more distance. This is a big commitment. Things didn't work out that great last time. What if something happens again? What if Mikey starts dating someone else? I feel a tear break from my eye and roll down my cheek.

Mikey swipes the tear away. "What's wrong?"

I lean slightly into his touch. "I don't know. I just don't think I could handle not having you in my life. What if something happens, and you want to fire me? What would that do to our friendship? At least if we took out the complication of manager, we could be okay."

He lifts my chin so that I'm looking in his eyes. "Why would I ever want to fire you? You are the best manger Sienna has ever seen. Hell, I'd go so far as to say you're the best manger out there, period."

"But what if we start seeing other people?" I ask, throwing it out there.

He closes his eyes and takes a deep breath. "I'm not going to lie. It's bound to happen one day, but it's going to be difficult, no matter what. It won't change if you're my manager or not."

I nod, not able to find words. He's right, though. That day will happen. He's going to find someone new to love, and I'll just be the manager. Will I be able to keep my emotions in check? I hope so.

Mikey leaves shortly after our conversation, and I sit on the couch contemplating life.

Mikey and I are best friends now, but is that all I want? I told myself I would keep my emotions in check, but I don't want to. Not anymore. I want Mikey. I don't just want him as a co-parent, or a friend. I want him as my partner, my lover. He's done more than enough to prove to me that he's changed, permanently this time. And I can't deny the truth anymore: I'm still in love with him, and I will be until the day I die.

After some soul-searching, I give Leah a call and convince her that we need some girl time.

"I feel like shit. I drank way too much last night. But I'm here, and I brought treats," Leah says, bringing in a box of cupcakes from our favorite shop.

I take the cupcakes from her, setting them down on the counter before giving her the biggest hug. "I missed you. Why does it feel like forever since we hung out last?"

"We are both busy ladies. You're a new mom, and I'm a drunken mess." She laughs.

"So, tell me what's new. You look…" I pause for a second, trying to think of the word. "Different."

She smiles grabs a couple bottles of water and heads to the living room. I plate up a couple of cupcakes and follow her.

"Well, I've been hooking up with this guy for a little bit." She takes a bite of her cupcake and continues. I hate when she talks with her mouth full, but I've gotten used to it. "It's not serious. We're more like fuck buddies. It happens pretty much every time I go out drinking, which has been a lot lately, since you've been so busy with CeCe."

"I'm sorry," I sigh. "I've been a shit friend."

I feel so bad for not being able to go out with Leah like I used to. I know it might sound stupid, but I never realized a baby was going to change my life so much.

"Don't," she demands. "You have not been a shit friend. You are a new mommy figuring out a whole new life. If anyone has been a shit friend, it's been me. I should be here more often. CeCe needs to know her Auntie Leah better."

I push her shoulder and turn on the TV. "I still love Mikey."

"Well, yeah. You're always going to love him, in a way. He will always hold a special place in your heart."

"I know that, but I'm still *in* love with him," I clarify.

Leah's eyes widen. "Oh?"

I sigh. "Yeah. I realized after our movie marathon that my feelings for him were stronger than I thought. Then today, after talking with him, I figured out that I still want to be with him. Everything is perfect right now, but what happens when he tries to move on with his life? I'll just be the manager, and I don't think I can deal with seeing him with someone else."

"Have you told him how you feel?"

I grab my cupcake and play with the wrapper. "No. Can we even make a real relationship work?"

"In life, nothing is guaranteed. But you have to try, don't you? He did the big gesture to woo you last time. Maybe now it's your turn. Tell him how you feel. Open up to him."

I look at Leah with tears in my eyes. "I think you're right; I've always been so afraid of rejection and not being enough. Mikey broke me last time, but he's proven he's a different man now."

Leah wraps her arms around me and pulls me in for a hug. "Good. Now let's work on a plan."

MIKEY

Today, I'm meeting Dustin and Tia at the studio. It's my first-time hearing Dustin's new music and I'm pretty excited. I knew he was a talented kid from the moment I first heard his music, and now I'm going to be touring with him. It feels great to be a part of his journey and help show him the ropes.

When I get to the studio, I see my precious little daughter in her baby vibrating chair. I remember the first time I put her in it, she freaked out so bad, and I panicked. I thought she either hated it, or that I hurt her. I picked her up and tried bouncing around, but she was losing her mind. Tia came into the room laughing and told me about the vibrating button. As soon as it was on, CeCe was super content.

I kneel down next to the chair and give her a gentle kiss on the forehead. "How's Daddy's little girl?"

She makes a little noise and goes back to batting at the toys hanging over her head.

"You made it!" Dustin says, walking into the room. "I'm excited for you to hear some of my new stuff. I'm working on one, maybe two, tracks today, but I can show you some of the stuff that's already recorded after if you have time."

He sticks his hands in his pockets and looks a little intimidated.

"I've got the day off, so I'm all yours. And you can chill, dude. We're friends. No need to be nervous," I tell him.

He gives me an awkward smile. "Thanks, man. Sorry. This is still new to me. I'm working with my idols. I never thought this would be my life."

"No worries. I get it. I was in your shoes once. Now I'm just an old man." I laugh.

"*So* old!" Tia states, coming into the room.

I give her a hug and don't want to let go; it feels right having her in my arms.

"Thanks for that," I joke and grab my chest. "I think you broke my heart."

"You don't have a heart," she chuckles. "More like I bruised your giant ego. It needs to be taken down a notch anyways. I see the way your social media following is blowing up. I'm surprised your head could even fit through that door."

I love how easily we can joke now. And that smile. Man, what it does to my heart. I'm happy that it seems to be a permanent fixture on her face now.

"Okay, guys, we're wasting time. Dustin, get your ass in that booth," A.J., the producer, demands with a smile.

We all laugh, but Dustin listens and gets his headphones on.

The first track is fire. Its old rock mixed with a bit of new, something entirely different then what's out there right now, but so pleasing at the same time. I give Dustin some tips to make it sound better and I swear his smile gets bigger every time.

"You're good with him. Maybe you should get into producing," Tia tells me, while leaning on my shoulder.

I smile. "Maybe one day, but I love to be behind that microphone much more."

She nods. "I know. When I watch you sing, it's like the whole world disappears and it's just you and the music. Nothing else matters."

"That's exactly how it feels. It's my happy place. The only other time I feel that happy is when I'm with you and CeCe," I tell her.

Tia's eyes widen. Fuck, I think I crossed a line. But then they soften and she smiles.

"You're our happy place too," she murmurs.

I can't stop thinking about Tia. I'm still madly in love with her, but I can't push her back into a relationship. Things are fantastic right now, but what happens when she gets a new guy? I don't want to think about it, and frankly, it's none of my business. I fucked everything up. She will forever be the one that got away. Thankfully, she will also still be in my life, but just as a friend.

My birthday is today and I'm excited to see Tia and CeCe. I had to go out of town yesterday for an appearance on *Jimmy Fallon*, which I'm still thinking was a dream. My new album, *Forgetting Everything*, released last week and is topping the charts. Tickets went on sale for the first half of the tour yesterday and most venues are already sold out. Life is looking up. I have everything I ever wanted when I was a kid. Well, everything except the girl.

"Happy birthday," my mom cheers as I walk into her house.

"Thanks, Mom," I say, pulling her into a bear hug.

I hear a little giggle and turn to see CeCe on the floor of the living room.

"I thought we changed the time." I look out into the backyard and see Leah and Crystal, but not Tia. "Or did I read your message wrong?"

My mom smiles. "Nope. Message was right. *You* were supposed to come later."

"Okay…" I have no idea what is going on, but I can tell something is up.

"You play with your daughter; I have a couple of things I need to do."

My mom leaves and I wish I could read her mind. I always know when she is up to something, and this is clearly one of those times.

I sit on the floor next to CeCe and pick her up.

"I missed you so much." I give her a big kiss on the cheek, and she giggles.

"Happy birthday, son," my dad says as he comes in from outside, and I get a whiff of the barbecue.

"Thanks. Something smells great. What are you making today?" I ask him.

He smiles. "Everything. I might have gone a little over the top." He lets out a boisterous laugh. "But it's not every day your son turns thirty."

I groan. "Don't remind me. I feel old."

He laughs again, and this time CeCe joins in.

"See? Even my daughter is laughing at me."

My mom comes back in with a giant smile. "Okay, everything is set up. Please bring CeCe and come with me."

I look at my dad with so much confusion. What the fuck is going on? He doesn't say anything, but he has a shit-eating grin on his face and nods for me to follow my mom.

"I really hope they aren't offering me up as a human sacrifice," I mock whisper to CeCe, and my dad laughs. "If you need a virgin, you definitely got the wrong guy."

When I enter the backyard, I see Jay sitting with a guitar, and a small sound system is set up. Tia is standing beside him, behind a microphone. She is fidgeting with her dress and picking at her nails. She is wearing a long, flowing red dress and her hair is curled, floating beautifully over her shoulders.

When she notices me, she lights up with the biggest smile. My mom gets me to sit in a chair that is set up in front of Tia.

"I want to thank everyone for coming to Mikey's birthday party today," Tia starts. "But I want to say a few things to Mikey first." She looks straight into my eyes. "Our time together has been crazy; we have had ups and downs and everything else in between. We have hurt each other and loved each other fiercely. I can't predict the future, and I don't know if we will last forever, but I want to try again. When I think about my future, it's only you I see, so to show you how I feel, I want to sing you a song."

Jay starts playing and all the air leaves my lungs when she starts singing a soulful rendition of "Make You Feel My Love" by Adele. I've heard her sing to CeCe a few times, but I am blown away by her raw talent.

I see her start to choke up a little and blink back tears as she finishes the song. I feel all her love being poured out.

"So, what do you say, Mikey? Can we give this one more try?" she asks.

I stand up and my mom is standing right there, ready to take CeCe. I don't have any words, so I grab Tia's face and land my lips on hers. I hear everyone cheer, and I chuckle a little before deepening the kiss. I move one hand to her waist to pull her closer. I break the kiss and move my lips to Tia's ear.

"I've loved you since the day I met you. I'll always be yours." I give her one more soft kiss.

Once the party is over, I take Tia and CeCe home. We put CeCe to bed and quietly shut the door.

The moment we're in the living room, I grab Tia by the waist and crash my lips to hers.

"That party lasted way too fucking long," I whisper against her lips.

She giggles as my hands roam her body.

"I've missed this," she whispers with a heavy breath.

Fuck, she has no idea.

"Me too, sweetheart," I tell her.

I pick her up, and she wraps her long legs around my waist. I kiss her as much as I can while we make our way to the bedroom.

Gently, I place her on the bed while pushing her back and lifting up her dress. I place kisses along her perfect skin. I've missed being this close to her. We have been through so much and I want this to be perfect for her.

As I get closer to her center, I take a moment, calming myself. My dick is pressing so hard into my pants that if I don't calm down, I'll blow before I even get inside her.

I slowly pull her panties off and move back, gliding my tongue through her folds. God, she tastes perfect. I didn't realize how much I've missed her taste until now.

"Yesss," she hisses, and fuck, those noises are not making things easier.

Sliding two fingers inside her, I can already feel her muscles contracting. She is so close.

I curve them just how she likes them and pick up a good pace. Her mewling is getting louder, and I wouldn't be surprised if she wakes CeCe up. I pull her bud into my mouth, giving it a tiny bite, and she loses it.

"Oh. My. God. Mikey!" she screams, and I smile.

I love making my girl come undone. And I'm just so happy to call her mine again. I pull myself up and start taking my clothes off.

"Please tell me you have condoms," I say as I pull my shirt off.

"Yes, in the side table," she giggles, taking her dress off.

I stare at her. How did I not notice she wasn't wearing a bra? I'm a fucking idiot. As soon as I put on the condom, I climb on top of Tia, placing my face between her breasts.

"I've missed you," I whisper.

Tia giggles. "Are you talking to me or my boobs?"

"Both," I growl before taking her perfect nipple in my mouth.

She quickly pushes me back, and I'm confused.

"I'm breastfeeding. These…" She motions to her breasts. "…are off limits for now."

I pout. Fuck.

I nip at her neck. "The moment you are done, they're mine again."

I crash my lips on hers, wondering if she tastes herself on me. Slowly, I slide into her. God, I love being this close to her.

"Fuck," she hisses once I'm fully inside.

Lifting her legs to my shoulders, I slowly start to pick up my pace. Nothing has ever felt as right as this does.

"I love you," I choke out as I'm just about to lose it.

"I'll love you forever, Mikey," she moans as her orgasm crashes over her.

She arches her back and I'm gone. I pull out and go to the bathroom to clean up. When I come back, Tia is curled up and looking so peaceful. I wrap my arms around her and pull her close to me.

"I've missed you so much," I whisper into her hair, as we drift off to sleep.

"You did amazing!" Tia says, kissing me as I walk offstage.

"I wouldn't be here today without you," I tell her, stealing another kiss.

I grab CeCe from her arms. She looks so cute with her little headphones.

"And do you think Daddy did good?" I ask her.

Her giant smile says it all.

The tour has just started, and it's been going amazing. My family has been making it so much better.

I was nervous about the tour, because I've always done drugs when I was on tour and I was scared of the temptation. But, with Tia with me, I know the temptations won't be around.

The tour has been labeled a dry tour, and no alcohol or drugs are allowed backstage or on our tour buses. If people want to go to a bar or party afterwards, that is up to them, but everyone has been great with not bringing that shit around me. Eventually, I'll be able to face that stuff and be okay, but right now I don't want it to be around me. It's still too soon, and I don't need the added pressure.

My counseling is going amazing, and my relationship with Tia is perfect. I'm so happy we were able to come back together again.

My life is finally complete. I got the girl, the daughter, and the fame I always wanted. I couldn't ask for more.

TIA

SIX MONTHS LATER

The first half of the tour went fantastic. Now, it's time for the second half. I'm so happy the first show is in Sienna. It's nice to be home for a show.

Life on the road with a baby is the craziest thing. CeCe is ten months old now, and boy, can that girl boogie. If you take your eye off of her for a second, she is gone. We keep her in a stroller a lot of the time just so she doesn't escape. We also hired a nanny to come on the road with us, since Mikey and I are both very busy on show nights, but I keep CeCe with me as much as possible. I am her mom, after all. She is loving all the attention she's getting and is already such a diva. Her daddy plays into that, of course.

The past six months have really been a blur. We're in a different city most nights, on the road a lot, and hardly have any down time. When the break finally happened, it was nice to be in our own bed for a change. We moved into Mikey's house just before the tour started. My lease was up on the apartment, and since we weren't home much anyways, it just made sense.

Crystal and Olivia are doing great! They found a great babysitter, and Leah still fills in when needed. I am extremely proud of Crystal; she could have given up so many times, but she is stronger than anyone I know. I was sad when I had to miss Olivia's birthday, but I made up for it over Christmastime.

Mikey surprised me for my birthday and threw a party with the closest people to us. I was kind of expecting him to propose, but it didn't happen. I'm not upset; our lives are perfect right now, so why mess with a good thing? It's just that everyone around me lately has been acting weird, and I can't help but think something is up.

Tonight, I'm excited to get to go to the show without CeCe. My dad is still up here and volunteered to watch her while I'm at the show. She is on solids now and drinks milk from a cup. I stopped breastfeeding last month and it wasn't even a fight. It was like we were both ready to be done. But it's my first time leaving her, so I think I'll be texting my dad a lot.

"Why do I need to dress up?" I ask Leah for the hundredth time. "I want to be comfortable; this show isn't any different just because we are in our home city. I still have to do my job."

"Because I'm dressing up, and we are going out afterwards, so stop bitching and do as you're told," she insists.

I roll my eyes and step into the sparkly red dress. It's surprisingly comfortable, and I know Mikey will love it.

"I'm wearing my fancy flats and there's nothing you can say to change my mind," I tell her while pulling them from the back of the giant closet.

"You can wear the flats, but let me do your hair."

I sigh, but agree. I mean, there isn't really any other choice. Leah pretty much always gets her way.

After a lot of pulling and teasing and so much hairspray that I couldn't breathe, we are ready and headed towards the venue for the sold-out show. Mikey said he would meet us there and not to worry about making sound check. He assured me that he had it all under control. I probably wouldn't have listened, but Leah took her sweet-ass time getting me ready.

"You look amazing," Mikey tells me, when I walk into his dressing room.

I smile and saunter over to him for a soft kiss. "Thanks. Leah told me I had to dress up."

"You know I love you in red," he growls, and grabs my hips. "I can't wait to get you out of this."

I giggle. "Your sex drive has only gone up since you turned thirty. Isn't it supposed to slow down?"

"How is that possible when my girlfriend is so fucking hot?" He play bites at my neck and I let out a squeal.

My alarm goes off. Play time is over.

"You are going to have to wait," I tell him. "It's time to give Sienna the show they've been waiting for."

He gives me a pout, then slaps my ass. "The show must go on."

I roll my eyes and follow him out the door.

Dustin just finished his set, and the crew is changing out the equipment for Mikey's band. I always knew Dustin was super talented, but he is blowing up. His album beat Mikey's on most of the charts, and everyone is saying he is the one to watch.

I watch as Mikey gets himself hyped up doing his usual pre-show ritual. I could watch him do this every night, and most nights I do. He's joked that it's creepy how I watch him all the time, but I know he loves it. He always has been an attention whore.

Dustin comes over and gives Mikey a fist bump. "You are going to rock like you always do."

"Fuck yeah," Mikey agrees. "I'm so fucking ready."

With one more kiss, Mikey saunters onto the stage for thousands of screaming fans. He loves writing and recording, but performing? That's where he thrives. It's what he lives for, to see all those people singing along and enjoying the show.

I stand just offstage like I do every night, but tonight Leah is with me, dancing along. This show feels so much more relaxed than the others. It's probably because my best friend is making me forget about my responsibilities and just enjoy life.

I'm lost in Mikey's new song, "Don't Fuck It Up," when I feel hands on my shoulders. I start bouncing up and down as soon as I see Jay and jump into his arms.

"What are you doing here?" I shriek.

It's been so weird not seeing Jay every day. Things have sure changed a lot.

"Well, I couldn't miss a show in the city I live in, and besides, I'm performing with him." Jay holds up his guitar.

My brows pull together, and I'm trying to figure what is going on. "I didn't know about that."

How did I not know about this? I am Mikey's manager. I should know what is happening at his shows.

"I know." Jay gives me a smile, like he knows something I don't know.

"What is going on, *Jeffery*?" I demand.

He shakes his head and puts his hand on my shoulder. "You'll see."

I'm about to tear into him when Mikey starts talking. "I want everyone here to give a huge round of applause for my good friend, who you may or may not know, Jay Coldheart!"

The crowd erupts. Of course they know who he is. But no one expected him to be here tonight. Jay waves at the crowd, touches a few hands, and blows out kisses. I roll my eyes. Always the cocky bastard.

"Jay here has agreed to help me perform a cover that I have never tried before. I haven't always been a huge fan of country music, and I know most of you here are probably in the same boat." The crowd cheers in agreement. "But my awesome manager and girlfriend has been opening my eyes to new music, and I hate to admit this, but not all country music makes your ears bleed."

I laugh and feel another hand on my shoulder. I turn to see my dad and CeCe with the cutest earmuffs on to protect her delicate ears. Mikey's parents are also there, along with Crystal, Olivia, Melly, Corey, Tyler, and pretty much everyone I care about.

I hear the music start, and my attention is drawn back to Mikey. "I want to dedicate this song to the love of my life, Tia."

The crowd goes crazy again. The second he starts singing, I know the song: "Yours" by Russell Dickerson. I feel the tears start as he sings, I've always loved this song, and I can't believe Mikey is performing a *country* song. I never thought I'd see the day.

"I want to invite my beautiful girlfriend on to the stage," Mikey says while his mom pushes me forward.

What is going on? I never go on stage. I am more of a backstage kind of girl. I walk out and it's deafening how loud the crowd is. Mikey grabs my hand and pulls me in for a gentle kiss, his lips just whispering over mine.

"Tia, I have loved you for so long, and our relationship has had so many ups and downs, but I couldn't see my life without you in it." He drops to a knee and I cover my face. Is this really happening? "Life without you wouldn't really be a life. Please say yes and be my wife."

I laugh a little because he rhymed, and my sense of humor is that of a twelve-year-old. I freeze for a second, not responding, then I hear the crowd chanting, "Say yes, say yes, say yes!"

I nod my head up and down like a crazy person. "Yes!"

Mikey places the obscenely huge ring on my finger, then stands, pulling me into his arms, and plants a very inappropriate kiss on my lips. I melt into him and don't even care that there are thousands of people watching us. I am so lost in this moment I almost don't even hear the cheering. Mikey walks me offstage and Jay starts performing an old Broken Hearts song.

"I can't believe you surprised me like that," I tell him once we are offstage.

"It wasn't easy, baby," he says, not letting me out of his touch. "I had to get so many people to help. You're hard to surprise since you always have to be in everyone's business."

I shove at him. "It's my job."

He kisses my head. "I know, and you are amazing at it. Now, I am sorry to do this, but I have to go perform one more song." He puts both hands on my face and gives me a kiss that steals my breath. "I love you."

I nod as he walks back on stage. I am going to marry that man. This day was perfect, and I can't wait to see what our future holds.

The End

Thanks for Reading!

I hope you enjoyed *Secret Smiles*! If you did, I'd love if you would leave an honest review.

Playlist

I love to listen to music while writing and get inspiration from certain songs. Here is my list for *Secret Smiles*, in no particular order.

1. "Beautiful Lies" by Jana Kramer
2. "Drag the Lake" by Amity Affliction
3. "Aftermath" by Royal Tusk
4. "Losing My Life" by Falling in Reverse
5. "Feels Like I'm Dying" by Amity Affliction
6. "Ghost" by Bad Flower
7. "Wonderful Life" by Being Me The Horizion
8. "I Hate It" by Underoath
9. "In Case You Didn't Know" by Brett Young
10. "Yours" by Russell Dickerson
11. "Make You Feel My Love" by Adele

Love in Sienna Series

1. *Secret Smiles* (Tia & Mikey)
2. *Hidden Kisses* (Leah & Johnny)
3. *Guarded Hearts* (Crystal & Dustin)
4. *Whispered Desires* (Shae & Tyler)

AND KEEP READING FOR
A SNEAK PEEK AT

LEAH AND JOHNNY'S STORY

Also By Laura John

Standalone

Monster in the Shadows (Dark Romance)

One

JOHNNY

"Yes! Oh, my God! Harder!"

I move in and out, giving her everything I've got, wishing she would just shut the fuck up. I know I should be thinking about how hot her tits are, but she isn't the woman I want. The woman I want wants nothing to do with me. So, I'm fucking a chick who's name I don't know, wishing it was Leah.

"That feels *so* good, Johnny! I'm so close!"

Well, that makes one of us. She sounds like a fucking dying cat, and it's really getting on my nerves. Why do some girls feel like they have to be so loud? I mean, if it's authentic, fine, but I know this isn't the best sex of her life—or if it is…well, I kind of feel sorry for her. Could she please just shut the fuck up?

"Right there! Yes! Oh my, God!"

My thoughts drift to Leah. To her long dark hair, what it would look like spread across my pillow. I think about her tits and what it would feel like grabbing them and sucking them into my mouth. I wonder what she would taste like as I sucked on her pussy, lapping up her juices.

The more I think about Leah and picture her instead of the chick I'm fucking, I realize I'm an inch away from coming. I give a couple more thrusts and picture Leah's lips around my cock. With that image, I blow.

Pulling out, I go to the bathroom to take care of the condom.

"What the fuck are you still doing here?" I bark at the stupid chick still naked in my bed.

"I was hoping we could cuddle or go for round two." She pouts, her red lipstick smeared all over her face.

Fuck, I didn't even look in the mirror. I hope I don't have too much on my face.

"I don't double dip, sweetheart, so get dressed and get the fuck out." I walk back into the bathroom and wash my face. It wasn't bad, but I don't want any memory of this chick. I just needed to get my dick wet and she was more than willing to spread her legs for me.

Everyone wants a taste of Johnny William Crown, famous baseball player and legendary pitcher, but that may all be over soon.

"Get your head out of your ass, Crown!" Coach Gibbs hollers, his face turning red. "You know I will fucking pull you if you don't smarten the fuck up. I don't know what the hell has been up with you these past few weeks, but you need to get over it NOW."

He throws his hat and storms out of the dugout.

I run a hand over my face. He's right. My head has been fucked up for the last several weeks, ever since my best friend Mikey's birthday party. I'm terrified that I'm going to lose baseball, the only thing that matters to me, but if I don't pull my shit together, it won't matter because I'll be fucked anyway.

I start jumping up and down and chanting lyrics from my favorite song. Mikey and I started doing this when we were kids. It's a way to get our heads into whatever we're doing.

"I'm doing this for you, Mom," I say, looking up at the sky.

The rest of the game is fantastic. I play like I haven't played in weeks, like the old Johnny is back. I play how I would want to if my mom was actually here watching.

"Great game, Crown."

"Way to throw."

"About fucking time."

"The legend is back."

Everyone is pumped that we won. I wish I could be that excited, but what's the fucking point?

I slump my way to my truck. Thank fuck tomorrow is a day off. I just want to get to my bed and pass the fuck out.

I start my truck and crank some Slipknot. Knowing I shouldn't, I shoot Leah a text.

Me: I can't get you out of my head. Just one night.

Leah: You're an asshole. Lose my number.

Me: I'm sorry for everything.

She's not wrong. I am a fucking asshole, but when I met her, I felt something I had never felt before.

I've never had a girlfriend. I've never *wanted* one. Girls are just there to scratch an itch. And love? Fuck that! Love is for pussies. I just need a girl once in a while to suck my dick and get me off. No need for feelings. But the second I laid eyes on Leah, I wanted something else.

"Hey, handsome. Care if I sit down?"

I look up and see a goddess. How have I never seen this woman before? Her jet-black hair is cascading down her back, and those cut-off jeans and crop top are showing me everything I like to see. Curves, a stellar ass, and tits that I want in my face right now.

I give her my best panty-melting smile. "Be my guest."

She giggles and cozies up next to me. I like a girl who isn't afraid to get what she wants.

"So, what's your name, sweetheart, and how have I never seen you before?" I say.

Her smile could light up a fucking room, and it makes my heart do a funny flip. That's new. I was starting to think I didn't even have a heart anymore.

"Leah," she purrs.

Leah. I like it. And her voice. It's so sultry. I wonder what it would sound like screaming my name.

"So, Leah, tell me about yourself."

"I'm a lawyer, I don't take shit from anyone, and I like to be in control."

My eyes widen a bit. Man, this girl has balls. I fucking like it.

"Well, I'm Johnny, I'm a pitcher for The Sienna Grey Wolves, and I bet I could get you to give up control to me for one night." I give her a wink and I see her shiver.

"I don't give up control." Her back straightens, a power move, but it doesn't work on me.

I put my drink to my lips. "We'll see about that."

I take a long pull before resting it back on my knee, never losing eye contact. Her eyes are chestnut brown with flakes of gold floating around, I wonder if they get darker when she is about to come.

She licks her lips, and my eyes automatically are drawn to them. They are perfect, kind of plump, a natural berry color, and I want so badly to see them wrapped around my dick.

"So, are you a hermit or something? I would have remembered if I'd seen you around before. A girl like you isn't easily forgotten."

She lets out a loud, but girly, laugh. "Definitely not a hermit. Maybe we just go to different places." She shrugs.

"Maybe." I raise an eyebrow at her before letting my gaze travel her body. "With those legs, I'm guessing you love to dance. What's your favorite dance club?"

She gives me a flirtatious smile and moves in closer. "Thank you for noticing." She looks up at the sky as if thinking really hard for an answer. "All That Jazz. They have the best deejays and the drinks are awesome."

"You have got to be shitting me. I'm there all the time. In fact, I was just there with Mikey a few weeks ago."

Her face lights up. "I was there that night! I saw him for like three seconds. I was with my bestie, Tia."

I place my hand on her thigh, stroking it gently with my thumb. "Well, clearly that place is too big if I didn't see the most beautiful girl on the planet."

She rolls her eyes. "Does that pickup line work for you often?"

I narrow my eyes. "I don't normally need pickup lines. I just ask if she's down to fuck and we leave."

Leah's breath hitches, and she starts to blush. I love that I have this effect on her. I lean in, plant a kiss on her neck, and feel her body shiver under my touch.

"So, do you want to fuck?" I whisper in her ear.

She grabs my face and slams her lips into mine. Most girls I'm with are timid as fuck, but not Leah. She knows what she wants and takes it.

I grab her hips and help position her so she's straddling me. I'm instantly hard from the way she is moving her hips.

"Honey, you'd better slow down unless you want me to fuck you in front of all these people. But I'm down if you are." I smirk at her.

Her face turns the perfect shade of red. "Oh, my God. I'm so sorry, I'm not normally that forward." She pauses, looking around to see if anyone is paying attention; of course, they're not. "I think I need a drink."

She stands up and walks off.

I shake my head, trying to get my thoughts straight.

Fuck, who is that woman? She is strong, confident, and sexy as fuck. I want her. Just for a night. A long, hot night.

I sit for a minute and finish my drink. No use wasting good alcohol. After a couple of minutes, my hard-on is down to just a slight chub, and I'll be able to walk without it being painfully obvious.

Making my way to the kitchen for another drink, I see my girl standing next to a cute blonde and my best friend.

Wait. Did I just say my girl? What the fuck? She isn't my girl. She's just a girl I'm going to fuck. I give my head a shake before I slap Mikey on the shoulder. I'm so glad I was able to make his birthday bash.

"This is Johnny Crown," Leah beams, grabbing me. "And Johnny, this is my best friend in the entire world, Tia."

I look at the tall blonde.

"Nice to meet you," she says with a half-smile.

I stare at her for a second. "Do I know you from somewhere?"

I mean, she is a blonde and I love blondes. She probably just reminds me of a girl I fucked once. The more I look at her, the more I think it was just the hair. She doesn't really look familiar to me.

"I don't think so. Must just be a familiar-looking face," she says.

"I didn't know you were going to be here," Mikey mumbles.

What's up with him? He doesn't even look at me. Just keeps his eyes on the girl, who I'm assuming is his new girlfriend.

"I got back last night and knew I had to make your party, man." *I grab Leah by the waist and pull her snug against me.* "And damn, am I glad I did."

Leah giggles, and I smile. I'm going to have so much fun with this one.

"I'm glad you made it, man, but if you'll excuse me, I want to spend some quality time with my girlfriend." *Mikey grabs Tia's hand and walks away.*

I put my truck into drive. That's enough of memory lane for now. At least those are good memories. That night turned to shit fast; I just hope my whole fucking life isn't ruined now.

Acknowledgements

There are so many people I want to thank.

Firstly, my husband. I would not be releasing this book without him. He has been my biggest support, and always encouraging me to keep going. His unconditional love has been needed while I have been going crazy writing.

Second of all, my alpha and beta readers: Amanda Carol, BJ Steele, Claudia Tobias, Eloise Gibbs, and Rebekah Vasick. These ladies are the real MVPs. They helped me cut the crap and add things to make this book strong and amazing.

Next, my amazing friends who read the first few chapters of *Secret Smiles* and encouraged me to continue my writing. Natasha and Jen, thank you for pushing me to keep going.

Next, my tribe, the Chadettes. These ladies kept me sane. They were always there to listen to me complain about ANYTHING. I am so lucky to have found these amazing women and be able to call them friends. Love you guys.

Next, my AMAZING editor and formatter, Carmen Richter with CPR Editing. Carmen had some health issues during my editing process, but never once let me down. She made this book the polished piece you have today.

Next, my amazing friend Kierra McKay for proofreading for me. Love you, girl!

Next, my amazing cover designer, the FANTASTIC Harper! She was so amazing to work with and really brought the perfect designs to life! I couldn't have asked for better covers! Aren't the guys on all the Sienna books hot?!?

Next, the amazing author community. When looking for pointers, I came across some fantastic authors more than willing to help me with all my questions. Maria Luis, Jessa York, and Alley Ciz are just a few who helped me with my million questions.

And lastly, you. Thank you so much for taking time to read this book. It means the world to me, and I truly hope you enjoyed it.

About the Author

Laura John is a contemporary romance author with a love for music. She lives in Alberta, Canada with her husband, two kids, and one loveable fur-baby. She loves karaoke, makeup, and of course, a good glass of wine. She mixes her love of words with her love of music and hopes to transport you into a world you don't want to leave.

You can find Laura online here:

Facebook Page: www.facebook.com/authorlauraj

Reader Group: www.facebook.com/groups/lauraslovelyladies

Instagram: @authorlaurajohn

Goodreads Author Page:
www.goodreads.com/author/show/19182589.Laura_John

Amazon Author Page: www.amazon.com/author/laurajohn

Made in USA - Kendallville, IN
1225184_9781689215541
01.14.2021 1431